BROTHER OF THE CHEYENNES

BROTHER OF THE CHEYENNES

Book Two of the Rusty Sabin Saga

by

MAX BRAND

Skyhorse Publishing

First Skyhorse Publishing edition published 2013 by arrangement with Golden West Literary Agency

Copyright © 2012 by Golden West Literary Agency.

Brother of the Cheyennes first appeared as a six-part serial in *Argosy* (3/17/34–4/21/34). Copyright © 1934 by the Frank A. Munsey Company. Copyright © renewed 1961 by the Estate of Frederick Faust. Copyright © 2012 by Golden West Literary Agency for restored material. The name Max Brand® is a registered trademark with the United States Patent and Trademark Office and cannot be used for any purpose without express written permission.

Skyhorse Publishing books may be purchased in bulk at special discounts for sales promotion, corporate gifts, fund-raising, or educational purposes. Special editions can also be created to specifications. For details, contact the Special Sales Department, Skyhorse Publishing, 307 West 36th Street, 11th Floor, New York, NY 10018 or info@skyhorsepublishing.com.

Skyhorse® and Skyhorse Publishing® are registered trademarks of Skyhorse Publishing, Inc.®, a Delaware corporation.

Visit our website at www.skyhorsepublishing.com.

10 9 8 7 6 5 4 3 2 1

Library of Congress Cataloging-in-Publication Data is available on file.

ISBN: 978-1-62636-064-8

Printed in the United States of America

Publisher's Note

Brother of the Cheyennes is the second book of the Rusty Sabin trilogy, which begins with *The White Indian* (available now from Skyhorse Publishing). The third installment, *The Sacred Valley*, will be published by Skyhorse Publishing in 2014.

BROTHER OF THE CHEYENNES

Chapter One

To Bill Tenney, strength was more than virtue, and Bill Tenney was strong. He had never ridden at a buffalo hunt; he had never shot at an antelope; he had never faced war-like Indians. Hence he could not be called a good plainsman, but he carried as sure a rifle as ever was brought out of Kentucky, and in a rough-and-tumble he was perfectly at home, particularly when knives came out.

He looked like a timber wolf—lean in the hips, heavy and somewhat bent in the shoulders, big-headed, and with a long, narrow muzzle. Behind his thin lips one could almost count the teeth, and his hollow cheeks made it hard to imagine the over-laid and intertangled masses of strength that were beneath his clothes. His nature, also, was very like that of a wolf. He was a skulker who bided his time, but when he struck, the blow was remembered.

He was an idler and a prowling thief, with twenty pounds of stolen gold dust and little nuggets in his money belt. The weight of it, pressing on his abdomen, assured him quietly and constantly that he was a man of mark. The trouble was that he had been marked by others, when he purloined that gold from the little trading post down the Tulmac River, and since he knew these plainsmen were very patient on the trail, he was afraid that the pursuit might follow him, even up here to Fort Marston, at the head of steamboat navigation on the Tulmac.

Tenney's original intention was to fade out into the Great Plains. Had he done so, he would have entered obscurity and safety at once. But even a wolf may be dangerously curious, and it was curiosity that involved Bill Tenney in all the danger that followed.

The whole town was equally curious, for that matter, and, from the fort, all the soldiers except a few sentinels had come down to the dock. The military stood somewhat apart, with Major Arthur Marston looming above them on a dancing black horse. The major knew how to set himself off in his best uniform, and whenever his horse stopped dancing it could be secretly encouraged with a spur prick in the tenderness of the flank. Apart from the soldiery, the rest of the crowd offered a picture stranger and more mixed than one could have found in an Oriental bazaar. There were the ordinary townsmen—saloonkeepers, professional gamblers, and shop owners; there were trappers and traders in deerskins; there were at least a score of Indians, most of them muffled in blankets, and nearly all of them highly decorated with paint, in honor of the day. For they, like the rest—like Bill Tenney—were expecting the arrival of the good ship *Minnie P. Larsen*, with the man known as Red Hawk, and his White Horse, on board. That father of Red Hawk, Wind Walker—he who had been the bane of so many of the Cheyennes—would also be on the steamboat.

For a week, the *Minnie P. Larsen* had been sticking her nose into mud banks, not far down the stream, and horsemen had brought to the fort long before this day full news of her cargo and passengers. The tidings had gone out over the plains, and that was why the Indians were there. If the *Minnie P. Larsen* had taken a few more days, the red men, at least, would have been present by hundreds, to await her arrival. For White Horse was one of those half legendary figures that had been talked about, during the last few years, at every trading post and every campfire.

With the story of the famous white stallion there was linked the tale of Rusty Sabin, the red-haired white man who, as a boy, had been carried off and raised among the Cheyennes until, under the tribal name of Red Hawk, he had trailed and literally walked down White Horse. The story of Red Hawk did not end there, but went on to a far stranger climax in which, as the champion of the Cheyennes, he had taken the war trail against the great enemy of the tribe. That enemy was Marshall Sabin, but Red Hawk's plans were frustrated when he discovered, as they struggled together, that they were father and son.

It was not such an entirely unique tale. All the elements of it had appeared many times before on the plains, but never had they been gathered together so compactly. And that was why a brief, deep shout of excitement broke from the crowd when the twin smokestacks of the *Minnie P. Larsen* appeared from behind the bend, streaming a double cloud of black.

She steamed through the current rapidly, until she reached the narrows just below the dock of Fort Marston. Here the compacted waters went at her with a rush, and threw high furrows off her bows, and, with the impact of the river and the redoubled labor of the engines, the *Minnie P. Larsen* trembled until the great gilded letters of her name shook into flame.

This slowing of the approach gave the crowd a chance to pick out on the low forward deck of the river boat the shining figure of White Horse, which had been brought from its quarters in anticipation of landing. When he saw that form of brightness, Bill Tenney jumped up from the stump on which he had been sitting and stared, his wolfish head thrust out before him. A young fellow beside him could hardly keep from dancing, so great was his excitement, but Bill Tenney was silent and motionless, because of the very intensity of his emotion.

Something like a voice rose up in him, and he fixed his soul with a determination to have that horse for his own. Once that beauty was his, he might laugh at all dangers of pursuit. He would be as free on the surface of the earth as a hawk is free to be the pirate of the air.

The youngster beside him was saying: "That's Red Hawk . . . that's Rusty Sabin. That's the medicine man of the Cheyennes, all right. The redhead with the long hair blowing. That one at the head of White Horse. Look there! You can see his hand on the mane of White Horse."

Not a very big or imposing figure, that of Rusty Sabin, beside the magnificence of the horse. Bill Tenney's nostrils quivered as he looked. If Tenney were a wolf, yonder man was little better than a coyote. The battle, felt Tenney, was already more than half won, and his great hand was already reaching for the bridle.

The chatter of the youth beside him drew his attention to other particulars of the picture. About White Horse, besides Red Hawk, there were four other figures. The huge man—that must be Rusty's father, the scourge of the Cheyennes. Yes, and now two crop-headed Indians close to Tenney began to talk rapidly, stretching out their arms and pointing.

"Those are Pawnees," said Tenney's companion of the moment. "Dog-gone' glad they are to see Marshall Sabin. He's the man who the Cheyennes call Wind Walker. A mighty lot of Cheyenne hair the Pawnees have raised, with Wind Walker to lead 'em. But look at them Cheyennes, yonder . . . them with the long hair. They're happy, too."

"Seems like I've heard the Cheyenne hunting grounds are a long sight north of here," said Tenney.

"Yeah. But around here the Cheyennes are friends of these Comanches. They're always visitin' back and forth. Them are Cheyennes, all right. You could pretty nigh pick 'em out by the size of 'em. Nothin' bigger grows on the plains, except the Osages. And they're all legs."

"If they are Cheyennes," said Bill Tenney, "what's that one saying? The one that's blowing puffs of smoke to the ground and the sky, and is now holding out his pipe in front of him."

"I dunno much of the Cheyenne gabble," said the other. "Wait a minute! I can make out a bit. That Injun is askin' Sweet Medicine . . . which is the name of the boss Great Spirit of the Cheyennes . . . to bring Red Hawk safe and sound out of the medicine boat of the white men, and lead him back to the tribe. This here Red Hawk . . . this here Rusty Sabin . . . he's a big medicine man among the Cheyennes, you know."

"Medicine man? How come?" asked Tenney.

For he was eager to pick up every crumb of information. He could not tell what would and what would not be useful later in the stealing of White Horse, upon which his heart was fixed.

"I dunno," said the excited youngster. "But the Cheyennes figger that Sweet Medicine will make the wind blow and the rain fall however Red Hawk asks him to."

"Who are the other three, standing together, near the two Sabins?" asked Tenney.

"That must be the Lester family. The news is that Rusty is bringin' the Lesters south with him, here, because old man Lester ain't so strong in the lungs. That must be him . . . the skinny-lookin' *hombre*. That's old lady Lester, hangin' onto him. And that's the girl. I reckon that's Rusty's girl. Yeah, you can see she's a kind of beauty, by the way she holds her head. Look at a lucky *hombre* like Rusty Sabin, that's got the finest horse and the prettiest gal on the whole plains."

"Married?" said Tenney.

"Not as I know of."

"What a gent has he can always lose," said Tenney through his teeth.

In so speaking, he was a prophet.

As the steamer came slowly closer, against the pressure of the swift yellow run of the water, a number of men put off from the bank in canoes, to paddle as far as the edge of the slack water, inshore, and so gain a near view of the steamer and its passengers.

Bill Tenney had no canoe of his own, but he promptly borrowed the first one at hand. Bill Tenney had never been one to see any harm in borrowing.

When he reached the edge of the shallow slack water, he could see the people crowded on the forward deck almost as clearly as though he were aboard the ship. Turning the canoe, it was easy for him to keep pace with the laboring steamer. He could see the huddled groups of emigrants from the East, now staring with frightened eyes at Fort Marston, which to them was the portal of the great and naked West. No doubt they were already wishing themselves back on their rocky New England farms. But these and the traders and plainsmen, who could be distinguished by their clothes, were nothing to Bill Tenney. His entire attention was fixed upon the splendor of White Horse.

While the great mustang had run wild, he had been the king of the prairies. White men with companies of chosen horses, and whole tribes of Indians, had chased this famous stallion. But Rusty Sabin, single-handed, and on foot, had worn down the giant.

Bill Tenney looked again, with a more savage attention, at the owner. He saw a man scarcely in his middle twenties, his red hair blown by the wind, his face lean and brown, not even handsome. In a word, the fellow was hardly above middle height, and, although he was strongly made about the shoulders, the rest of him was decidedly slender. Small men, to be sure, have done many great things, even in the West, where measures are large, but Rusty Sabin had by no means the look of the hero and the conqueror. His expression was gentle, almost dreaming; his smile would have won the trust of children.

Bill Tenney's thin upper lip lifted in a sneer of contempt. No matter what Rusty Sabin's reputation—no matter what the legends about this Red Hawk of the Cheyennes—Bill Tenney was prepared to swear that the repute had been falsely gained. He was sure it must have been won by good fortune and easy chance.

As for Rusty Sabin's father—ah, that was quite another matter. That long-haired giant looked the full part of what he had proved himself to be, a king among men.

Bill Tenney had just reached this conclusion when trouble struck the *Minnie P. Larsen* and threw the first trick of the game into Tenney's hands.

Chapter Two

There was a snag in the swiftest part of the current. It was just large enough to reach the surface of the stream, and its presence was made known by the water that sprang into the air from the face of it, as though from the prow of a boat. The pilot of the *Minnie P. Larsen*, therefore, swung the head of the steamboat away from this danger. All should have gone well, except that the head of the boat was pushed over a little too far, and instantly the force of the current did the rest. It caught hold of the nose of the *Minnie P. Larsen* and swung it with a sudden thrust. The ship trembled, heeled enough to bring a yell from the crowd on deck, and then came broadside on against a hidden sandbar.

Bill Tenney could hear the groaning of the timbers. He saw the river boat heel far over, until almost the entire width of the deck was visible. The top layers of a big pile of cases spilled over the rail into the water. People fell and skidded, yelling. But Bill Tenney's eyes were for White Horse alone. He saw the stallion flung, staggering, regain its footing with cat-like speed, and, to avoid crashing headlong into the railing, the horse leaped right over the side of the boat and into the boil and sweep of the swiftest current.

Then, out of the wild outcry on the ship, Tenney heard one mastering voice of agony. He saw Rusty Sabin dive over the side after his horse. They were lost, horse and man, and Tenney knew it.

The people on the *Minnie P. Larsen* knew the same thing, and acted on it, for when Rusty's father tried to lunge after his son, Tenney saw several men fling themselves on the giant and hold him back. He was lost under a twisting heap of humanity, still struggling.

What about those expert canoe men along the shore? What would they do? Well, they knew too perfectly the force of that current and the numbers of sharp-toothed snags that would shear like knives through the paper-thin birch bark. They kept to the edge of the slack, shouting to one another, paddling hard to see the disaster, but not to intervene in it.

Then Tenney saw the head of White Horse break above the surface of the churning water, far down the stream. It was as bright as a piece of wet satin. He saw the red flare of the nostrils, and with bewilderment, with a mighty leaping of his heart, he noted that the ears were pricked forward.

No fear was in the great horse. Heading upstream, fighting with all his might, he was striving valiantly to work to the edge of the current and gain the slack. Perhaps courage came to him from the sight of his master, who appeared for a moment above the surface nearby. But the swift, rolling water would soon have them both under. They were gone, all at once, and White Horse, the animal that might have given wings to Tenney's savage ambitions, would surely be battered—stifled—drowned.

There was as much evil in Tenney, already born or darkly breeding, as one could expect to find in a man, but there was a strain of courage in him, also, like the flash of steel in thick night. He drew in his breath with a groan, flashed the blade of his paddle, and shot his canoe right out into the tumult of the stream.

What did he think to do, that thief in fact, that murderer in the making? Well, there was no room in him for thought, but only for emotion. By that paddle stroke he had thrust himself out of the audience and onto the stage of a tragedy, and a certain greatness of heart in him matched the danger of the moment and its bigness. The river had three lives in its grasp, and he alone could save himself and the others by skill and strength and lucky chance.

Certainly in Tenney's mind there was little heed for the man; it was for White Horse that he drove the canoe, kneeling in the bottom, amidships, while the little craft staggered and pitched. He steadied it with speed, as he put his might into the long handle of the paddle.

He gained rapidly, of course. Man and horse were blotted out before him, then they appeared again. The horse was not far away. The man was a little closer. And then Tenney saw, out of the blindness of desire that filled him, that he had no means of effecting a rescue. He had flung himself madly into the conflict, like a man who is incapable of swimming but who goes to the rescue of a drowning soul. For how could he reach a hand to the horse and still manage the canoe?

A snag, like the pointed nose of a shark, lifted out of the water just before him. He veered past that point, which would have spitted his canoe like a spear. And now he saw that Rusty Sabin, his hair floating dark red on the water, had reached the stallion and was holding to it by the mane. The only effect was to cause the pair to whirl slowly and to shift farther out toward the center of the river.

There are things to be dreaded more than death. The loss of that which is dear to us is far more terrible. Vaguely Bill Tenney realized this as he shot the canoe onward, still making his endeavor after he had lost the hope of making the rescue. But if he were to die, it was somehow better to die there, near the man and the horse. Men talk of hell for the wicked, but White Horse and Rusty Sabin, brave, gentle, merciful—might they not draw after them one companion into a brighter afterlife of hope?

That, too, was in Tenney's brain, but more than all else, the blind persistence of his first impulse—to do something, somehow.

He was coming down too fast. In another instant he would be beside them. So he backed water strongly, and the riffle that followed threw a heavy wave into the boat.

The desperately set face of Rusty Sabin showed above the water. As the canoe swirled in the stream, Sabin's hand gripped its rear. His other hand gripped the mane of the stallion. And suddenly Bill Tenney found that he was indeed linked to the pair. An indivisible trio, they would now live or die together.

All that can be said is that he was not afraid. As he felt the pull of the weight behind him, he could understand that behind the gentle, dreaming look of the fellow he had marked on the deck of the ship there was that mysterious power that had enabled him to become great in the eyes of both red men and white. He was a white Indian, into which the strength of the two races had been breathed.

Big Bill Tenney felt this, and then all thought, all feeling went out of him as he bent his efforts toward pointing the nose of the canoe up the stream. Body, brain, and spirit, he turned himself into a machine of vast labor.

In the might of his grasp, the strong ash paddle became a supple thing. He wanted an oar of iron for such work as this. The pull of every stroke sent a numb tingling up shoulder and neck and into the base of his brain. The shore grew hazy; the other canoes that were racing down through the slack water were blurred before his eyes.

They were shooting blindly down the stream. The first snag that lay in their path would be the end of them. He kept uttering one word, as the breath gushed from his body: "God . . . God . . . God . . . God!" Over and over, not knowing what he was saying.

He forgot what was behind him. He forgot the purpose for which he was striving, except that he had to edge the bobbing, swaying, ducking point of his canoe farther and farther toward the edge of the sweeping current, and closer to the slack. There is a divinity of labor; a blind god. For his worship men need use only the power of the body. And in that black ecstasy Bill Tenney fought on.

They reached the bend. The water foamed and shouted more heavily than before; its rushing noises seemed to be streaming through Bill Tenney's soul. The spray whipped his hot face. His shirt at the armpits and down the breast had split open from the force of his mighty effort.

He could hear voices, thin as the rays of starlight, but they gave him no hope. The shore was blotted out from him. A force pushed behind his eyes, making them bulge out, and a constant strain drew back the corners of his mouth and made his face hideous.

Then a thin arm grasped his shoulders and froze his arms to his sides. The force of that grasp bit into his hard muscles. He was drawn suddenly forward in the canoe, before he realized that a line had been flung over him.

He gripped the sides of the canoe. Before him, he saw the length of the braided rawhide, trembling and swaying. Little by little, as his eyes cleared, he was aware that he had so far succeeded in his efforts as to bring the canoe close to the verge of the strong current, and now, where the current narrowly rounded the bend, the men on shore had managed to wade far into the slack water and make a successful cast with the lariat.

After that, his brain cleared rapidly. He saw the crowd on the shore gathering to a greater size. He heard their cheering. Men were galloping their horses down from Fort Marston.

Hell, said Bill Tenney to himself. *Looks like I been a damn' hero or something.* He wanted to laugh in derision.

Looking back, he saw the head of White Horse above water as he was being towed in toward safety. Rusty Sabin's hand was white with the force of its grip, on the upper edge of the canoe; the other hand still clutched the mane of the stallion.

And then it was all over. Even Bill Tenney's strength was gone, so that he could hardly get out of the canoe and stand erect on the shore. The labor had been with his arms, and yet his knees were shaking.

Men came swarming around him. Their eyes were big. Their lips were smiling. They looked on Bill Tenney with a sudden bright love. For in spite of our envies, our hates, our malice, our greed, our cruel self-seeking, when one man serves another and puts his own life in danger, the whole world of men become brothers.

Tenney suppressed the sneer that kept trying to work onto his lips. These men felt that he had wanted to be a hero; they could not know that he had simply wanted to steal a horse. Yes, and he would have it yet.

Burnished by the sun to blazing silver, the great stallion stood on the shore, his head bent low down, for his master's grasp was still in his mane. And Rusty Sabin's other hand was fixed on the stern of the canoe.

The man was senseless, Tenney saw with a peculiar interest, but the grip of the hands that had saved White Horse was still strong, like the locked jaws of a bulldog. They had to be worked free gradually. Then Rusty Sabin's body lay inert on the ground.

Chapter Three

O ut of the crowd there came forward those two big Cheyennes who had been pointed out to Bill Tenney on the bank by the dock. Other men were bending over the prostrate, senseless body of Rusty Sabin, but the two Indians brushed past them. One of them was a monster who was naked to the waist, and clad only in moccasins and deerskin leggings. Bigger than Tenney, he suddenly lifted young Sabin in his arms. Under that burden the immense muscles of the Cheyenne's arms and shoulders stood out like cast bronze. He was a heroic figure.

The burden-bearer began to speak in a voice that paused, from time to time, filled with emotion. A white man near Tenney translated the speech, softly, not for the sake of others but to impress the words on his own mind, and Tenney never forgot the meaning of the phrases, a kind of prayer.

"Sweet Medicine, all-seeing spirit . . . what are you doing on the other side of the mountains? Lift your head and see what has happened. This is where he lies. Here is Red Hawk . . . his body cold against my breast. Give him back to us, Sweet Medicine. Is he not the son of your spirit?"

Before the last phrase had ended, Rusty Sabin—Red Hawk— stirred in the mighty arms that supported him. Instantly he was lowered to the ground, and there he stood erect on his feet, though wavering. With one hand he grasped the wet mane of White Horse, and the stallion suddenly lifted his head and neighed with a sound like that of a dozen trumpets, all his sleek, shining body trembling with the effort.

The sound of that neigh carried Bill Tenney away like a strong wind. It seemed to bear him off from danger. In a moment he could feel himself swept over effortless leagues. That was what the great stallion could do.

The effect of the neighing, also, was to lift Rusty Sabin's head. He shook back the hair from his face and looked about him wildly for an instant. Then he saw Tenney, and came straight up to him. Tenney noticed that White Horse followed like a dog, high above the head of his master, staring into the face of the stranger. Ah, for the time when that stallion would follow Bill Tenney in like manner, and look upon all other men with such eyes.

The two big Cheyennes stood a little back of Rusty Sabin. By their manner, it was plain that they considered that another miracle had been performed and that Sweet Medicine, their Great Spirit, had actually interposed to call his favorite back from death. They stared with great eyes on the white man called Red Hawk. And their bearing gave Bill Tenney clearly to understand that the stealing of White Horse from such a man would be a most difficult feat. Here were men ready to die for Red Hawk— and these Cheyennes seemed men indeed.

But Rusty Sabin himself, as he stood before Tenney, suddenly lifted his hand. He advanced one foot, and stamped with it lightly on the ground. His face was pale. Water still dripped down his body. But his eyes were kindling and speech was apparent in him before it reached his lips.

He uttered first some phrases in a guttural tongue that Bill Tenney could not understand. Then he appeared to recollect himself. When he spoke again, it was as though he translated his thoughts into a foreign tongue. Yet he was speaking English.

"I was lost, and the Underwater People had laid their hands surely upon me," he said, referring to his Cheyenne religious beliefs. "White Horse runs faster than the wind. He is strong as the mountain goats that leap among the high places. When he leaps into the rivers, they fly in white foam away from him. He beats the dry bed of the stream with his feet, and leaps up to the farther shore.

"But White Horse also felt the hands of the Underwater People. They were drawing him down. The blue sky and the golden sun spun around above us. Breath that is dear to the body of man began to fail us. And at that moment, where all other men feared, we saw one who feared not. He came . . . his canoe was like a winged bird that lives in the air, close to the river. It was like the water ouzel that sings where the spray flies. The sweep of his paddle was like the beating of a wing. He lived and laughed in the danger.

"He came to us. He gave us his hand. With a mighty strength, he drew us out of the water. The dear breath . . . the air that is life . . . he poured again through our nostrils. He gave back to us the blue sky, the wind, the flying clouds, the wide green earth, and the buffalos that herd upon it. For us, once more, the teepee shall be raised and the women bring wood to the fire. The pot seethes with tender tongues and back fat and strips of choice meat. The sacred smoke of the pipe again fills the lungs. The voices of the wise old men break upon the ear. The young men are singing. The drums still beat. The women are chanting. And the good warm sun falls on the face and the breast."

He paused in his half chanted recital. Then, taking a deep breath and straightening himself so that he seemed taller, and so that Bill Tenney lost a sense of his own advantage in inches, Rusty Sabin ended briefly, but in a voice that came from his heart: "Ah, my brother." He offered his right hand.

Bill Tenney was a trifle slow in answering that gesture. For one thing, the extravagant poetical words of the speech had bewildered him more than a little. For another thing, he felt vaguely that he was being approached in a ceremonial manner, and that, if he took the hand of Rusty Sabin, he was committing himself to a sacred pledge. Pledges and holy things meant very little in the life of Bill Tenney, yet he hesitated because of Rusty Sabin's blazing eyes.

He remembered, then, that he had wanted to steal this man's horse, and that, therefore, nothing could be more valuable to Tenney than to have Sabin's confidence. So he took the hand with a sudden gesture.

The grip that was returned to him was surprising. His own enormous strength could hardly brook that pressure. Madmen have a strength beyond their physique. Was this fellow a little touched in the brain? No, he was smiling now, and most calmly. The ecstasy seemed to have left him the moment that his hand closed over Bill Tenney's hand.

"I am very happy," said Rusty Sabin quietly. "In the world there are more men than there are wild ducks, even when the ducks fill the sky. But there are only a few friends."

With that, he held up one hand and slowly closed the fingers together. Bill Tenney had a queer feeling that his own soul lay within the grip.

There was another ceremony that followed, a ceremony that seemed, so far as Rusty Sabin was concerned, almost as important as the first, for now he turned to the two Cheyennes and introduced them to Tenney. Their names had no meaning for Bill Tenney. He merely knew that he was being presented, and from the scarred fronts of these men he could guess that they were men of considerable importance among the warriors of their tribe.

The body of the one who was naked to the waist showed the dim, silver gleaming of half a dozen great scars, besides those huge breast scars that told of his tribal initiation. The other, probably, was just as well adorned under his buckskin shirt. Each of them in turn took Bill Tenney's hand, in imitation of the white man's style, and pumped it ardently up and down several times, then took a long stride to the rear. This was important, also. For Tenney had a distinct feeling that he had been inducted into the friendship of the entire Cheyenne tribe.

Chapter Four

A great many other things had been happening since the *Minnie P. Larsen* had heeled over against the sandbank. Righting herself at once, with the full thrust of her engines driving her ahead, she had slid rapidly forward until her nose touched the dock. The strong hawsers then drew her in beside the floating platform that kept pace with the sudden changes in the height of the stream.

Even before the ship was made fast, several of the passengers were on the dock, but first of all sprang a huge man whose bulk seemed no weight to his lightness of foot.

Major Arthur Marston marked this man well. The major, though he was only in his early thirties, already had made for himself a considerable name. That name was perhaps better established in Washington than it was on the plains, because in the capital city the major had certain friends who had pulled vital strings for him. He had been able to secure federal backing for the erection of the fort that bore his own name, a compliment that was rarely paid to soldiers during their lives.

Besides, the man certainly had done some distinguished Indian fighting. The motto of Major Marston, when it came to Indian warfare, was: "Be thorough." He believed completely in the old adage that the only good Indians are the dead ones, and he lived up to his belief. Midnight attacks on Indian villages were his forte, and, like the Indians themselves, he counted all scalps, no matter of what origin.

If the hail of bullets that the major directed happened to strike down women or children, he expressed regret for the moment, but he was sure to include all the fallen in his list of *enemy killed.*

His troops hated him with all their hearts, but they respected him because he was always successful in whatever he set out to do.

The major was a fellow with a fine eye for a good military position, but he was even keener in spotting a pretty face in the distance. That was why he had picked out Maisry Lester, on the forward deck of the boat as it came in toward the dock. He had at hand good informants to name the principal members of that interesting group, and even before White Horse had plunged over the rail, the major spotted all five of the group of travelers to which Rusty Sabin belonged. He knew that it was Rusty who dived after the stallion. He knew, also, that it was Rusty's father who strove like a giant to follow his son, and was barely subdued by force of numbers and was thus prevented from making the leap.

But these things were of small account. What chiefly mattered to Major Marston was the agony of Maisry Lester. Her torment pleased Marston almost more than her beauty, because it showed that she could and would be true to her lover. That lover had been stolen away by the river. She would grieve heartily for a time, and then. . . . Well, the major, like all good strategists, was a fellow who was able to look far into the future. Already he could see himself sitting close to that brown, rosy loveliness and making it smile.

All this must be understood in order to interpret the perfect calm and mildness of Marston when he saw Marshall Sabin, as he leaped from the boat to the dock, suddenly pluck a cavalry trooper out of the saddle and drop the man on the ground, then leap into the empty saddle.

The major issued not a single order to apprehend the giant, but as Marshall Sabin, with set teeth, and with hair wind-blown over his shoulders, galloped his stolen horse furiously down the riverbank, Major Marston followed. The officer's long-striding black gelding quickly overtook Sabin, and a few of those who looked after the pair expected to see the major attack the horse thief. Instead, they saw the major ride straight on, for he was seeing on the river, toward the first bend of the stream, some very odd things indeed.

He was seeing both White Horse and Rusty Sabin as they were taken in tow by a canoeist who must have had the courage of a madman. He saw the other paddlers, too, as they streamed their canoes down the slack water in pursuit, but carefully avoided coming near to the boiling verge of the central current. He saw still other men, on foot and on horseback, gathered at the bend. Then he lost sight of all that was happening.

When he hove into view again, after his black had labored through a stretch of deep, soft sand, he saw Rusty Sabin, alive and on his feet, talking to his rescuer.

The major was not pleased. The charming scenes in which he had pictured himself and Maisry Lester, and in which he had been consoler, tempter, and lover, now vanished. He hated Rusty Sabin with a sudden, deep, quiet hate. The man had been about to lose his life, and now he was restored to the two possessions for which he was famous—the loveliest of girls, and the greatest horse on the prairies.

The major felt that he had been insulted. His own life and fame were made to appear empty and thin, compared with the wealth of this youth. In a world properly adjusted, thought the major, such things could not be, and an officer in the United States Army surely ought to take precedence in every way over mere civilians.

It may seem strange that the major should have burned with so much emotion about a man and a woman to neither of whom he had as yet spoken a word. But for years Marston had been master of all he surveyed, and few men can be given the power of a tyrant without becoming tyrannical.

His second thought was that since he could not directly supplant Rusty Sabin, he would at least use him as an entering wedge to make the girl's acquaintance. And so he came straight up to the group, flung himself out of the saddle, and confronted Bill Tenney's wolfish face. The man had a dangerously bright eye and a calculating look, but the major grasped his hand with a hearty force.

"As fine a thing as I ever saw," he said to Tenney. "A thing that ought to be written in brass. You'd be an honor to any race. You're worthy of a command, my friend. Tell me your name, because I want to remember it."

For an instant the thief steadied his bright eyes on those of the soldier. There was more to this officer than one could detect at the first glance, he decided.

"I'm Bill Tenney," he said then. "I didn't do so much. Things just . . . happened."

The major laughed this modesty aside, and next wrung the hand of Rusty Sabin.

"We've heard of you, Sabin," he said. "You and White Horse have ridden pretty far into our minds. If you'd passed out of the picture in the Tulmac, just now, it would have been a black day for the fort. Come on, my friends. You're going to sit at my table, and we'll celebrate. We don't have enough wine to drink it every day, but this is a special occasion."

Here Marshall Sabin came up, his borrowed horse panting and straining under the crushing weight of the huge man. Dismounting as actively as any youth, the man known as Wind Walker laid a hand on the shoulder of his son. Major Marston, watching closely, saw them look at one another with a wordless smile. And again savage jealousy entered the heart of the major. For this red-headed fellow—this younger Sabin—seemed to be surrounded by nothing except faith and affection. What a welcome would be awaiting him, for instance, when he eventually returned from the shadow of death to the Lester girl?

But the major knew how to keep his emotions out of his face. He seemed the most cheerful man in the world, as he headed the procession back toward the fort. And he insisted that Rusty, after his terrible ordeal in the water, should ride his black horse, since there was no saddle on the back of the white stallion. He insisted with such force that out of courtesy Rusty had to mount the good gelding.

White Horse followed beside him, showing a great deal of impatient and jealous anger, throwing his glorious head about, with flattened ears and open mouth, and sometimes threatening to attack the horse that dared to carry his master. Even White Horse loved this man.

The major took heed, and his cold hatred multiplied, even while his smile widened.

Richard Lester and his daughter met them first. They were riding borrowed horses, with troopers on either side of them. And the major kept his head high and his smile steady, although the hate and envy poisoned him. For the girl, as she came closer, dawned on his mind like a sun on a dark land. And when she threw out one hand in greeting to Rusty, she looked to Marston like a shining statue of victory.

Yet they all had the true frontier restraint. There was no embracing. She and Rusty barely touched hands. Their eyes did the rest. But that was enough to suggest to Marston that he was in the presence of a passion as great and enduring as it was quiet.

Yet, in this human world, all things are humanly possible. And so the major did not feel defeated. Rather, it was a challenge to his generalship. The battle would be hard, but victory would be all the sweeter if he could separate this pair. In the meantime, he was meeting the Lesters, father and daughter, and pressing his invitation upon them.

That was how it came about that for lunch, that day, in the major's own rooms at the fort, were gathered a thief, a white man who was Indian by rearing, the half-wild giant who was the white

Indian's father, a man named Lester, who was looking forward with a consumptive's hope to the blessings of a mild climate, his wife Martha, full of fear of the new land, and his daughter, Maisry Lester, looking half Indian herself in her dress of supple doeskin, her eyes never straying far from the man who had been brought back to her from death.

The major presided as the genial host, pouring his interest into the affairs of the strangers. Within his jurisdiction, under the very shadow of the fort, there was a big vacant cabin that he hoped the Lesters would occupy. And not far down the street, in the town, there was another place that would exactly suit the two Sabins. They could have it for a song. It was the very place for Rusty to set up his forge, since it appeared that he was a well-qualified blacksmith.

"A most interesting occupation," said the major. "I respect craftsmen with skilled hands. And as a matter of fact, there is not a single real blacksmith in Fort Marston. Every hour of your time will be filled, from the start."

Everyone was charmed by the major's cordiality. His generosity amazed and delighted them. Soldiers were not always popular figures on the plains, but the major seemed a delightful exception. And amongst them who could know that the only face at which he never glanced, that day, was the only one of which he was really thinking each moment?

His smile was turned mostly toward the stern, reserved face of the older Sabin, or toward Rusty, who, when the great platter of venison was placed on the table, absently helped himself to a large joint, holding it with his left hand and in his right using a knife to slice off large bites. Manners of this sort the major had seen among the Indians—even among some of the wildest of the trappers and hunters—but never before at his own table. He pretended to make himself oblivious to it, but he took keen heed of the embarrassment that almost stifled Mrs. Lester, and of Maisry's crimson face when Rusty licked the meat juices from his fingers as he ended this part of his repast. But the white Indian seemed totally unaware of the critical looks directed at him.

When the wine was passed, Rusty took his glass in both hands, smelled it cautiously, tasted it, and put it down in haste. His face, at the same time, retained its Indian gravity. There was only a slight twitching at the corners of his mouth to indicate how repellent he found the sourness of that good claret.

And the major rejoiced. By little things are great results achieved. Bad table manners and barbarous ignorance of civilized foods may seem a small handicap. But with these and similar advantages, he felt that he could go a great distance on his chosen way.

He drank, in the meantime, to all of his guests. He made a cheerful little speech to give them an even warmer welcome, so much so that Bill Tenney, the thief, began to lose all suspicion of this man. Bill Tenney began to feel that he could spread his elbows at the board, and he began to believe that he could not possibly overstay his welcome in Fort Marston. He began to tell himself that no matter how much time he needed to make his preparations for the stealing of White Horse, that time would be at his disposal.

Chapter Five

To Rusty Sabin, the first days in Fort Marston were a whirl of confused excitement. He tried not to think of that time when, as Red Hawk, he had walked like a chief among the great Cheyenne tribe. It was in the world of the whites that he lived, now. That world was one of labor, and every moment of his day was taken up with his work in the blacksmith shop. He had opened it where the major had suggested. Behind the shop there were two rooms, one for himself and one for his father. His father, Marshall Sabin—Wind Walker, to all the Indians of the plains—spent his time as one lost in thought, rarely speaking except when one of the visiting Pawnees came to see him, and sat cross-legged on the floor of his room. It was Rusty who did the cooking during the day, washing the soot and grime of iron dust from his hands before he attended to the food.

Up the street, huddled close to the thick wall of the fort, was the big cabin that the major had turned over to the Lesters. But Rusty had little time even for the girl he loved, the pain of work so starved and burned and exhausted him. It was the gold he had brought from the Sacred Valley of Sweet Medicine that paid the way of the Lesters. It was that gold that furnished the cabin and bought the food they ate, but he did not begrudge that.

His father said to him, in one of his rare moments of speech: "Rusty, you have enough gold to make you quite a well-to-do man. Why do you leave it all in the hands of the Lesters? Richard Lester is a good man. I know that. And I know that someday you'll marry the daughter of the family. But oughtn't you to keep your money in your own hands?"

Rusty looked up, considering. "There is blood on it, Father," he said at last. "Two men died because of it. White men can use it . . . but not Cheyennes, because it was taken out of the Sacred Valley."

"White men? You are a white man, Rusty," said Wind Walker.

"Yes . . . yes," answered Rusty. "I am your blood and my mother's blood, and that makes me white. But all the Cheyenne days and nights are in me. You white men have a god who died on a cross. He never comes back to you. But I have Sweet Medicine. He is the god of my tribe. He gave me the sacred arrow. I have seen him twice . . . in the shape of an owl. That is why I am a Cheyenne, Father."

To this speech the father was about to make an answer, but suddenly he closed his lips and said nothing. For he knew that the long years his son had spent among the Indians could not be undone in a moment. Besides, Rusty now pulled up, by the thin horse hair string that supported it about his neck, the little green scarab that his dead mother had once worn in her hair. And the sight of it so moved Marshall Sabin that speech would not have been easy. He could not even think of that scarab without remembering that day when Rusty, as the champion of the Cheyennes, had rushed against him, and how the father had been saved from murdering his own flesh and blood only because he recognized the green scarab that hung from the youth's throat. So Marshall Sabin was silent.

Only after a moment, when the terrible vision had died out of his eyes, was he able to say: "Money makes trouble, Rusty. Money is a poison finer than thin air. Be careful."

Once every day Rusty used to give himself a sight of Maisry Lester. She would stand close to him, sometimes, holding up her face, her eyes melting with happy nearness, and sometimes she would touch him with her hand. But he could not understand this gesture, for, as he had told his father, the greatest part of his spirit was that of an Indian, and Indians rarely give caresses. Yet when he saw her, he wanted to lay down at her feet bleeding carcasses of venison and thick-rooted buffalo tongues, and raw, heavy pelts from newly killed game.

Most of his time was spent in the blacksmith shop, because there was much work to do. His long apprenticeship in the shop of a brutal but skilful mechanic had made him a master workman, and all of his strength and ingenuity were repeatedly taxed by the jobs that were given him. For caravans were constantly outfitting at Fort Marston, for the long trip across the plains, and although those inland voyagers were handy men with all sorts of tools, there were certain things that could only be done by an expert. Long iron couplings had to be welded together; tires had to be shrunk on wheels; and a thousand other metal details had to be passed through the hands of a competent workman like Rusty Sabin.

The result was that Rusty made good money, but the sad part of it was that he could not keep the cash. He was as free-handed as an Indian, and Indians are generous because they attach no value to possessions. Those two big Cheyennes, Broken Arrow and Little Porcupine, who had been the first to lift him from the edge of the water on that day when he first came to Fort Marston, were still waiting around, and their very patent hope was that sometime their great medicine man, Red Hawk, would return to their tribe. Morning or afternoon, therefore, they would come into the blacksmith shop or stand about for a time in the acrid, swirling clouds of smoke, with their heads deeply muffled in their long buffalo robes. For they did not wish their faces to be seen in this shameful scene where all men could behold a famous brave and worker of magic, like Rusty, laboring more diligently than the commonest squaw. Every day, they came and stood by, watching somberly. Every day, one or the other of them would say: "Father, have we come to the time of our return?"

And when Rusty would shake his head and bid them go on without him, they would silently stretch out their hands, and he would give them money. Then they would go down the street, with the money gripped in hands that were extended before them, as though they were holding live coals. They had no idea of values, and of course they were plundered right and left. Sometimes they would come back again, during the day, for more money, and Rusty never refused them.

They felt no gratitude for these gifts. Their reasoning was simple and effective; Rusty, who they thought of only as Red Hawk, was the favored son of the Great Spirit, Sweet Medicine. Upon Rusty, therefore, Sweet Medicine would continue to shower favors. It was only right that Rusty should divide his spoils with the members of his foster tribe. Broken Arrow and Little Porcupine belonged to the tribe. Therefore, why should they not take Rusty's gifts?

They thanked him no more than a child thanks its parents for their care. Instead of feeling gratitude, they felt merely a blind love, such as children know for a parent. In the meantime, they and the other beggars in the town kept Rusty's pockets empty. Sometimes he did not even have cash enough on hand to buy food for himself and his father, who still spent his time in that stone-like, meditative trance.

The blind giving of money to Indians as huge and as powerful as that pair, Broken Arrow and Little Porcupine, was not at all safe, in a town where whiskey could be bought.

A terrific furor broke out one afternoon, down the street, and the word was passed through the open door of Rusty's shop that Broken Arrow and Little Porcupine had gone on the warpath. They had cleared the other patrons out of a saloon, and were now holding high revel inside, defying the entire town.

Rusty Sabin went there in haste, empty-handed, angry. He was hardly noticed by the crowd that filled the street. The people of

Fort Marston had been intensely curious about Rusty when he first arrived, but, when he fitted himself quietly into the part of the town blacksmith, their curiosity died out. No longer was there about him that wild splendor of bearing of old. He had neither the size nor the clothes of the usual frontier hero, and he was quickly being forgotten.

Attention at this moment was too thoroughly fixed on the commotion inside the saloon, from which rang the yelling and whooping of the happy Cheyennes, with the crashing of glassware thrown in, now and then. In addition, a squad of cavalry had come clattering down from the fort, with sabers and carbines. They were forming up as though prepared to charge the saloon, but they were in no haste. The Indians, they knew, had plenty of guns, and, when it came to hand-to-hand fighting inside a room, a gigantic Cheyenne was apt to be on a par with the finest fighting men in the world. So there was a long-drawn moment of suspense, and in the midst of it Major Marston himself appeared on the scene.

It was just the sort of stage that, ordinarily, he would have liked—a chance to show off his generalship and courage, with plenty of spectators ready to applaud him. But this looked like bad business. A direct charge on the saloon was going to cost lives, and plenty of them. The only safe dodge would be to burn the Cheyennes out, and that, of course, would mean the total destruction of the saloon.

The major began to pull at his mustache with his gloved fingers, totally baffled. Every moment he was cursing his luck, because the townsmen were beginning to laugh. And it was just here that Rusty Sabin stepped briskly through the crowd and headed for the door of the saloon. Many voices shouted out to him a warning, but Major Marston said, loudly enough to be heard by those nearest to him: "The fellow's either drunk or a fool. This is on his own head!"

In fact, Rusty went to the door and knocked on it.

The answer was a rifle bullet that split the boards and whirred past his ear. Yet he did not even duck aside. He merely shouted several angry words in Cheyenne, and these were followed by a silence that amazed the crowd. The laughter died out. Men and women and children stood agape.

Presently the door was opened and the two mighty Cheyennes were vaguely to be seen, rifles in hand, inside the threshold. A few more harsh words from Rusty Sabin, and they stepped out. They gave into his hands their rifles.

A wild shout of astonishment broke from the watchers, and Major Marston swore softly under his breath, because he could see slender Maisry Lester, hurrying up to the verge of the crowd, where she could see this strange performance. Not only the rifles, but even their knives were surrendered by the two Cheyennes to Rusty. He took them without abating his severity. He spoke again, and the warriors hung their heads. Broken Arrow, that mighty man, dropped to one knee, and, lifting his muscular arms, he began to appeal in a broken voice. But Rusty turned grimly from this prayer.

"Where's the owner of this place?"

A fat fellow with a mist of beard on his face came waddling forward. "I'm Tom Wayling, and I own that saloon," he said.

"Go inside," said Rusty. "Find out the cost of the damage, and I shall pay it."

Tom Wayling stood on the threshold, looked over the ruin inside, and then shrugged his fat shoulders. "I'm still wearin' my hair on my head," he said, "and I reckon that's all the pay I want. Me putting red pepper into their drinks was kind of a fool joke, anyway, and I guess it had oughta cost me some money. You keep your coin, Sabin. If it wasn't for you, they'd've cleaned out the whole place. It might have been burned down."

This generous speech brought a good laugh from everyone except the two guilty Cheyennes. These, with their heads muffled in their robes and their shoulders stooped, went slowly up the street ahead of Rusty, who marched behind, beating them with stern words. In that instant the stature of the white Indian, in the eyes of the townsmen, increased by inches. He might be a blacksmith in Fort Marston forever, now, and never lose the reputation that he gained that moment.

Something else was happening as Rusty intervened to save Wayling's place. For behind the blacksmith shop big Bill Tenney had slipped quickly into the shed that held White Horse.

The great stallion, danger in his eyes, lifted his head and turned toward the stranger. Bill Tenney, bent on haste, with set teeth, snatched the saddle from the peg on the wall and flung it on the back of the big horse.

The next instant the saddle hit the ceiling and a white tornado rushed at Bill Tenney. He dodged and fled, and, as he reached the door, a striking forehoof grazed his back and hurled him headlong into the little corral outside. That would have been the last instant of Tenney's life had the force of the blow itself not saved him, sending him rolling over and over, right under the lowest bar of the fence.

As Tenney gained his feet again, staggering, White Horse was rushing up and down inside the fence, raging to get at the thief. But Tenney laughed, a gasp in his voice. As he saw the sun flashing on the satin coat of the famous horse, as he watched with awe the stallion's angry front, he did not feel that he had been defeated. He had merely been taught a lesson that he would profit by the next time.

And that was why Bill Tenney lingered on in Fort Marston until danger overtook him.

Chapter Six

That very night, sorrow found Rusty Sabin. He had finished his day's work and had gone to the rear of the cabin to clean up when his eye caught on a piece of paper that lay on the table that he himself had made. In the twilight, it lay like a spot of pale moonshine on the table, and he carried it curiously to the rear door before he could read it. It was his father's hand, and Marshall Sabin had written:

Dear Rusty:

I've got to go. The Cheyennes call you their father. The Pawnees give me the same name. I am going back to them.

I thought that I could find something to do here, but when I think of farming, my hands feel empty. The truth is that I have been too long on the plains. I want to sit in a teepee again and listen to the Pawnee talk. I want to listen to the braves again when they call me Wind Walker.

Many times, I shall be hungry to see you, but, if I remain here, I'm only a burden to you, and when you marry, you will have burdens enough.

One thing more I ought to tell you. Perhaps I'll be on the warpath once more with the Pawnees, before long, but I shall never lead them against the Cheyennes again. Be sure of that, and send that word to your own tribe.

Give my love to Maisry, and marry her soon, because you must remember that young girls—the best of them—have a new mind at least once a year.

We shall meet again. Forgive me for going without speaking to you face to face, but I was afraid that the resolve would go out of me if we talked together.

Affectionately,
Your Father

When Rusty had read this letter, he crushed the paper together between his hands. He had had two fathers in his life—Spotted Antelope, among the Cheyennes, who he had first shamed so terribly and then honored so greatly, and then his own white father. But Spotted Antelope was dead, and Marshall Sabin was gone now. And half of Rusty's world seemed suddenly to have shrunk away from him. He wanted to sit by the hearth and pour ashes on his head and cut off his hair and wail like a woman. Instead, he wrapped himself in a blanket and began to sway back and forth, for his grief was choking him.

When he looked up again, the thick of the night was around him. It made his breath harder to take. His heart seemed to fill his breast so that there was no space for air in his lungs.

He went out to the corral fence and called, softly, a single word. White Horse came like a glorious ghost through the starlight, whinnying in a voice no louder than that of his master. Through the perils of many a dangerous trail, the stallion had learned the soft note that answers human speech. When he saw Rusty's head, bowed on the top bar of the fence, the horse pulled the blanket away and snuffed at the long hair. He even nibbled at it, and then fled wildly across the corral.

Since he was not followed even by a rebuke, it began to be clear that the master was not bent on a game, so White Horse came stealthily back, lifted his head, and stared about him, pricking ears as keen as the ears of a wolf, and scenting the air. Since it seemed that no danger was near, he pressed his soft, damp muzzle against the side of Rusty's face and pushed impatiently up, trying to lift the fallen head. And at last, with a sigh, Rusty turned away from the corral, covered his head again, and left the place.

Even White Horse could give him no comfort. Even White Horse, calling eagerly after him, could not make him turn again, for he wanted to ease his heart. Therefore he went to the Lester house.

Music drifted out of it as he came near. When he came to the door of the big cabin, which was open to the warm airs of the night, he was able to see Major Marston playing a guitar; it was the major's voice that drawled through the melancholy Negro songs. The Lesters sat about enjoying the melody, Maisry with her head back and her eyes fixed on starry distances.

Rusty waited until one of the songs had ended. Then he stepped across the threshold, one hand raised in a silent greeting.

"Great heavens, an Indian!" cried Mrs. Lester.

"Hush, Martha. It's Rusty," said Richard Lester, jumping up from his chair.

Already he was a changed man. Color was coming back into his face, and brightness into his eyes. The mild Southwestern climate was giving his starved body a chance to regain strength.

"Rusty?" exclaimed Mrs. Lester. "Then why don't you say something? Rusty, what's the matter with you?"

"I think I understand," said the major maliciously. "Among the Indians, you know, a brave must not speak to his mother-in-law, if he can avoid it."

Rusty sat down against the wall, just inside the doorway. He sat cross-legged, his robe pulled in a close hood over his head, which was bowed. Instantly Maisry was on one knee beside him.

"What is it, Rusty?" she pleaded. "Tell me what's happened? Is it something to do with White Horse?"

"Has something gone wrong in the blacksmith shop?" asked the major carelessly.

Rusty, still without speaking, held out the letter from his father.

Maisry read it aloud, exclaiming in her soft voice, now and again.

"Back to the Pawnees?" cried Mrs. Lester, her face wrinkling in disgust. "Back to those thieves and murderers? What can the man be thinking of? Is the whole Sabin family more Indian than white, Rusty? Great heavens, will your own children have the same insane spirit?"

"The blood of adventure, you know," said Major Marston. Aside, he made a deprecatory gesture to Mrs. Lester.

She felt that this was support.

"Do sit on a chair, at least," she urged Rusty sharply. "You'll have to begin to learn civilized customs."

"Please be quiet for a moment, Mother!" broke in Maisry almost impatiently.

She sat down beside Rusty, found his hand, and clung to it. "Will you go out and walk with me, Rusty?" she asked gently. "If we walk a lot and talk a little, you may feel better. Or have you had supper? Will you let me bring you something?"

"Ah, Maisry," he said, "I am so full of grief that there is no room for food in me. My belly is crowded with grief, and my throat is choked with it. There is grief between my teeth, and the taste of it is on the roots of my tongue. He has gone away from me. My father has gone away, and my house is empty."

"It's a thing all boys have to outgrow," said the major calmly. But, at this, Richard Lester frowned and shook his head.

"But I may take you," said Rusty to Maisry, rising suddenly to his feet. "Come home with me, Maisry. Come!" He drew her to her feet.

"Go home with you?" said Mrs. Lester, almost screaming. "Go home with you? Without being married? Is the man crazy? You know we have to wait till a preacher comes to the town for the marriage. Richard, say something! Do something! Richard, are you just going to sit there?"

"Maisry will tell him," said Richard Lester, looking down at the floor and shaking his head again, in pain and confusion.

"I can't go, Rusty," said the girl to Rusty. "There has to be our marriage."

At this, he made a sudden gesture, and the robe slipped entirely away from his head, showing the grime of soot and iron dust on his face. It was almost as thick, in spots, as streaks of Indian paint.

"I have made the gifts. Your father has given you to me," he said. "When I take you to my lodge and lift you over the threshold, you are my wife, Maisry."

"Oh, heavens!" said Mrs. Lester. "Do you hear him, Richard? Major Marston, Major Marston, are such things permitted under your eye?"

"Never!" said the major emphatically. "I'll stop it in good time, my dear Missus Lester."

Maisry was saying, "You know, Rusty, we have different customs. There's a ring given, and a minister reads from a book, and we kneel down together. But when we stand up, we are man and wife."

"Kneel?" said Rusty. "Why should I kneel, except to Sweet Medicine?"

"I shall kneel, then, Rusty, when the time comes, and you shall stand," said Maisry patiently. "But to go with you now . . . I can't do that. I want to. And my heart aches because you have an empty house. But before the end of the week a minister will be here. He's coming up from the next trading post. And then we shall be married."

"Maisry you might take better advice than you'll find in your own silly, empty little head, before you start fixing your wedding day!" cried the mother.

The major here shrugged his shoulders, but he said nothing.

And Rusty, after staring at Maisry for a moment, said: "Well, is it true that a girl changes her mind once a year?"

"Other girls may change. I shall never change," said Maisry quietly.

"So?" answered Rusty. He took a breath, deeply and gently. He smiled a little. "Your mind and your heart, Maisry, will they never change?"

"Never," she told him.

From around his neck he took the thin braid of horsehair, with the little green scarab attached to it. "My mother wore it," said Rusty. "When she died fighting for me, the Cheyennes took it away. I have worn it ever since. It has turned bullets and knives away from me, while fighting. It is a great medicine. Look, now. I put it around your throat. Now the thing is close to your heart, and while it is there, it is I. If ever you wish to stop thinking of me, send it to me, and when I see the green beetle in my hand again, I shall know that your mind has changed, as my father says it will change."

She took the green beetle in the palm of her hand and kissed it reverently, solemnly.

"I shall never change," she said.

He remained for a moment close to the door, his eyes scanning her face, little by little. Then, raising his arm in a silent gesture of farewell, he stepped out into the darkness.

And in the house behind him, Mrs. Lester was weeping heavily.

"Indian! Nothing but his skin is white! Richard, you must stop it! Oh, Maisry, how can you think of marrying a savage? Major Marston, tell us what to do? Tell us what to do?"

The major was thinking hard of several things that might be done, but he doubted that they would bear telling.

Chapter Seven

Bill Tenney had a bruised shoulder and a bump over one eye, after he landed on the ground of the corral. But in his heart there was a spirit of quiet content, and a resolution. He had bought a powerful, cruel Spanish bit with which, he told himself, he would be able to control even the savage head of the stallion, for Rusty always rode White Horse with no more than a light hackamore. And as for pitching, if a horse is hobbled or sidelined it cannot buck efficiently.

The next time he tried his hand on White Horse, he would work with the utmost skill that his experience had taught him. Nothing would be left to chance. In fact, already he could almost feel between his knees the barrel of the great horse, sleeked over and quivering with strength, sweeping him across the prairies like a bird across the sky.

He took his confidence of victory with him to Tom Wayling's saloon, and stood in front of the mirror, which the Cheyennes had cracked, as he swallowed a glass or two of red-eye, slowly. He wanted to brood on the future. He wanted to call up the pictures of the things that he would do when he had White Horse under him. He could see camps in confusion, men mounting their ponies to pursue a raider, and the plunder and the plunderer borne swiftly away on the back of the stallion. He could see himself laughing at pursuit, toying with it. He could see himself overtaking his enemy as surely as a heaven-directed bolt of lightning.

These images, pleasant to the mind of wolfish Bill Tenney, kept a smile working in and around the corners of his mouth.

Sinister laughter flashed in his eyes, and dimmed again. Certainly nothing was farther from his mind than the thought of gray-headed Dikkon Saunders, from whose trading post down the Tulmac River he had stolen the twenty pounds of gold. Even when he heard the quiet voice saying—"There he is, boys."—it was a moment before Tenney realized.

Then, from the corner of his eye, he saw four men closing on him, among them gray-headed Dikkon Saunders himself.

Bill Tenney lifted his whiskey glass, poured the last of his drink down his throat as though totally oblivious of the danger around him, and then leaped for the window. He reached it, too, and would have bounded out into the open night in another instant, but the swinging butt of a rifle in Saunders's hands clicked against his skull and dropped him in a heap.

When his wits came back to him, there was no longer the pressure of a heavy money belt across his loins, and he was being marched up the street of the town by a pair of long-haired plainsmen, each of whom securely gripped one of his arms. Weaponless as he now was, he would have put up a fight against these fellows, beyond a doubt, but before him walked a third man, and two more strode at his back. Therefore he said nothing, attempted nothing. A trapped wolf may lie still, too wise to struggle, and Bill Tenney could do the same. A great many of the townsmen came out to look, and they saw Tenney, so recently a hero, now walking in the swinging lantern light, under guard, and bound for the fort that was also the prison.

Only one face meant anything to Tenney. That was the calm countenance of Rusty Sabin, who stared straight ahead and seemed to see nothing as Tenney was led past the blacksmith shop. And Tenney wanted to turn and curse the man's indifference; this man who he had saved from the river. However, he said nothing here. Neither did he speak when he got to the gate of the fort, where the soldiers took him over. There only Dikkon Saunders and one witness were admitted. They brought out irons, and fastened Bill Tenney's hands together. Then they led him into a guardroom, long and dreary and empty, except for two tables and some benches, all covered with carved initials.

Presently an orderly came into the room, leaving an inner door open, and through this Saunders was marched into the presence of Major Marston. Bill Tenney recognized the major, of course. He felt that he would have recognized a representative of the law and of the Army merely by the cold detestation that ran through his own vitals. He lifted his eyes, once, and looked long and searchingly into the major's face. Then he dropped his gaze to the floor. It was not often that Tenney stared people in the face. His eyes were a weapon to be used as such.

The major, his hands in his pockets so that the stiff skirts of his jacket flared straight out, walked up and down behind the desk on the raised dais, which added to his dignity of command. He gave Tenney only a casual observance at each of his turns.

"Charge?" he said.

"Robbery," said the sergeant.

"The fellow looks like a stealing coyote. No, more like a wolf," said the major. "I've seen him before. Pulling something out of the water, that time." He laughed as he said this. "Go on with the charge, Sergeant."

It was briefly rehearsed—how Bill Tenney had entered the trading post when only two men were there, backed them into a corner with his leveled rifle, and broken open the cash box. The money had been found again on his person. It was exhibited in the money belt.

The major picked up the belt, whistled as he felt the amount of the burden, tossed it down with a crash on the desk, and then continued his promenade, laughing a little. It pleased him to administer justice. He was delighted to be the only judge in the district, and these impromptu duties helped to fill out the measure of his self-importance.

Still chuckling, he said: "Only a mad wolf will steal by day-light. You should have known that, Tenney. Now you're going to be taken down where you'll cool off. We have some rooms down there beside the river that raise mold about as fast as the prairies grow grass in the spring. You're going to have a chance to enjoy a quiet rest down there. You're going to have a chance to think things over. I'll be thinking, too. I'll be deciding what to do with you. But before you're put into such a cool place, we'll warm you up. We'll give you the warmest shirt you ever wore in your life. We'll give you a red shirt, Tenney." Laughter stopped his speech again. His eyes were actually merry as they danced over Tenney. Then he said: "Take him out in the yard and give him the whip."

"How many strokes, sir?" said the sergeant.

"I don't know," said the major. "I'll have to see about that. Get a blacksnake, and bring in one of the teamsters."

They took Bill Tenney out into the central yard of the fort and tied him to a post. They stripped him naked to the waist, and tied him by the manacles that held his wrists. The post was so low that he had to bend over a bit, and that made the huge muscles in his back stand out. Those muscles sprang in ridges from the small of the back, and rippled away in rapidly undulating waves over the shoulders. The man did not seem naked somehow. He was clothed in his strength. And his long hair fell down over his face like a mask of darkness.

The teamster was a wide-jawed brute with the face of a frog—a hunchback with arms that were vastly long and powerful. He chewed tobacco, and spat a thin jet through his teeth between each of the whip strokes that he deliberately laid on the back of Bill Tenney. The teamster loved this work. First, as he slicked the blacksnake through the palm of his left hand, he said to the major: "You want blood, or no blood, Major?"

"Which hurts worst?" asked Major Marston.

"I dunno," said the teamster. "It's sort of a matter of what you want. I've seen mules that sure hated the flat whang of the whip and the welt it raised on 'em. And I've seen mules that don't mind a thump, but that rear and tear when the blood begins to trickle down. There's mules that I always keep a raw spot on, on each side of the tail. Once I get 'em raw, I keep 'em raw. Then, with just a little flicker of the lash, they try to climb out through their collars. And there's still others that I keep one big welt on, and when it comes times to make 'em scratch, I give 'em a little tap on the old welt, and they groan like they was human."

The teamster laughed. The major laughed, also.

"Try it plain. Try a few welts, first," said the major.

The teamster tried a few welts. They stood out red and round on the back of Tenney. First there was a white streak with blue edges. Then the white turned crimson and began to swell. The sound of these strokes was like the falling of a rod. Tenney did not stir. He got his hands on the top of the post, and gripped until the big muscles of his arms stood out and trembled. That was the only thing about him that moved.

Suddenly the major called out with a strange ring in his voice: "Blood! Blood, man! Tap the red, and let it run a while."

The teamster, without pausing in his swaying motions, spat yellow through his teeth and turned his wide, horrible grin over his shoulder toward the major. At the same time, the whip struck with a different sound; there was a smart popping, and instantly a trickle of red flowed down Bill Tenney's back. A shudder ran through him at the same time. And the major, marking this with a cheerful eye, shouted: "That's it! Let him have it, now. Let's see the red come out of him."

Every stroke of the whip sliced the flesh, and in a few moments Tenney's back was crimson. The red ran down over his trousers. But after the first slight movement, he did not stir.

The major kept drawing closer and closer, until a flicker of thin red drops flew off the end of the lash and streaked his face. At that, he leaped back with an oath. He pulled out a handkerchief and scrubbed at his face.

"All right!" he called finally. "Let up on him now. We'll just have his dirty back washed clean. Get some salt and water and pour a little vinegar into it. We'll clean the wounds the whip made, for him."

They brought the acrid solution, and mopped Tenney's back with it. As the torture struck into his flesh, the salt soaking in, the vinegar biting him, he permitted his shoulders to jerk upward, once. Then he remained still, even as he was freed from the post. His shirt was pulled over his head again, and dragged violently down over his tortured body.

He stood up straight and shook the long hair back from his face. His running sweat had clogged the hair in long, ugly locks. He was utterly colorless. At several paces, the sound of his breathing was audible. And his eyes rolled with a yellow fire as he stared at the major.

Major Marston laughed again as he stepped closer. "You don't like it, eh?" he said. "Having dreams of stabbing me in the back one night, are you? But I know how to turn wolves like you into dogs, and dogs into curs. And I make the curs crawl and lick the hand that beats 'em. Now take him away, and put him in the coolest and the deepest room you can find."

Chapter Eight

If Rusty Sabin's face had been empty when he saw Tenney as he was marched past, it was because Rusty was seeing before him, very clearly, a distant thing that meant more than the realities at hand. He was seeing duty, on which he would never turn his back.

Afterward, he went through the crowd and found his two Cheyennes, shoulder to shoulder. He laid his hand on the naked arm of Broken Arrow, and his fingers moved rapidly. There are few Indians who cannot read the sign language of the plains by touch, in the midst of darkness.

As Rusty left the spot, Broken Arrow and Little Porcupine did not follow him at once. It was some time before they appeared behind the blacksmith shop, and then they had with them three strong-bodied ponies.

Rusty stood in the starlight and made them a brief speech: "I lay in the river, and the Underwater People took hold on me and were pulling me down. Then my white brother came and drew me out. That was a thing that you saw. Also, you have seen him taken captive by his enemies. They have brought him into the fort. Therefore, we must follow him and bring him out again."

After this, there was a breath of silence in which the chill of fear could sink into the soul like the starlight into staring eyes. But finally Broken Arrow said: "The war chief of the white men is in the fort. His best warriors are around him. They have many guns and their eyes never close."

"Sweet Medicine shall help us," said Rusty Sabin confidently.

45

"Then we may go safely?" asked Broken Arrow.

"A man with fear in his heart is never safe," answered Rusty.

Little Porcupine had not spoken before. Now he said: "Where we were closed in the place of the firewater, we never should have come out alive except for Red Hawk. If he asks for our lives now, they are not ours . . . they belong to him."

"Go up to the gate of the fort," said Rusty. "You can look between the big bars. Perhaps you will see where they are taking my brother."

The two left him at once, and Rusty turned back into the blacksmith shop with a lighted lantern. The smell of the smoke reeked from the blackening walls. He picked up the fourteen-pound sledge whose handle was already well polished by his grasp as he swayed the heavy hammer. He glanced toward the bin that he had filled with discarded horseshoes. Then he spread out his hands and stared down at the palms, where the skin had grown thick.

He might be leaving this place and this life. If he managed to take Tenney from the fort, doubtless he would have to flee with him, and in that case there would be no return.

Writing was not easy for him, but he sat down and laboriously spelled out a letter.

> I go back to my people, perhaps. I go for a little time or for a long time. The Green Beetle will tell you every day that my heart remains with you. Farewell.

On the outside of the letter he wrote **Maisry**, and stuck the paper into a crack of the wall, where it would surely be seen by the first eye. It did not occur to him, at the moment, that people should be identified by two names instead of by one.

Afterward, he got his knife. It was eighteen inches long. He had forged it himself, of the finest steel, and while he was totally unskilled with rifle or pistol or the bows and arrows that had still been in use among the Cheyennes in the days of his boyhood, he was expert in the wielding of that long, heavy blade, whether thrown or used hand to hand. He looked down the blue, curving shimmer of the steel for a moment, now, and then freshened his grip on the handle.

He was still holding the knife when the two Cheyennes returned. Their faces, to an ordinary eye, would have been considered totally expressionless, but to the observance of Rusty's every feature of them bespoke excitement.

Little Porcupine said briefly: "They tied your white brother to a post and beat him like a dog, and the white war chief stood close by and laughed. They beat your brother till his back was red, and then they took him away. And the white war chief is still laughing."

Rusty closed his eyes. When he opened them again, a thin fingertip of light was running rapidly up and down the edge of his knife as it wavered slightly in the fierceness of his grip.

Together, they went all around the fort, walking quietly and apart. When men walk together, they all see the same things. When they go one by one, each man looks for himself.

When they had joined each other again, each gave his report, but not a single detail was useful to Rusty Sabin except that Little Porcupine had surely seen the war chief walking up and down behind an open window on the river side of the fort.

Rusty, looking wildly around him, found no inspiration in the dark of the night, so he sat down, cross-legged, jointed his pipe, filled it, sprinkled tinder from his pouch on top of the tobacco, and then kindled the smoke. He blew out puffs that were faintly visible in the starlight, and then he held up his hands, the pipe fixed upside down in one of them. He would hold up his arms in this manner until the ache of weariness turned them to lead and made them fall, unless, before that time, Sweet Medicine brought wisdom to his mind.

Broken Arrow whispered to his companion. "Be very still. He prays to Sweet Medicine."

Then, gradually, all the sounds from the village died out of Rusty's ears. He no longer heard the barking of the two dogs, one of them yipping in soprano and one howling a deep bass. A jangle of strings, and the sound of two men singing, also faded from his ears. The lights blurred and went out.

In the intensity of his concentration he felt himself swept far away, and once more he was before the great pillar at the mouth of the Sacred Valley of the Cheyennes, praying to the Great Spirit, Sweet Medicine. He thought of the wide, whispering wings of the owl that had flown over his head on that day, long ago. And it seemed to Rusty that the same whisper stole through his ears again.

Then, blindingly bright, he saw the face of the major, laughing. He had marked Major Marston long before this, on the outskirts of his attention, and he had not marked him with favor. The major's superior airs were perfectly patent. If Rusty paid no attention to them, it was because he chose to overlook those annoying mannerisms that always drew attention, subtly, from the rough manners of Rusty and to the major's gentility.

Above all, there had been the day when the major had walked into the blacksmith shop, accompanied by Maisry, and sneeringly remarked: "Well, there have to be some honest laborers in the world. Every man cannot work with his brain."

These words floated back into Rusty's recollection. And then he thought, also, of Tenney under the lash, his back flowing crimson.

Still the face of the major persisted before him. And suddenly Rusty's arms dropped.

"*Hai*," whispered Little Porcupine. "There is no answer?"

"There is the war chief of the whites," said Rusty. "That is the answer."

"Is the name of the man an answer to this prayer, my father?" asked Broken Arrow.

"It is the answer which was given to me," Rusty said briefly, as he stood up.

"What does it mean?"

"The Sky People," said Rusty sternly, "do not always speak out clearly. They give a sound, they give a vision, and wise men know its meaning."

"We wait for you to tell us, father," said Broken Arrow humbly. "Our minds are empty, but our hands belong to you."

Rusty began to pace up and down. His arms still ached at the shoulders. The darkness of his moment of prayer was gone. He could hear the singing, the barking of the dogs again. The slamming of a door not far off startled him.

What was the meaning of the thing he had seen? And still it persisted in his brain—the face of Major Marston, laughing!

He stopped short. "We are to go to him," he said.

Broken Arrow uttered an exclamation. "Go to him?" he said. "Break open the gate or leap over the wall? Father, if all the Cheyennes were gathered together here, it still would be a mighty day of work for them to do that thing. How shall we come to him?"

"By the open window, behind which you saw him walking," said Rusty.

"It is high up the wall," said Broken Arrow.

"We shall climb to the place," said Rusty. "A voice has spoken to me from the sky. Shall we not follow it, brothers?"

Chapter Nine

The wall, as it turned out, was high indeed, up to the window behind which the major still strolled back and forth, now and then singing a note or two from some Negro melody. But the face of the wall, for greater strength, sloped outward, toward the base, and the stones of which it was built were so huge and so roughly bound together that there were ten thousand small fingerholds and toeholds scattered across the face of it. Little Porcupine, when he had examined the wall, uttered a whispering laugh.

"See," he said. "Already Sweet Medicine is with us. He has given us a ladder and a path up the height."

It was not even necessary to strip away the moccasins so that the toes could get a better grip.

Little Porcupine was the first up the wall, and, grasping the sill of the window, he waited until the other two were beside him.

Inside, Rusty could see a big, comfortably furnished bedroom, with a fireplace built into one wall and a range of books along a shelf. When he looked at those books and considered the millions of words that must fill them, his heart shrank a little. A man who had read so much must surely have mastered some strong medicine—even something as strong, perhaps, as the power of the Sky People of the Cheyennes.

The major, contented by his thoughts, kept smiling as he walked. He kept his hands folded behind his back, most of the time, but occasionally he made a gesture as though snapping a whip before him. And once, as he did this, he actually laughed aloud. So that it was clear that he was remembering the flogging of big Bill Tenney. When Rusty was sure of this, a terrible rage blinded him. He shuddered so that he seemed about to fall, and the powerful arm of Broken Arrow steadied him in his place.

Then Rusty whispered in the ear of his companions: "I go first. Follow when I give the sign."

At this moment, the major was at the farther end of the room, about to turn. Before he had swung around, Rusty was standing inside the window, with his arms folded high on his breast. The major started and actually sprang back a pace, when he turned and saw this unexpected sight. Then he exclaimed: "The blacksmith, eh? Now, how the devil did you get there, Sabin?"

Rusty smiled in his turn, and almost without malice. "When a friend calls to a friend," he said, "the call must be answered."

"Am I your friend, Sabin?" asked the major, his eyes working over the blacksmith's still sooty face.

Rusty shrugged his shoulders at that apparent sneer. "My friend," he answered, "is now closed up in the fort. His back is raw . . . from the whip. I have come to talk about him."

"Ah. So he's your friend, is he? You shouldn't have friends among thieves, Sabin. You know what they say . . . 'birds of a feather flock together.' Eh?"

He laughed as he made his point, but Rusty answered. "He has given me my life. Shall I call the hand that saves me unclean?"

He made a gesture, as he said this, and the major's lip twitched as he saw the grime on the fingers.

"Some people like dirty hands as well as clean ones," remarked Marston. "What can you say to me about Bill Tenney?"

"He took the gold of another man," said Rusty. "Therefore he was tied to a post and flogged. What else will be done with him?"

"He may be flogged again," said the major. "I don't know. I haven't decided what to do with him, yet. There are too many thieves and scoundrels in this part of the world, and we must teach them lessons. I have to be the teacher . . . and I don't really mind the work. I may keep Tenney in irons, and send him down the river to the first prison. I don't know. I haven't decided what to do. Have you any ideas about it, Sabin?"

Curiosity and malice joined equally in his voice. "I will give you money . . . I will give you horses, if you set him free," Rusty answered.

"Buying him, are you?"

"Money buys all things from the white men," answered Rusty confidently.

"You'll give horses for him?"

"Yes."

"You'll give White Horse?"

At this, Rusty started violently and lifted his eyes toward the ceiling as if he might find the answer written there. Then he replied: "White Horse is not mine to give away. He stays with me because he loves me. How could I give him away, except to his old freedom?"

There was such obvious sincerity in this speech that it troubled the major. He had looked upon Rusty as a wild man—a freak—a strange creature of fortune. He saw now that there was something else in the man, and a profundity of goodness and justice that made his own soul seem both small and evil. And to a man of the major's pride and self-sufficiency, this discovery was merely an injection of poison. He had scorned and derided Rusty before; now he hated him with a whole and perfect hatred. For he understood now that Maisry saw in this man not merely a striking figure of the frontier—a romantic hero—but a man whose soul was of the true steel of integrity. If Rusty Sabin's manners were still, very often, those of a wild Indian, his spirit was both wise and brave.

Rusty had previously made the major feel the superiority of civilization over the barbaric life. Now he made sure that his only superiority was that of greater place and power. The major was not abashed by that discovery. He was simply offended. So he said: "You're willing to give away anything for Bill Tenney, who saved your life. You're willing to give everything except the things you care about. Well, Sabin, you may have bought off other white men with your gold, but you can't buy me off. I represent justice, out here on the plains, and justice is going to run its course with Bill Tenney. The man's a wolf, and he has to he treated like the beast that he is. In the meantime, it's late and I'm going to bed. You had better get out of here by the way you came."

To his amazement, Rusty merely shook his head.

"You're not going?" demanded Marston, thrusting out his jaw a little.

"We have only begun to talk," answered Rusty gently. "I am asking you to be generous and kind to a helpless man. You have hurt him and shamed him a great deal. Pain of hunger is bad . . . pain of fire is worse . . . but these things can be cured and forgotten. Shame is a sickness that never leaves the soul of a man. You have shamed my brother. Now you must set him free and let him try to be a man again in his own eyes. For that, he will need much time and many great deeds."

The temper of the major snapped short. He pointed suddenly at the door and exclaimed: "Get out!" He added: "I've had enough of this damned nonsense! I've given you enough hints, and now I'll give you facts. Get out of this fort!"

The major, as anger and enthusiasm grew within him, squared himself close to the window, confronting Rusty. Rusty now spoke one deep-voiced word in Cheyenne, and instantly two long, naked, copper-colored arms leaped through the window square, and two mighty hands fastened on Major Marston.

He tried to yell, but one of those hands was grasping his throat, shutting off the sound. He tried to wrench his revolver from the holster at his hip, but Rusty Sabin caught his wrist with a grip that was iron-strong from the swinging of heavy sledges. The major stopped struggling. Rusty touched the hand that was throttling the white war chief, and that hand fell away.

Major Marston, for a moment, was fully occupied in getting his breath again; after that, as his eyes cleared, he stared at Rusty. There was plenty of courage in the major; he showed it now in this time of high danger.

"Well?" he demanded briefly.

"My brother has had the whip until his back was red," said Rusty. "There will be no whip for you, if you do as I say . . . if you send at once for Bill Tenney."

"I am to send for the guard, and let him see you all in here?" demanded Marston.

"Open the door just a little, speak through the gap, and no one will be seen," said Rusty. "I shall stand behind you with this."

As he spoke, he drew out the blue, glistening length of the knife. The major's glance dwelt on the curve of the blade. He could almost feel the cold of the metal in his warm flesh.

So he walked to the door, with Rusty stepping like a shadow behind him, and, opening the door a bit, he called out. The half sleeping orderly at the end of the little outer chamber jumped to his feet and saluted.

"Send for Bill Tenney . . . the fellow who was put in the cellar this evening," commanded the major. "Have him brought here at once." He closed the door and turned slowly. The white in his face was the white of the shame that would be his next morning, when the town would awaken to the discovery that Tenney was gone. They would have many things to guess about that disappearance, and none of their guesses would be favorable to the major, because he knew that he had won the respect but had never gained the love of the frontiersmen.

"Sabin," he said, "are you being wise? Are you thinking of things to come? Are you remembering that you never can show your face in the fort again? Are you realizing that one day I may have *you* at the whipping post?"

Rusty, for answer, merely shrugged his shoulders and sighed audibly. "A man must go where his friends require him," he said.

It was a remark that the major made nothing of, however, and a moment later they heard the trampling of feet and the jangling of chains in the outer room.

The two big Indians had stepped back into a shadowed corner. The major now pulled the door wide, with the point of Rusty's knife gently pricking the skin of his back between the shoulder blades.

"Send him in alone," commanded Marston. "I want to examine him."

Bill Tenney strode across the threshold. The major closed the door behind him and locked it.

As for Tenney, one glance at the Indians, and the sight of the long knife in Rusty's hand, told him what was happening. He lifted his manacled hands to smash Marston's skull with the weight of the irons, but Rusty raised a finger, and Little Porcupine caught Tenney's arms. The thief stood still, breathing hard and muttering: "Let me have him, Sabin. By heaven, I've earned a chance at him, and I gotta have it. Leave him and me alone. Irons or no irons, I'll handle him."

"We've made a bargain," answered Rusty. "He sets you free, and then he's safe from us . . . for tonight at least."

Tenney began to nod. "Aye, it's better," he said. "Choking him ain't the way. I gotta have time to think out the best way of murdering him . . . and when I've thought it out, I'm gonna do the trick."

"You have the key of the manacles?" asked Rusty of the major.

Marston silently pulled out a bunch of keys, selected one, and turned the oiled lock. Tenney's hands were instantly free, and he extended his arms above his head in a great gesture, opening and closing his fingers. As he straightened, the blood-stiffened shirt on his back gave out a crackling noise. Rusty motioned to the Cheyennes.

"Tie him," he commanded, indicating the major.

A blanket, quickly slashed into strips, offered the means of binding the major. He was wrapped like a mummy, with his hands against his sides. A gag insured his silence, and he was bound to the foot of the bed. Only when the work was done did Broken Arrow say in the Cheyenne tongue: "You know, father, that dead enemies make long nights of sleep?"

He held poised above Marston's throat the glittering blade of a small knife. The major, feeling himself trussed and ready for the slaughter, and unable to voice a plea for mercy, turned his desperate eyes toward Rusty and thanked his gods when Sabin shook his head.

We keep faith," said Rusty simply. "Even with liars."

Chapter Ten

The major lay perfectly still for a time. He felt that he was lying there endless hours, but each slow second had for him all the timelessness of the moments when a man faces death. The major was facing worse than death. He was being shamed, and mingled with his agony there was a vast incredulity, for he felt that this thing he was suffering could not be.

His four tormentors had slipped out the window of his room and had climbed soundlessly down in the outer night. He had heard only one soft thump as their feet struck the ground. Now they were gone. In his imagination, it was as though the wind were blowing them, sweeping them toward the horizon from which they would never reappear. He thought of himself as a pillar of fire—reaching for them—failing hopelessly to catch them.

To make his madness complete, he could not rid himself of that profound sense of a certain nobility in Rusty Sabin. The man had said that he would keep faith, even with liars. Well, if Rusty and his damned nobility ever came into the hands of the major, there would be an end of both.

All this while, he was making vague, struggling efforts to loosen his bonds. The material of the blanketing had been wrapped very tightly around him, almost tightly enough to stop the circulation of the blood in his arms and his legs. But there was a slight give in the woolen fabric, and, as he strained from the shoulders and the hips, he could feel the bonds that fastened him to the bed yielding a trifle. But it was a slow business.

He tried to work his tongue back behind the gag and so spit it out, and his tongue began to ache. It gathered in a great bunch at the top of his mouth and closed the air passages. For a frenzied moment he was sure that he was stifling himself. Then the tip of the tongue got a purchase and thrust the gag a little forward until it wadded hard and firm behind his teeth.

Not a particle of air was entering his lungs now. He could feel his face swelling, his eyes thrusting out. But still he persisted. And in a silent outburst of savagery he told himself that it was better to stifle with rage and a gag than to be discovered tied like a helpless dog in this fashion. The thing would never be forgotten, not while he lived. Men on the frontier did not forget. They would laugh forever at what had happened to the dignity of the military.

Straining his jaws so wide that they threatened to crack, a final convulsive effort of the tongue thrust the gag out. Still he could not breathe, however. For an instant he felt that his lungs were bursting, that the imprisoned air would never leave them so that new oxygen could enter. But finally he could gasp, and then he could breathe, and suddenly the gasping shout came, tearing his throat.

"Help! Help! Orderly! Damn you, where are you? Help!"

There was a hasty trampling of feet, a wrenching at the outer knob of the door.

"Break it down, you fools!" yelled the major, regaining his full voice.

A metal crash of musket butts smote the door to the ground. The sound was like the boom of a big gun. And in a moment the excited faces of his men were above the major.

They cut him free; they helped him to his feet. Even before he was erect he was snarling orders.

"Call the trumpeter. Sound 'Boots and Saddles'. Turn out the command. Some of you head straight for the blacksmith shop. Get your hands on Rusty Sabin. Get him dead or get him alive!

The damned white Indian! Take hold on him. I'll make the man who gets him!"

They fled with these orders, but they did not run so fast that they were unable to exchange glances on the way. There are jokes in every military command, but few to equal the sight of a commander, stretched on the floor of his own room, tied fast in strips of his own blankets. And the major was not especially loved by those under him.

By the time he had buckled on his saber and revolver and clamped his hat on his head, he could hear in the central yard of the fort the bugles sounding the thrilling call to horse. He could hear the entire stretch of the barracks resounding with suddenly roused life. Then he rushed down from his room to lead the manhunt.

* * * * *

As Rusty and his three companions had reached the ground, big Bill Tenney grasped Sabin's arm and muttered at his ear: "Partner, now we're quits, and on the level." He was amazed by Rusty's reply.

"Brother, so long as I breathe, I shall always owe my life to you."

The thing stunned Tenney. In his world, there is nothing that cannot be bought and paid for, and often at bargain prices. But a gift to Rusty Sabin seemed to be a thing that could not be repaid, even if its own weight and value were returned over and over again. That was a fine point for puzzling over, and there was no time now for pondering. Instead, they were forced to race across the town, across the main street, and then, taking the way behind the houses, they came to the rear of the blacksmith shop. No one had seen the escaped prisoner, up to this moment, and there at hand were the four horses, waiting, bridled and saddled. They mounted, but, even as they were putting their feet into stirrups, the note of a bugle rode thin and sharp across the air.

"'Boots and Saddles' 'Boots and Saddles'!" said Bill Tenney. He turned in the darkness and shook his fist at the sound. "I'll boot and saddle you, damn you! Rusty, the major's loose, and the fort's been warned. They'll be piling after us like devils, and we gotta ride. Are the nags good?"

"They're as tough," said Rusty, "as Indians know how to pick out. And Indians know."

They jogged a short distance from the shop, into the starlight. Then, with loosened reins, they fled. All saving Rusty. He, with a word now and then, had to teach White Horse that this was not a race but a ride, in company. And Bill Tenney, looking aside to the dim shimmering of the stallion, marked the mighty sweep of that stride, so light and reaching that it seemed to be buoyed up by the beat of invisible wings.

A terrible yearning came over Bill Tenney's spirit, and a great pain stabbed into his vitals. He could not understand that pain. It had never tormented him before in all his days. It was a thing of the spirit, and yet it was almost physical agony. He wanted that horse, but the stallion belonged to Rusty, and Rusty Sabin was his friend.

It came suddenly to Tenney that never had he had a friend before. He had known many men; he had roughed and played and gamed and fought and companioned with them, but they had not been friends. They had been picked up and thrown away like gloves, soon worn out in heavy weather. But between him and Rusty something else had happened. He had risked his life for Rusty, and Rusty had risked his life for the thief. The double payment did not cancel out. No, for Tenney now felt that there was an overplus on both sides. Between them was a strange tie.

He wanted White Horse. He would have it at any cost. But he could not help wishing that the theft would be made at the expense of any man in the world other than Rusty Sabin.

They were well out on the easily rolling waves of the prairie, by this time, and Tenney called: "Ain't any use burning ourselves out, Rusty! They can't find us now!"

"Dogs!" called Rusty in answer. "They have dogs for the trailing." And the steady, swift gallop continued.

Then, confused like the blended voices of many church bells, and beating all on different notes, Tenney heard the chorus of the dogs awaken from the direction of the town. The two Cheyennes instantly increased the gait of their horses. Rusty pulled the stallion over to Tenney, saying: "We still need luck. I thought that it would be at least an hour or so before the major was found. It might even have been till morning. But the luck was against us then, and it seems to be against us now."

"Why?" answered Tenney. "This nag of mine is jumping right along. And God knows that they ain't gonna tag you on that White Horse."

"I'm with *you*," answered Rusty. "If they take you, they'll take me."

Tenney blinked at that. The stars actually whirled into streaks of thin radiance before his eyes. He couldn't understand it. What was the use of having the swiftest horse on the plains, if the rider anchored himself by fanatic loyalty like this?

Aye, but the talk was well enough. It would be time enough to prove such statements if ever the men of the fort came close on their heels, and if the Indian ponies faltered while White Horse was still full of running. Yet a cold uneasiness remained in Tenney's breast and the sense that heretofore he might, perhaps, have been living only on the surface of this human world, divorced from all insight into the depths of great emotions.

Chapter Eleven

They rode all night. They struck a vast intertangling of gullies that the rains had ripped out of the heart of the plains. No better hiding places could have been wished than these labyrinths, but they were useless to men who were being trailed by dogs, and always, sometimes dying down to a dreadful whisper, sometimes blown loudly along the wind, they could hear the music of the hounds.

Rusty could remember them well. Bloodhounds, and a few common mongrels and fox hounds, were at the nose of the pack. Greyhounds were the far-striking missiles, as it were. And in addition, there were a number of powerful brutes, cross-bred between greyhound and mastiffs, and strong enough to fight bears, savage enough to kill men. They were regularly exercised and trained by capable handlers at the fort, and the dog pack was, in fact, Major Marston's contribution to Indian fighting. No trails were blind on which the dogs could run, and more than once he had been able to follow a party of raiders to a great distance, striking them when they were blinded by their sense of security.

The two Cheyennes, as the dawn came gray over the plains, were plainly worried. They said: "The white war chief has many men, father. He has two horses for each man. His heart is angry, and he will drive his men like eagles across the sky. We are not going fast enough. Is Sweet Medicine to give us strength, or turn us into clouds?"

There was no irony in this. The Cheyennes had seen Rusty in so many strange scenes that they had in him a more than implicit confidence. Rusty answered with a vague gesture, because his heart was beginning to grow heavy. Turn them into clouds? Well, White Horse, at any moment, could go blowing over the round side of the earth, beyond pursuit. But with the other ponies it was a different matter.

They had left the entanglements of the badlands, now, and the sweeping prairie was before them. And as the dawn grew, the condition of the horses could be studied. They were very far spent, indeed. Their heads were down, their backs were beginning to roach up, and their bellies to pinch—all sure signs of exhaustion. Moreover, their fierce eyes were beginning to dull.

They came to a wandering rivulet, and there Rusty ordered a halt to let the horses drink a little. Not enough to weigh them down, only time enough to loosen the girths for a few moments, and so perhaps give the ponies new heart.

But when they mounted again, the far tremble of the dog chorus was drawing nearer, across the green waves of the prairies, and the horses, as they trotted forward, had little more life than before.

Rusty drew up again. "There is only one way," he said. "Two of us must face the danger . . . two of us may escape. Broken Arrow and Little Porcupine, draw away to the right. I go with my white brother, to the left. If I am lost, give your hands to Standing Bull. He is my friend of friends. Farewell! Go quickly."

So they split into two parties, and gave up all hope of making a real battle. Four armed men may fight against numbers. Two men are soon lost.

But as they parted, the four men looked at one another with eyes that went deep. In turn, the two Cheyennes took big Bill Tenney's hand. Then Broken Arrow bowed his head before Rusty.

"Father, pray for us," he said in his own tongue.

Rusty looked up, and raised both hands to the sky. "You behold us, Sweet Medicine," he said. "Give us the thing that is in your heart."

After that, they divided. The two Cheyennes were soon lost over the wavering green. And from the rear, the noise of the dogs came gradually beating, nearer and nearer.

"Are they following the Injuns, or are they taking after us?" asked Bill Tenney anxiously.

Rusty shook his head, and continued to listen. "They are following us," he said finally.

"Damn them," groaned Bill Tenney. "And damn a short-legged worthless runt of a horse like this here." He beat the mustang as he spoke, but the pony failed to rock into a responsive gallop. Instead, it stumbled heavily, fell to a walk, and then raised a mere dog-trot. Its sides were heaving bellows. Its nostrils could not widen enough to take in enough of the life-giving air.

"We are ended, brother," said Rusty, calmly, as he halted White Horse.

Bill Tenney stared at him with wild eyes for a minute. Then he jerked the mustang to a halt, in turn, and flung himself out of the saddle. A jerk on the reins, and the heavy thrust of his shoulder forced the pony to lie down.

"If they get me, they're gonna pay for me . . . and pay damn' big!" shouted Tenney. He shook his fist toward the increasing chorus of the dogs. "They're gonna pay blood for blood, damn their rotten hearts!" he shouted.

Rusty slipped from White Horse. He stood with his arm around the head of the great stallion, and absently stroked the face of the horse. Then he said: "This day is my day, brother. It was your day when the river was taking me. It was taking White Horse, also. As you drew him safely to the shore, so he will carry you away from danger now. Take him, friend." He smiled as he spoke.

Bill Tenney, staring, could see no bitterness in his companion's face. "You're talking, partner," said Tenney. He began to breathe like a man who has been running with all his might for a great distance. "You don't mean what you say. Besides, how would I be taking your horse and riding off? How would I . . . ?"

Here the beauty and the glory of the stallion filled his eye and his soul, and silenced him to a gasp.

"One day," said Rusty, "Sweet Medicine will be kind to me again. He will bring me back to you and White Horse, and then I shall take him. Take him now. Take him quickly, because they are coming close. And I must tell White Horse that you are a friend, or else he will not carry you."

The noise of the dogs, creeping closer and closer, made a riot in Bill Tenney's brain. He seemed to see a campfire, with men seated around it, and he seemed to hear a deep man's voice saying: "And this here hound . . . this gent called Tenney . . . he takes the horse that his partner offers him, and he just rides off and leaves Rusty Sabin alone to be grabbed. And the soldiers, they sure murdered Sabin, after they got hold of him."

"Quick!" urged Rusty.

Here a thin trickle of tired-looking dogs came over the crest of a low, green wave of prairie land, and behind them rode the heads and shoulders, the horses of several riders. Thirty men were soon cantering on that trail.

"My God, they've got me," groaned Tenney, and he flung himself hastily into the saddle.

Under him the stallion crouched low, and, when that set of lithe steel springs reacted, Tenney knew that he would be hurled into the sky. Good rider that he was, he knew that he could not sit half a minute on the frantic back of White Horse. But a few words from Rusty made the big horse stand straight again. He turned his head, blowing his breath, shining his angry eyes at Tenney, till Rusty took the man's hand and laid it on the stallion's face.

"Be to him as you are to me," said Rusty.

As a child speaks to an animal—a child not sophisticated enough to believe that beasts have no understanding—so Rusty spoke to the stallion.

Out of the distance they heard the dim shouting of men who saw, at last, the prey they had toiled for so long.

"Take him easily," said Rusty. "Speak to him a great deal. He will serve you now, and carry you. Start now, brother."

He held up his hand, and Bill Tenney seized it with a frantic grasp.

"I'm wrong," said Tenney. "I shouldn't do it. I'm a hound. But . . . my God! What'd they do to me if they got me a second time? Rusty, so long! Good bye. God bless you."

He turned the stallion. White Horse made a few steps, then he halted, looking back toward his master. But a shout that came cheerfully out of Rusty's throat made the big animal break into a canter—a gallop—a racing stride that kept the chunks of turf dancing in the air about his head like little flying birds. Rusty watched him going like a streak that diminished in size, then the wavering surface of the prairie covered him from view.

From the other direction, the beating hoofs of the many horses thundered down upon him, and before them the dogs strained forward in full cry. He looked down at the mustang, which still lay as if dead on the ground.

Bill Tenney had intended to use that living breastwork and fight from behind it, forgetting that he could be surrounded and picked off from the rear. But Rusty had no intention even of making resistance. He was not good with a rifle; he never had been good. Indians are not famous marksmen with firearms, although among the Cheyennes there were always plenty of warriors who could surpass Rusty with firearms of all sorts. And so White Indian simply faced the advancing charge, and with his eyes he selected the form of Major Marston, riding first of all.

Far to the rear there appeared other horses—undoubtedly the reserve herd out of which the major would have remounted his men, if the goal had not been reached. But what would he do now? To follow White Horse would be an act of perfect folly. The two Cheyennes were gone far away, and were beyond pursuit. And out of four men there remained only one for the major's wrath to consume.

Then the dogs came in, leaping furiously at Rusty. He shouted and raised his hand, and they shrank to either side of the human quarry. And there was the major, towering above him on horseback, reining his excited, tired horse, glaring down at the calm face of Rusty.

The soldiers, too, were sweeping up.

A voice from a young lieutenant called: "Shall we go on, sir?"

"Go on after what?" snarled the major. "After a streak of lightning? Don't be a damned fool, Wells."

Lieutenant Wells strained his eyes at the point, far away, where a dissolving point of white could still be seen. He made no answer, for it was plain that they might as well try to catch birds out of the sky with their bare hands as to hunt for White Horse.

"You weren't man enough to keep your horse, eh?" said the major to Rusty. "You let him take your horse away from you, eh? That's what he is, eh? The fellow whose hide you saved?"

But a sergeant broke in to say: "There wasn't no fight, sir. I seen it all. He just give Tenney his horse. He give him the stallion. I watched, and I seen him standin' at the head of the horse. I never seen nothin' like it."

"Keep still!" commanded the major angrily.

It would have been better the other way. It would have been a great deal better to take Rusty Sabin back to the fort and spread word that, like a coward, he had permitted his companion to take away the horse by force. But this thing of voluntarily giving up so famous a stallion, would it not make Rusty even more of a hero than ever, in the mind of Maisry Lester?

Aye, and in the minds of all the other men in Fort Marston, too. That was why the major glowered as he sat the saddle and stared down at Rusty Sabin. Quick and keen as his mind was, he did not know at once how he would be able to handle Rusty to the best advantage. But in his very soul there was an iron determination to wring out of Rusty enough wretchedness to make up for the shame that the major had endured the night before.

He could not see his way clear. There were legal methods, of course, but his own methods would be more to his personal taste. He had the desire to raise his quirt and slash Rusty across the face with it, right now. He wanted to flog this blacksmith all the way back to the fort.

Instead, he merely forced himself to smile, and commanded that for the return march the captive be mounted between two of the troopers.

Chapter Twelve

That bitter quandary kept the major's mind employed all during the long, slow march back to the fort. It was the position in which Rusty stood that baffled him.

The major, it is necessary to make clear, was a man who never gave up an objective, once he had settled upon it. And as a goal the winning of Maisry Lester was more firmly established in his mind than anything else ever had been. It was so deeply rooted in him that her name moved in his very blood. All that was simple and gentle and beautiful in the world was represented to the major by the girl. It seemed as though the very evil in him craved her because she was his opposite.

Now he had Rusty Sabin in his hands, but, if he wreaked his wrath on Rusty, the girl would never forgive him, no matter how he cloaked his proceedings in the name of justice.

He heard one of the soldiers behind him saying to Rusty: "That was a damned fine, crazy thing you done today, Sabin."

Every man on the frontier would say the same thing. Rusty faced years of imprisonment, for the crimes of entering a federal building by force, for an assault upon a United States officer, and for forcibly interfering with the course of federal justice. Any one of three crimes would be enough to lodge him in prison for a long term. The three combined were enough to put him in darkness for almost all the rest of his days.

But if this were done, the girl would never be able to look upon Major Marston without pain. And therefore the thing had to be managed in another way. Obscurely the major's good brain worked on the problem. In some way, he was sure, he ought to be able to arrange the affair so that he could seem to give Rusty the advantage, so that the major himself might appear really as a benefactor to the young man. By so doing, his reputation would be sweetened in the eyes of the girl, and a vast step forward in that direction would be made.

For a long time the plan was nebulous before Marston's searching brain, but little by little, during the long march, it gained in clarity.

It was toward the evening when they drew near Fort Marston and saw the big, square shoulders of the building rising. The major never saw that outline lift without feeling that it spoke the name Marston in a voice whose vibrations could be sensed around the world—Marston, a word that meant big and powerful and enduring.

Fort Marston would become a city one day, the major hoped and believed. The railroads would come out here, bringing wealth and noise and soot, and people would pool around Fort Marston and make the name of its founder immortal. No matter how occupied his mind might be, there was a smile on his lips as he saw the gross, formidable outlines of the fort growing up out of the plains.

He sent riders on fresh horses ahead of him. He sent a special messenger to inform the Lester family that Rusty Sabin was "safe in the hands of Major Marston." If Maisry had half a brain—and she had a whole one—she would be able to interpret that as a message from a friend, one who would intercede between justice and her lover.

The whole maneuver that followed would be complicated, difficult in the extreme. But he would manage it.

Some of the difficulties began to appear when the cortège entered the town, for the entire population of Fort Marston, as a matter of course, had heard about the return from the advance riders. They knew the entire story of what had happened by now, and they thronged the way. There were no cheers for the soldiery; there were simply multitudes of shouts for Rusty Sabin.

"Good lad!" screeched an old woman as she ran out from the others and followed along at the side of Rusty for a few steps. "A better or a finer thing wasn't never done. You'll be teachin' brutes how to make themselves into men! More power to you, Rusty Sabin!"

And all who heard this shouted and cheered Rusty.

The major wanted to curse, but he made himself smile. He was pale with rage, but he kept that smile enduring like one cut in rock. He hated these townsmen.

Then he saw the Lesters in front of their house—the father and the daughter close together, the mother at a little distance from them. It would have pleased Mrs. Lester well enough, the major knew, if Rusty had been thrown into jail for life. Anything to prevent the marriage of her daughter with a half-wild man. But the anxious, tense faces of Richard Lester and his daughter told the major how keenly they were suffering.

Well, if all went as he planned, he would have her for his own, one day. And more than once she would stand like that, with just that face of suffering, waiting for his return. Good women, the major felt, always love where they should love. If only a man can wangle the marriage, everything else follows as a matter of course. And a girl like Maisry Lester—why, she would as soon deny her God as her husband.

These were Major Marston's thoughts as he got Rusty Sabin inside the fort and had him placed in the guard room. When he looked at Rusty's manacled hands, he wanted to hang the man by them from the high walls of the fort, but he made his tone gentler as he said: "I must pursue certain courses, in order to fill out my duty to the law, but I intend well by you, Sabin. You'll be surprised before the end, by what I intend to do for you."

After that, he went straight as a homing pigeon to the Lester house. Maisry, standing straight and still in a corner of the room, turned a white face toward him and could not speak. Richard Lester had his face bowed in his hands. Only Mrs. Lester was at ease, and almost florid in her talk.

"It's a good day for this town when you took charge of things, Major," she told Marston. "There'll be an end of the scalawags and the wild men. The decent people are going to have a chance to call their souls their own, and to lead their own lives."

But the major got to Maisry at once, saying: "I want to speak to you in the next room, Maisry. I have something important to tell you."

She showed him into the next room. It was a storage place, with sacks of flour on the floor, hams and bacons hanging up from the low ceiling, and various barrels and boxes of dried meat and fruit, for the Lesters were buying during the cheap season, in order to have supplies for the next winter. They sat down close together on a pair of boxes. The girl had a look of one in church during a funeral service for a dead friend.

The major said: "This is a serious business, in a way . . . and yet it's a business to laugh about, also. To begin with, I've grown mighty fond of Rusty, during the trip in from the place where we caught him."

"Fond of him?" breathed Maisry, looking up suddenly, a shadow of disbelief in her clear eyes.

"Well, he was pretty scared when we came sweeping up," said the major. "Seemed to think that we were going to eat him. And as we came back toward the fort, I talked to him a lot. The fact is . . . he's a simple fellow. There's no real harm in him. I like him. I like him so much that I've told him I want to do what I can to help him out. And what do you think he asked me to do?"

She shook her head. She seemed dazed when the major talked of the kindly feeling he had for Rusty.

"Why," went on Marston, laughing a little and touching his mustache with the tips of his fingers, as though to make sure that it was there, "why, he's a bit superstitious, you know. He feels he's had all this bad luck . . . lost White Horse and put himself in prison, so to speak . . . all because he gave up his luck. And do you know where he thinks his luck centers? In that green beetle that he gave you."

The major laughed again, but the girl, startled, drew the little scarab from the bosom of her dress and fingered it anxiously.

"He asked me to beg you to send it back," said the major casually.

"But he couldn't have done that!" exclaimed Maisry. "Of course he couldn't have done that. You were in the room, Arthur, when he gave it to me. You heard him tell me never to send it to him unless I wanted to be rid of him."

"Well, that's true . . . I remember the scene perfectly well," answered Marston. "I wonder if that's really in his mind? I never thought of that. I wonder if he really wants to be free from you again?"

"Free . . . from me?" said Maisry. She looked away from the major, envisaging disaster.

The major went on in a tone of gentle sympathy: "I don't know. But I suppose it's the wild life calling him back again. Towns are too small to hold red Indians . . . too small for white Indians, as well, I suppose."

She was rigid. Her lips were purple-gray.

"And then, I dare say, he feels his luck is wrapped up in the green beetle," went on the major. "You know, the Indians have their medicine bags, and they think their souls are sewed up inside the leather. And. . . ."

"Don't," breathed Maisry. She took the green beetle from around her neck and made a gesture to give it to the major, but, catching her hands back again, she pressed the little scarab between them, close to her breast. "If he's asked for it, it means that he doesn't want to see me again," said Maisry miserably. "Or else it's because he expects to spend all his life in prison. . . ."

"Not that," answered Marston. "I've told him that, after all, I'm going to take the law into my own hands and set him free."

"You are? Set him free?" said the girl eagerly.

"I've got to," said the major. "The fact is, Maisry, it makes me sick at heart to see you like this. When I rode past you with Sabin, this evening . . . and when I saw your white face . . . I knew that I would have to turn him loose."

"Ah," she said, "how good and how kind you are. How really good and kind. Then, if I send him the green beetle, he'll have a chance to come to me?"

"Aye, if he wants to. Of course he'll have the chance," said Marston.

She put the scarab suddenly into the major's hands. "It seems like giving away life and breath," she told him, trying to smile. "But take it to him at once. Tell him that I love him, and that I am waiting for him. Will you do that for me, Major?"

He stood up. There was nothing but blackness in his heart. "Tell him? Of course I'll tell him," he lied.

He crushed the scarab with the grip of his fingers, and felt as if he were squeezing Rusty Sabin's very heart.

Chapter Thirteen

A light heart makes a brisk step, and the major's step was like that of a colt on a spring day. He went back to the fort with his head in the air. Once in a while, his heels hit a bump and he stumbled, but he recovered almost with a leap. The major's smile kept his mustache spreading and contracting.

To be sure, the sentry at the gate silently and deeply damned the major's heart, as the officer entered the fort, but to Marston the opinions of subordinates were matters of no importance whatever. The only people he cared to impress were those who were above him, or those who could be used only after they had been flattered. He never cared to be right, but always to be successful. And now, as he advanced on the road of his success, his handsome face was flushed a little and his eyes were luminous. He had the appearance of one who moves with a great heart toward the accomplishment of some magnanimous purpose.

When he got to the guard room, he took the prisoner by the arm and marched him off to his own quarters, unescorted. There, in the same room where he had confronted Rusty Sabin the night before, he unlocked the manacles and set Rusty free. Then he stepped back to take stock of what he had done.

Rusty, stunned, looked up from his freed hands into Marston's face and waited for the explanation. The major took the long knife that had been removed from Rusty when he was captured and gripped the handle of it, hard. There was such passion in the man that he was half tempted to drive the long blue steel straight into Rusty's body, but he merely smiled and presented the weapon to its owner. The major took a fierce and quiet joy in mastering his hatred and covering it with his smile, and in keeping his eye as gentle as though there was arising in his heart an intense affection for this man.

Rusty took the knife as though it had been a sword of honor. Now he was waiting, with wide eyes.

"You are free," said Marston. "The fact is, I've been fighting myself all the time since you were taken. The law commands me to punish you. But when a man has sacrificed himself for the sake of a friend, as you have, why then I have to listen to a law higher than that of men. I've made up my mind, and you're going free."

Rusty, like one trying to clear his brain after receiving a heavy blow, shook his head a trifle. The thing seemed impossible. More than once he had seen on other days the sudden malice come darkly into Major Marston's face. But there was a fundamental simplicity in Rusty Sabin's soul that prevented him from searching other men too deeply. There was such a well of trust in him that it was apt to be invested in any man. So he puzzled only a short time over this matter of the change in Major Marston, and then he said, simply: "What shall I say? I have done you harm . . . and now you befriend me." He took a breath, adding: "A kind act can be a weight on the heart. My heart is heavy because I have not known what a good man you are."

The major did not laugh aloud, but inwardly he was merry enough over the success of his deception. "I have to be two men in one," he explained. "I have to be the head of the military and the law, but, besides that, I hope that I can be a man, now and then. And that is why you're going free. You understand, though, that after you've left the fort . . . after you've escaped from it . . . you mustn't be seen in the town again?"

"That is true," agreed Rusty thoughtfully. "Then I shall have to write a letter to Maisry, before I go. . . ."

"There's bad news from her," answered Marston, shaking his head. "By the Lord, I think what she told me made me pity you, you poor fellow."

"Bad news? From Maisry?" echoed Rusty Sabin, incredulous.

The major took Rusty by the arm and walked up and down the room with him, slowly. He said: "You know how girls are, my friend. They change their minds quickly."

"Once a year!" exclaimed Rusty as his father's words struck up the memory in his heart. "Once a year, a girl will change her mind. . . ."

"Who would think that it began with the blacksmith business?" remarked the major, making a sweeping gesture with his hand.

"That? That disgusted her?" asked Rusty, finding it difficult to comprehend.

"And yet what can a man do that is more honest?" asked Marston.

"The smoke and the grime and the soot," said Rusty.

"Well, I suppose so. It might have been a little more clever if you had always washed your face and hands before you let her see you."

"A clean heart . . . that is better than clean hands."

"Well, a white girl has a good deal of pride. She likes to see her man stand out among other men."

"Ah, yes . . . yes," murmured Rusty.

And as he spoke, he looked up at the major's bright uniform, with its epaulets, its trim, closely fitted collar, and at the handsome face above it. The major was a big man too, and, as for the strength of his arm, it was said that he had once cloven the skull of a Comanche, with a stroke of his saber. Cloven it to the chin.

"Yes," added Rusty. "A man like you . . . a chief . . . a war chief. But I shall see Maisry before I go. Perhaps when I stand in front of her . . . well, when I touch her hand with my hand and her eyes with my eyes. . . ."

"I wish you could," said the major heartily. "That was what I begged her to do. I told her that I was setting you free, and she cried out against that. 'I never want to see him again,' she said."

Rusty's head jerked back. "Did she say that?" he asked.

He withdrew his arm from the major's hand and stood stiffly erect. His face, at a stroke, had become impassive except for a very faint smile that pulled on the corners of the mouth. With such an expression, a wild Indian would face the torture, surrounded by his enemies. And at sight of it a keen thrill of pleasure ran through Marston's heart.

"I'm sorry!" he exclaimed. "I didn't want to tell you that. I begged Maisry to see you again. I pleaded with her. I pointed out that you're new to the ways of white men . . . that perhaps you could become something more than a blacksmith. . . ."

"Yes," said Rusty with dignity, and he made a slow gesture toward the window.

Somehow, at that gesture, the major was suddenly able to see the wide waves of the prairie over which the sky stretches its longest arms. He could see a single file of Indians on the warpath, half naked, their knees lifted by their short stirrups, and at their head rode the young chief and medicine man, Red Hawk, known among the whites as Rusty Sabin. Yes, Rusty could be something more than a blacksmith, if he chose.

"The mind of a girl is like the wind," went on Marston. "Maisry has changed like that. She blew with you . . . for you . . . and now she's blowing against you. So much that she doesn't want to see you. Bill Tenney . . . he's a part of it."

"Because he is my friend?" asked Rusty.

"You see, he appears to be a bit of a ruffian. A thief . . . that sort of thing. That's what seems to disgust Maisry."

"I understand," said Rusty Sabin.

"So," continued the major, "she asked me to bring back to you something that you would understand. Something that would make you realize that she doesn't wish to see you again. . . ."

Here he paused and looked down. Real emotion had overcome Marston, at this instant. Perhaps to every liar there comes one cold moment in the telling of the lie. However, he recovered himself at once, and, with a frown and a shake of the head, he took out the narrow little horsehair lariat, so finely braided, and offered it to Rusty, with the scarab hanging from it.

The smile, he saw, remained carved on Rusty's face, but the face was gray-green with agony. Rusty took the green beetle and drew the loop of the string over his head. The scarab itself he dropped inside the neck of his shirt.

"This is ended," said the White Indian. "I shall not see her again. To you, oh, my friend, I give thanks. I give you my hand and my friendship."

A vague, cloudy glimpse of a troubled future rushed across the mind of the major. He saw this stony face of the White Indian turned passionate with anger. He saw a death struggle that locked the two of them together. Then the image went out of his mind, and he was shaking Sabin's hand.

Rusty descended from that room as he had gone the night before.

The major remained for a time, contemplating his triumph, his heart great and fierce with joy and victory, knowing well that this freeing of the prisoner would gain him popularity all through the town, and knowing that above all it would give him strength in the house of the Lesters.

And meanwhile, Rusty, in the dark of the night beneath, had dropped upon his face and was digging his fingers into the ground. He lay there for a long time, then he stood up and ran, because the thought of Maisry worked in him and drew on him until he wanted to rush to the Lester house and crawl before her on his knees, begging her to give him her love again.

That was why Rusty ran, shadowy and swift, out of the town of Fort Marston and into the dark of the plains. He ran until, when he glanced over his shoulder, the lights of the town had drawn together in a single huddle, like the brightness of one eye with many shining facets. There he paused, and, standing with folded arms for a long moment, he stared until the tears in his eyes caused the thin rays of light to shatter into many colors.

After that, he filled and lighted his pipe. On his knees he blew the four ceremonial puffs to the four quarters, then to the Underground People, and to the Sky People, whose dancing footfalls cause the stars to tremble on the curving fields of heaven. After that, with lifted hands, he called aloud, and, with every word, his voice grew louder because the greatness of his agony was passing out into the sounds.

"Sweet Medicine, you once loved me. But I left my people and went far away from you, among the white men. All the time, you kept my heart drifting back to the teepees of the Cheyennes. While I lay in the white man's house, my ghost walked among the lodges and looked in at the red fires and smelled the buffalo meat stewing in the pots. The dogs came and licked my hands. The children cried out around me, also. The braves stood close and smiled on me. But I stayed far away from them all, until you sent your anger on me. The soul of my mother was locked up in the green stone with my soul. Yet I gave it away . . . and then your anger came on me.

"You took from me White Horse. Even the Sky People must know him. They must see him flying across the dark face of the earth as we see a shining cloud blow across the face of the heavens. But you took White Horse away from me. He no longer waits for me, stamping and neighing . . . he is gone, and I am alone.

"You turned the heart of my woman against me . . . you made her despise me . . . you made her tremble with disgust. My father, also, you snatched away from me, drawing him out and away into the night. Therefore, I am alone.

"I was so happy that every hour I was laughing. Now there is nothing left and I am returning to you. I am afraid of you, Sweet Medicine, and therefore I am coming back, with my hands held up, asking for help. Be kind to me. Open my breast and take the sorrow out of my heart. Blow into my nostrils happiness like a spring day.

"And I shall leave my white brothers. I shall not return to them. I shall give them up . . . deny them and cast them out of my thoughts. They have been false to me, and they have lied to me. They have scorned me because you took your strength away from me. Give it back to me now, and I shall make men honor you again because of me. I shall do great things. I shall lead the warriors, and make them sing your name aloud, all night long.

"But the white men I forget . . . I turn my back on them. Their lights now die as I turn my back on them. I shall find a wife among the Cheyennes . . . I shall take a mate among the Indians. Sweet Medicine, teach me to be a good Cheyenne, and to forget my father and my mother. The tribe shall be my mother, and you shall be my father. Hear me, Sweet Medicine. And open my breast and kill me quickly, or take the pain away."

After that, he went on across the prairies, jogging steadily. And, as he jogged, the stars in the sky jerked up and down before his eyes.

He was a great medicine man. That he knew, because it had been proved many and many a time in the past. And he had seen Sweet Medicine in the guise of a gigantic owl, in the Sacred Valley. He knew, therefore, that he had been a mighty spirit on this earth. To him had been given the fairest of women and the greatest of horses. But now there was only misery and doubt in his breast, and Sweet Medicine, to whom he had prayed, would not open his breast and take from him the sickness of grief.

Now and again, in his eyes, there was a stinging. Perhaps his whole soul had been weakened by his stay among the white men. Perhaps, when he rejoined the Cheyennes at last, they would find his softness and would despise him again, as they had done long ago when his courage had not been great enough to permit him to endure the tortures of the initiation.

The greatness of his doubt caused him to stop running, and he continued to walk forward, very slowly. He was in the center of an emptiness no less great than his grief. Only his loneliness was as vast as his sorrow.

Chapter Fourteen

The joy which had been in Bill Tenney as he rushed the great stallion across the plains had gone out of him, after a time. For the blood-stiffened shirt rasped against his back, and every fold of it was a torment. Therefore he halted White Horse.

That was not so easily done. For when he took hold on the reins of the hackamore and gave a stout pull, the stallion bored out his head and doubled his pace. The slight humping of the back gave sure signal that pitching was about to start, and Tenney had a dizzy picture of the monster hurling him to the ground, and then flinging away into freedom.

So Tenney stopped pulling on the reins and talked gently. The talking did far more than the hauling at the reins. Gradually White Horse came back into the hand of the rider, so that a mere touch on the reins was enough to check him to a walk.

After that, afraid to dismount, Bill Tenney gradually worked the torment of the shirt off his welted back, rolled it, and tied it to the side of the saddle by a pair of the dangling leather strings. Then he could go on with a greater comfort; he could even forget his pain somewhat.

With that forgetfulness, however, there began another torment that was of the mind alone. He had let his friend fall into the hands of the soldiers in his place. But long before, he had planned to betray that friendship. The whole logic of his life taught Bill Tenney to take what he could, without remorse. But all other things he had taken by craft or by sheer daring, and on this occasion he had received a free gift.

He began to tell himself that his brain was softening, and that he was a fool.

He had White Horse under him; he was equipped to defy the dangers of the prairies. If the ways of this part of the world were strange to him, he would soon grow used to them. And he had a rifle and enough ammunition to assure him of food for a long time. He had lost the gold that he had stolen; he had gained a thorough flogging; but all of these payments were more than made up for by the possession of the stallion. Therefore, why should he not be happy? Why should he be tormented by a sense of loss.

"Rusty," he said aloud, "is just a poor half-witted fool."

He was sorry that he had spoken those words aloud, because they awakened in his mind undying echoes that rolled continually through his brain.

"A poor, half-witted fool. A poor, half-witted fool," he repeated.

But half-wits do not venture into a fort crowded with armed men, for the sake of a friend. Fools are not apt to defy the law and give up the prospect of a marriage, for the sake of a friend.

Somewhere in Bill Tenney's soul hammer strokes were falling on an iron anvil. A new idea was ringing out: *Friendship is sacred. Friendship is sacred.*

"Damn friendship!" snarled Tenney aloud.

The stallion leaped suddenly ahead and nearly unseated him, and for an instant, with chilling blood, he felt that the horse had understood the blasphemy he had uttered. Aye, the whole world would detest him if it could hear what he had said.

He pacified himself somewhat by deciding that, when opportunity offered, he would return to the fort; he would kill Major Marston, and he would liberate Rusty Sabin. In this way, he would redeem his pride and his self-respect and so complete his payment to Sabin.

In this way he put his conscience to sleep, for the time being, and concentrated his attention on the stallion.

He had watched, during the early part of the ride, exactly how Rusty had managed the stallion, and he had heard the terms of the ordering. But it seemed that between the horse and his real owner there was little need of speech. By a gesture, Rusty could control his mount. It was as though some electric current from Rusty's brain flowed down through the rawhide reins and touched the brain of the animal. As for Bill Tenney, he had to experiment, and only in that manner could he work out carefully one possibility after another.

The horse reined across the neck, of course, but Tenney discovered that he responded to touches, not to jerks and hauls. A lifting of the reins was enough to make him increase his gait, and lifting the reins higher at any time was enough to send him away like a bullet, at full speed. Above all, the animal seemed to be studying his rider, keeping his head a trifle turned so that the brightness of his eye could be seen as he looked back. To urge him with the flat of the hand or with the heel was instantly to invite trouble. And the best way, plainly, was to treat him as a partner, a traveling companion with a proud volition of his own and plenty of brain to work out every problem of the trail.

This investigation of the stallion's properties kept Bill Tenney thoroughly employed until he struck one of those patches of badlands through which he had been guided by Rusty, during the night. And in the bottom of the first gulley, he struck a rivulet of water that was too much for him to resist.

He was about to dismount, when he saw a huge buffalo wolf sitting on an eminence a quarter of a mile away from him, and obviously watching. It gave Bill Tenney an odd thrill to see the brute.

The wolf began to scratch with a hind leg, and Tenney, irritated, he hardly knew why, reached for his rifle. Instantly the wolf was gone from view.

He bathed his back slowly, carefully. The effect of the cold water was to make him groan with relief. He was feverish, of course, and the cold sopping cloth with which he squeezed or patted the water onto his bare flesh gave him the most exquisite relief.

Looking up from that occupation, he saw, not two hundred yards away, on the opposite side of the ravine, a second wolf as big as the first. But this one was showing itself with more caution, only the head and shoulders appearing. Again, Tenney snatched up his rifle and tried a snap shot, but the brute disappeared just as the trigger was pulled.

Well, if the wolves knew firearms as well as that, they signified hard hunting.

White Horse began to show a great deal of interest in this second appearance of a wolf. He danced away a step or two, and then stood beautifully alert, turning his head and looking anxiously up and down the shallow cañon that the stream had ripped out of the easy face of the plain. The clay bluffs looked as hard, almost as polished, as rock. And White Horse seemed to find danger in the very air that he snuffed.

Bill Tenney could remember what he had heard—that a horse of the prairies is more keenly on guard than a human hunter. Perhaps there *was* danger at hand. He was about to step over to White Horse and remount when a chorus of shrill yells struck his heart cold. The cries came from both up and down the valley. And now a troop of half a dozen Indians appeared from either side, racing around the bends and bearing down on him.

Chapter Fifteen

The first yell of the Indians seemed to run a spur into White Horse. He tore straight across the ravine, hit what looked to Tenney like a perpendicular slope, and went up it, enclosed in a cloud of dust that evaporated in the wind at the top, revealing that the stallion had disappeared.

Tenney had only had time to snatch the rifle out of its cover, but he did not use the gun.

When he was in Kentucky, he had heard a lot about fighting Indians on the plains. There were tales of men who had raised their rifles and waited, reserving fire, until the Indian charge split to either side, each brave feeling that the muzzle was pointed at his breast. He had always felt that he would be able to do the same thing. It was simple, easy, convincing, and, in the tales he had heard, it always had the same results. The Indians broke, and they kept on breaking.

But now he thought of other tales, of whole armed caravans that had been wiped out by a single attack. He saw more than he thought; he used his eyes and drew deductions. A lot of these Indians before him were as naked as Mother Nature, except for a small covering about the loins, and the sunlight played over muscles of solid bronze. Indians are supposed to be strong in the legs and weak in the arms and shoulders, but these fellows looked as though they were professional wrestlers, every one of them.

They made a pretty picture—for a man on top of a hill. It would have been a nice sight—if the red men had been going the other way. But they came on horses made beautiful by speed.

Most of the riders had rifles; some extended lances. A few carried in their hands nothing but short sticks.

Bill Tenney knew about the ones who carried sticks. They were the hot-blooded young devils who had sworn that they would touch a living enemy with the coup stick before they drew a weapon. Thereby, they would achieve the highest of all honors—for a mounted man to touch an armed footman who was uninjured.

Queer devils, these Indians—a little too queer for Bill Tenney's taste. Like all thieves, he was essentially a practical man. Now he dropped the butt of his rifle to the ground and, leaning on the barrel of it, waited for the charge to drive home.

Some of the riders did not go straight at him. Half of them swerved to the side and charged the steep bank up which White Horse had plunged, but none of them gained the top. Two or three pushed their struggling ponies halfway to the crest of the rigid slope, and then were rewarded with handsome tumbles that stretched them on the flat of the ravine floor below. But they rose, remounted, and seemed unharmed.

The half dozen who remained in the charge against Bill Tenney swooped about him. They came close so that he could see the silver glistening of the tribal scars on their breasts. Those scars came from the initiation festivals about which he had heard, when thongs were torn through the pectoral muscles by iron-willed young initiates.

The bodies all seemed young, all equally young, and the merest youth of the party had a face cast in a savage mold. The older men were like cruel masks, things designed to strike terror to the heart. Bill Tenney was afraid, but he was also resigned, watchful, ready for any chance if it was offered.

They weren't giving chances, however. Four of the fellows who bore the coup sticks rode about him and gave him smart whacks as they went on. The rest pulled out their horses in a swirl of dust. One of them threw a noose of rawhide rope over the neck of Tenney, pulled the loop taut, and seemed ready to drag the white man to death. Yet, with his horse turned, he waited for a moment.

The oldest-looking brave of the party, the one with the longest hair flowing down his back, came up and made his face more hideous with speech. He tried a harsh, rapid, guttural tongue, at first. But when Tenney shook his head the fellow growled: "White Horse . . . where get him?"

"Rusty Sabin give," said Tenney. "Red Hawk give."

"Give?" exclaimed the warrior. He took a stride nearer and grasped Tenney's throat.

"Red Hawk no give!" he declared vehemently.

Tenney shrugged his shoulders as he repeated: "Red Hawk give."

The elderly brave glared at him for a moment. The face of the old man was a living horror. The mouth kept twitching so that deep furrows sprang in and out along the cheeks. His nostrils kept flaring and contracting with each breath.

"Lie . . . lie," he muttered. "White men all lie."

"Red Hawk is white," said Tenney.

The brave fetched out a long knife with the look of one ready to use it. However, he shoved it reluctantly back into its sheath. He wore only the belt and the loincloth, but his body was as young as that of any of the other Herculean figures around him—full of slope and shine and the bulging of mighty muscles.

After that, he mounted, took the rawhide lariat from the hand of the fellow who had lassoed Tenney, gave the captive a jerk that half strangled him, and told him to start moving.

Tenney started. Walking would not do. These devils trotted their horses, or even loped them gently, and Tenney had to run uphill and down dale.

He ran till the soft green waves of the prairie washed up into the blue sky, and the sky rippled like blue water along the ground at his feet. He ran till his lungs were filled with flame. Finally he stumbled. The rope rubbed his throat, dragged him a dozen feet before he managed to scramble erect, and then he had a bad few minutes after he had loosened the rawhide around his neck. Those minutes were spent in trying to catch his spent breath again. He kept on catching it, but it would not really come back, and, all the while, the cruel old devil at the head of the party would not so much as turn in the saddle, and all the rest kept their backs likewise turned upon Bill Tenney.

He was gone, staggering in his stride, almost done in every way, before the warriors dropped the pace of their horses to a walk. And Tenney, at that, could still go on, held toward a straight direction by the tugging of the lariat every time he reeled to this side or to that.

But he uttered no complaint. He felt that it would be as silly to waste breath complaining to these men as to utter laments to hungry wolves.

After a time, his knees had strength once more. And also he was able to see that over the horizon the peaked tops of a group of Indian lodges were appearing. That was what made him think of White Horse. These fellows were likely to take him into their village and torture him to death. But if White Horse had been under him, a pale thunderbolt of speed, he could have galloped away from the best of them. He could have laughed at the best mounted of the warriors. As it was, he had to trudge on foot, into whatever trouble waited for him.

As the troop came nearer, a cloud of naked young boys rushed out of the camp on racing ponies and swirled around the returning war party, screeching. Nearly every one of these young devils carried a weapon of some sort. Knives, clubs, axes were brandished over the head of big Bill Tenney, and some of the rascals had arrows with blunted heads. With the latter they thumped his body soundly. When the blows fell on the raw of his still naked back, they gave intense pain. However, this was not yet death, such as he expected. He wondered, when the flames of the fire began to consume him, if he would be able to endure that agony, too, without screaming. And an immense pride and resolution filled his heart and swelled in his throat as he swore that he would die like a man.

In that moment he looked back along his life as a traveler sometimes looks back along a great road, and it seemed to him that he had never stopped at an inn of importance. It seemed to him that he could spend future days better, that he could find men of greater significance, that so far his work had consisted of idle gestures. He had been a thief, but a thief cannot really take anything. He can only steal money or worldly valuables—baubles. What is worthwhile is something else. He wondered what that something might be.

They went still closer to the Indian village. Then a cloud of the smallest children, intermixed with howling dogs, poured out around him, and the dogs leaped high and snapped their teeth close to his throat. They seemed to be howling, even when they were closing their teeth. He could feel the teeth in his flesh, as it were. But to be torn with teeth would be nothing compared with the soul-searing bite of the fire.

Then he was on the verge of the camp, and he saw that all the lodges were arranged in circles. Some of them were new and glistening white. Some of them were tanning with time, from rain and with sun. Thin cracks seared the leather, here and there. And the gaudy, childish paintings that decorated the tents were sometimes garishly fresh and sometimes crackling away to obscurity.

Here and there, he saw braves standing at the entrances to their lodges, cloaked in buffalo robes, sometimes with their faces almost completely hidden, and often with their stark features seen only through deep shadow. He saw the squaws, the old ones who were time-bent and work-worn, their hands dangling from their sides like the hands of laboring men—big hands, with fingers too thick to suggest femininity. There were the young squaws, also, still with the unmistakable signs of life upon them. And last of all, there were the girls. Cruelty was in their smiling, no doubt, and their beauty was not that of white girls.

White men only look at faces. They may joke about the bodies of women, but they only look at faces. Put the face of a saint on the body of a cripple, and the girl will marry well.

Well, it was different, here. These girls were modestly clad, and yet the supple flow of young bodies was apparent under the thin deerskins. And the picture was a whole. Those faces, often blunted, wide, too round, were to be observed rather for the expression than the fact. Tenney, near to death, noticed those women. And he held himself a little taller and stepped with a lighter and a longer stride.

He was ashamed of the red gorings on his back that told that he had been flogged. He was ashamed of the lariat that clasped his neck and led him along like a dog. Despite these things, he told himself that he could die like a man, if there were such women as these to watch while he was being tormented. He felt that he would be able to laugh in the midst of the flames as, windblown, they rotted away his body a little at a time.

Then, before one of the lodges, the party halted. He was dragged through the entrance flap. A strong jerk on the lariat laid him flat on the ground, and he was wise enough not to try to stir, not to struggle to sit up.

Chapter Sixteen

He lay for a long time. He was aware that there were two young braves in the teepee. They never spoke to one another. They kept watching his big body. Sometimes, as dust worked into the whip wounds in his back, the anguish it caused him blotted out everything in his mind, and sometimes the cold force of thought made him forget his torment.

Hanging about the neck of one of the braves was what seemed to be a dried up mouse skin. The other wore a shapeless pouch that could not be identified. One carried a short truncheon with a spearhead on it. The other was unarmed except for a knife at his belt. But Bill Tenney knew that he could not escape. Among white men he was almost a giant. But among these Indians, he was hardly more than a peer. He had seen scarcely a single mature man in the camp who he would not have considered at least his equal.

After a time, the tent flap was raised, and another man entered. At sight of him, Tenney started to a sitting posture, though one guard instantly balanced his javelin for the cast, and the other jerked out a thin-bladed knife. But they held their hands. Perhaps they understood the excitement of their captive, who saw before him another white man.

Not that the white man was capable of much active interference. He was old. His beard flowed softly and loosely. It was the beard of a man who is too lazy to shave. And his body had almost the same loose contour.

He was dressed like an Indian, below, and above the hips like a white man. Yet he was not a half-breed. The blue of his eye was too clear, and his skin, where it showed on the hands and about the eyes, was apparently merely darkened by a tan. He held in his hand a short, curved pipe. No weapon was on his person.

Behind him, there was a scuffle at the entrance. Then an Indian girl broke in. No, she was not all Indian. She had blue eyes, like the man, and her skin, instead of the dull copper, was a paler tint with a deeper glow shining through it. She was breathing hard; hands reached after her through the tent flap, and a savage face showed for an instant until the white man spoke.

He took the girl by the arm. She chattered at him, half savagely and half appealingly, until he released her. After that, her step was like a spring as she moved to the place where big Bill Tenney sat upright. The guards, he noticed, had lowered their weapons, strange smiles appearing on their harsh faces. And she, leaning over Tenney, burst out at him: "Is it true? Did you have White Horse? Did you get it from the Red Hawk? Did you get it from him? Did you lie, and say that Red Hawk gave you the horse?"

He had to think for an instant. It was hard to think. The dusky beauty of the girl closed up his throat. She was trembling, and, like hers, Tenney's flesh and spirit vibrated. He looked like a half-wit as he sat there. But he managed to nod his head and say: "Yes, he gave it to me."

"You lie!" cried the girl. "You murdered him! You killed him and took the horse! You sneaked up like a coward and killed him in his sleep. You could not have faced him. He would have laughed, and the breath of Sweet Medicine would have blown you away like a dead leaf. *You* could not face him . . . you *must* have killed him in his sleep."

Tenney shook his head. Words were still hard to come at. He merely said: "We were chased. My horse pegged out, and he gave me White Horse."

"*Gave* you?" cried the girl incredulously.

"Wait a minute," said the white man. "You know, Blue Bird, that Rusty is always the one for giving and giving."

"You look like a wolf. You look like a white wolf. Why would he give the horse to you?" exclaimed the girl.

"I dunno," said Tenney. "He's queer. I'd hauled him out of the river one time . . . out of the Tulmac. That's all I know about it. But he gave me White Horse, all right."

"And what happened to him?" she demanded. With this she clasped her hands and crooked a knee, and seemed to be sinking down toward the earth, in the ecstasy of her entreaty.

"I dunno," repeated Tenney. "The soldiers were after us. Major Marston and his lot. I guess they grabbed Rusty Sabin. There wasn't no fighting. They just sort of come up and took him. I seen it while I was riding away."

"You rode away and left your friend?" said the girl. "You rode off and. . . ."

She looked ready to go at his eyes with her hands made into eagle talons, but the white man caught her and pushed her rudely toward the exit. He called out, because her struggles were almost too much for him, and big dark-colored hands reached through the flap of the lodge and mastered her, bearing her away.

Still her outcries, and then her sobbing, reached Tenney's ears from a distance. And something in his thought magnified the sounds and multiplied them. He was full of ears. He could close his eyes, and to the end of time, he knew, he would remember clearly the sheen of her blue ones. He had been touched—and far deeper than the skin.

He heard the white man saying: "Well, it kind of looks mean for you, stranger. What might your name be?"

The fat white man with the beard was sitting cross-legged on the ground near him, stuffing his pipe full of tobacco.

"Bill Tenney is my name. What's yours?" he answered.

"I've got another name," said the white man. He finished filling his pipe, sprinkled some light-colored dust over the tobacco, and then picked a coal out of the fire that burned in the center of the tent and laid it on the bowl of the pipe.

Tenney noticed that, like a real Indian, the man blew four ceremonial puffs of smoke to the quarters of the compass before he settled down to the enjoyment of the pipe.

"I've got another name . . . somewheres," went on the fellow, "but among the Cheyennes I'm called Lazy Wolf. It's not a name I'm proud of, but I reckon it has to stick. Lazy Wolf is what you might as well call me."

"All right." Tenney nodded. "But what's all the excitement about Rusty Sabin, up here? What's it all about? Or is it because I had White Horse? Or is it because I let White Horse get away from me?"

Lazy Wolf puffed smoke out of his fat lips. He pulled down from his forehead a pair of spectacles that had been riding high, and, as they settled over the bridge of his nose, he took on an owlish aspect. Gravely he considered Tenney.

"I'll tell you plenty of things about Rusty Sabin and this tribe," he remarked. "But first I better get your straight story. How did you come by the welting, and who gave it to you? How did you come by White Horse? Tell me the whole yarn." He added: "I wanna do you some good, stranger, and it's going to be a mighty hard thing to wangle. These redskins want your hair, and they'll likely take it. But if you got any chance, it's because I'm willing to talk for you. Talk to me like I was wearing your own pair of ears."

Tenney blinked. He liked the truth little more than he liked justice and its courses. He was a good, thoroughgoing liar, as a rule, and the temptation was to start lying now. Yet an instinct worked in him to make him understand that this was the time for the naked truth, no matter how much shame there might be in it. So he simply said: "I stole twenty pounds of gold out of a trading post down on the Tulmac. I got up to Fort Marston. I seen a steamer coming in, and a white horse was lost off of it, a man diving in after the horse. I managed to fetch them both out with a canoe I grabbed. The man was Rusty Sabin. He shook hands with me and said he was my friend. Afterward, I was caught with the gold on me. They took me into the fort and tied me to a post and flogged me."

His lips pulled back far enough to show his teeth, as he said this. "Then Rusty and a brace of Cheyennes showed up and got me away from the major," he went on, "and we rode away across the plains. The soldiers followed on, with dogs to light the way for 'em, and my mustang pegged out. Then Rusty climbed down off White Horse and gave it to me. And I took it and rode away till this gang of Injuns stopped me." He paused. His face was hot and his breathing fast. A queer agony of shame, an entirely unfamiliar sensation, was burning through his blood. "Back there at the fort," he muttered rapidly, "they'd knocked the hell out of me. Anyway . . . I dunno . . . anyway, I took White Horse and I rode off . . . and I left Rusty behind me, there. . . ."

Here he jerked up his head and glared at Lazy Wolf in defiance, but the calm consideration in the eyes of the older man overwhelmed him, and by degrees he found his head sinking until his chin was on his breast.

"Well," said Lazy Wolf, "I'm gonna do my best for you. I believe what you're saying, by the shame that seems to be in you. But will these Indians believe you? I don't know. Let me tell you, these are Cheyennes. Rusty is the biggest medicine man that ever walked the ground, as far as this tribe is concerned. And that leads me on to tell you the other half of the story that you ought to know. The Cheyennes felt pretty mean when Rusty left them and found his father and went back to the white people . . . and not long after he went away, a sickness hit a lot of the people. The medicine men danced themselves black in the face and wore their craziest masks and whooped and hollered and ordered up steam baths every day, with plunges in cold water afterward, but the sick men got sicker and sicker.

"But pretty soon word came across the prairie . . . you know, news spreads far and fast over the plains . . . that Red Hawk was away down south on the Tulmac River . . . and with that it was decided that a part of the tribe would start south as fast as it could leg it and take along with it all of the sick people. And that's what happened. I came with the rest. I didn't want to come, but my daughter made me. You understand, she's pretty fond of Red Hawk, Tenney. So fond that I had to leave the tribe for a time. But when Rusty turned white, I went back to the Cheyennes, and now my girl, Blue Bird, has dragged me south. She's heard of a strange man who was riding White Horse . . . and that means, to her, that she's heard of the man who has *murdered* Rusty.

"The whole tribe feels the same way. It wants blood in exchange. It wants your blood . . . and it's pretty likely to get it."

He made a short, eloquent gesture. There could be no mistaking his grim meaning.

"These people are scared of Rusty," he went on. "They look up higher than the sky to see him. Besides all that, they love him. He's a gentle sort of a cuss, Tenney. Giving his horse to you . . . well, that's what he would do to a friend. All the ways he walked in the Cheyenne camps were kind ways. Men in trouble went to him. He talked to them like a woman. He has a soft voice. He has the softest voice that an Indian ever heard. The women of the camp turned into stone when he went by. When they saw Rusty, nothing about them lived except their eyes. But he wouldn't notice that. All he thinks about himself is that he's lucky. Well, Tenney, that's the man the Cheyennes think you've murdered. You can guess what they want to do to you, but they've sent me in to give you a last chance."

This last part of the recital was what killed the hope in Tenney.

"Even if you told 'em the truth," Bill Tenney mused, "even if you told 'em how he really gave me White Horse and stood there, waiting for the soldiers . . . even if they believed it, they'd want to kill me just the same."

The silence of Lazy Wolf was a death sentence to Tenney.

At last the squawman said: "The sick people who are dying in these lodges . . . the ones who've been kept alive by the hope of seeing Rusty and having him work a miracle over them . . . well, they're the ones who'll be extra set against you, Tenney. They say that Red Hawk's dead, and that means that *they're* all dead, too."

"What *could* Rusty do?" demanded Tenney, agape. "He ain't a wizard . . . and he sure ain't a doctor. How could he cure 'em?"

"I don't know," answered Lazy Wolf. "I'm telling you what a lot of Cheyenne Indians believe, not what I think." Then he stood up and said good bye. "I'm going to talk to the council, now," he told Tenney right before he left. "I wish I could say that I'm going to put everything right for you. But I'm afraid I've only got half a chance."

He turned to the entrance, paused there as though he wanted to say something else, and then hurried through the flap.

Chapter Seventeen

Big Bill Tenney sat up until he could endure no longer the eyes of the two guards that devoured him steadily, unwinkingly. Then he lay down again, and the slow hours went by.

This was his first visit to an Indian camp. He had always imagined them to be places of silence. Instead, this was a continual riot. The dog noises never ceased. Either there was a yelping voice in the distance, howling at the moon, or else an outbreak of snarls and fighting close by, or a whole tide of battling dogs would wash in crescendo and diminuendo across the area.

The dogs were not all. Most of the night, two or three children, near or far, were crying. And odd bits of music with no tune to it tormented Tenney's ears, music that was howled out by serenading braves to the ladies of their love, and accompanied by the banging of odd instruments. Now and then a random brave was even inspired to burst out into a war song or a battle yell that struck cold and hard upon the nerves.

Yet, at last Tenney was able to sleep, and he did not waken until long after sunrise.

He spent the hours of the sweltering day still in the lodge, with only a change of guards to amuse him, the new pair being a shade older and uglier than the first ones. It was late in the afternoon before Lazy Wolf appeared. He came in looking totally spent, and he sank down on a thick, folded buffalo robe and joined his hands together wearily, as he stared at the prisoner.

"I talked most of last night," he said. "I made 'em put off the decision until they'd slept on the thing. Then I talked to 'em again this afternoon. But no matter what I say, they've fixed on the idea that Red Hawk is dead. You're to be a sacrifice they'll send after him. Besides, they've got an idea that they may be able to wash away their disease in your blood. The sick and ailing ones are going to do the work on you. And . . . God help you, Tenney!"

One deep note of compassion came into these last words, and Bill Tenney heard them ring all through his soul.

"I've gotta die, have I?" he demanded.

"You've got to die," said Lazy Wolf. "The way the people are feeling now, not even the head chiefs of the tribe could handle them or change them, and the only big chief among the lot, just now, is young Standing Bull, who was Red Hawk's best friend. I spent a long time with Standing Bull, but he wants to tear you to pieces with his own hands."

"All right," said Bill Tenney. "I'm their meat . . . and I guess they'll spend a long time whittling me away."

Lazy Wolf sighed as he answered: "I've got to tell you the truth, and the truth is that they'll make you last as long as they can."

"Pardner," said Tenney, "you couldn't do a little thing like picking up that axe and braining me with it, right now, could you? Or passing that knife between my ribs, eh?"

"They'd shred me into mincemeat, if I did," declared Lazy Wolf. "I'm sorry, but that's the way they're feeling. I've come to say good bye."

He rose and held out his hand, but there was a sudden snarl from one of the guards, who leaped between and fenced the two white men apart from one another.

"It don't matter," said Tenney. "I'm thanking you for what you've tried to do. I'll tell you another thing, Lazy Wolf. I'm nothing for a gent to grieve about, at all. I been a thief and a crook and a damned mean man. I sort of wish I'd have a chance. Well, anything that the Injuns do to me will sure be coming. So long."

When he was left alone with the guards, Tenney's courage sank a little, but he took a firm hold on himself. It was the length of the trial that filled him with dread. To face death—to stand before a firing squad—why, a thing like that would be as nothing. But to drag through the frightful hours, always waiting and waiting—and then to feel his own body being plucked and torn and burned, bit by bit, the precious flame of life still cherished and kept active by the skilful fiends who operated on him—that was the prospect that made him shrink. But the heart of a brave man is always greater than his knowledge of it. He set his teeth and made himself smile.

He was still smiling a little, faintly and steadily, when a great noise of voices drew near, focusing on the lodge. He knew that they were coming for him. So he stood up and folded his arms and waited, facing the entrance flap.

He was not bound hand and foot. He was merely led out with a rope around his neck. He saw the night covering the village; he saw the lodges, vaguely illumined by the flutter and the flicker of the fires inside them. He saw the glittering of the stars, and the sky seemed to be turning slowly, like a vast wheel. But all around him, pressing close, were the Indians. The smell of them was different from that of a white crowd. The odor of wood smoke clung to them. And their faces were so hideous that it seemed to Tenney that they were illumined by ugliness as by a light.

Still, he was not able to take in the full terror of the moment until he had been led into a central circle, which was an open space in the middle of the camp, with the teepees all around, pointing their blunted fingers at the sky. In the middle of this space he was tied to a thick post. Two lengths of small iron chain were used to bind his feet and his hands to the pole. He could imagine why the iron was required. Flame would too quickly eat its way through cords or ropes.

In the four quarters of the circle, fires had been already kindled, to give light for the proceedings. Perhaps at the climax, the materials of the four fires would be heaped suddenly around him, and so the flames would eat their share.

Could he stand it? It came on Tenney with a fresh shock of surprise that the torture itself was not the thing that weakened him in prospect; it was the savage ugliness of these Cheyennes. They were, to be sure, the handsomest race of red men on the whole of the plains, but they were now hideously transformed by passion. Furthermore, the normal men and women of the race could not be seen so clearly. They were masked by five score or more of the sick who occupied the center of the area.

These last were a grisly lot. The disease, whatever it was, had withered them like famine. Their flesh had shrunk to the bone. Their skin was in many folds. Their eyes burned at the bottoms of black pits, and when they opened their mouths, it seemed certain that the teeth must clamp down afterward on the skin of the sunken cheeks. So starved by pain and suffering were they that there seemed to be nothing left in them except the ghost of life, and that ghost was now frenzied.

Off to one side, some drums began to beat in a steady rhythm, and this cadence threw the line of invalids into movement. What a dance! A Dance of Death. Fleshless knees were staggering; skeletal arms waved in the air. Those who could not walk crawled, and paused, now and then, to beat the earth with one hand. And at certain pauses and accents in the drumming, the whole crowd looked suddenly up and cast a hand toward the sky, shouting a few syllables.

In that shout the dim multitude on the verge of the firelight joined, and the roar of the voices surged in a wave over big Bill Tenney's heart and brain. He could pick out details, now. In the first place, every man, woman, and child was armed, and all with knives that they brandished at him in turn as they staggered by, their skinny breasts heaving so that sometimes the ribs looked empty—a mad, ominous dance.

At a little distance from the rest was one form so feeble that it had not yet been able to work its way into the line of the walking, crawling dancers. That meager body was naked except for the loincloth, and there was so little strength in the Indian that he had to wriggle slowly forward, snake-like.

Now and again, he paused and lay stretched out at full length, and, as he came closer, Bill Tenney could count the ribs down the back, and the lumps of the vertebrae. He could see the hip bones standing out like elbows, and the shoulder blades that did not even seem to be covered with flesh. Now the face of the crawling Indian turned up toward him, and he was shocked to realize that it was that of a mere boy, a child of fourteen years or even less, the skin drawn across his face as tightly as the membrane over the face of a frog.

Horribly he grinned, when he saw Bill Tenney, and stretched out a knife toward the prisoner. Literally, then, the sick were going to try to wash away their diseases in the captive's blood. And perhaps those shouts that they occasionally raised to the sky contained the name of Red Hawk, in whose honor all of this sacrifice was performed.

The crawling, wriggling boy now came to the line of the dancers. They stamped and jumped and sprawled and stumbled across him. But he advanced, until with one hand he could grasp the toe of Tenney's boot. Then, gradually, the youngster began to raise himself. It was a process of the most infinite pain. Tenney could hear the gasping breath, with a rattle in it.

Slowly the boy gained his knees. By the dreadful grin of hate and hope in the lad's face, Tenney knew that the knife would be buried in his flesh the next moment. Ah, if only that stroke would find the heart!

Then, out of the distance, a wild voice came toward the camp, shouting. And what it cried made the dancers halt in the middle of a gesture. The drums ceased their beating.

Chapter Eighteen

A rattle of hoof beats sped toward the crowd. A youth appeared, his bronze body flashing out of the night like a hurled spear as he raced his horse through the crowd and around the circle within, always yelling that same brief group of syllables that Bill Tenney had already begun to suspect stood for the name of Red Hawk in the Cheyenne tongue.

The effect of the outcry of this rider was to drive the audience completely frantic. The seated men leaped to their feet and turned to rush into the outer darkness, toward that point from which the jubilant shouts had already begun to issue. Proud chiefs with great headdresses of feathers sweeping down to their heels, men with the many brightly stained coup feathers bristling in their regalia, old fellows full of dignity but weak, one and all poured off, leaping and screaming, toward the unseen thing in the night.

Only the sick remained in place, and they gathered into a closely packed group. The lad who had drawn himself up on his knees, ready to strike the first blow at the prisoner, now turned a little and spilled down on the ground, where he lay inert, with his head on Tenney's feet.

Tenney, straining his eyes, first thought he saw a slowly stalking giant, tall and slender, a yard higher than the loftiest of the big Cheyennes. But now he was able to make out that the man was carried forward, literally standing in the mighty hands that supported him.

Before this advancing figure, borne along like an idol, came a scattering, scampering troop of young boys who cut enough

111

capers to fill the brains of ten thousand designers. Guns exploded. The very dogs of the Cheyennes added their voices heartily to the great moment. And out of the throats of the sick there went up a united screech of joy.

That scream was still piercing Bill Tenney's brain when he recognized the newcomer as Rusty Sabin! Tenney closed his eyes then, and the groan that came out of his throat made his entire body tremble a little.

When he looked again, he saw that Rusty was no longer being carried. Instead, he was walking slowly through the cluster of the sick. He had to go slowly, because the ground before him was covered by the meager bodies of those who implored his aid. They reached up for his hands. They clutched at his legs as he went by. Tenney saw a woman on her knees, alternately beating her breast and throwing out her hands toward Red Hawk. And so Rusty Sabin at last managed to get clear of them all and come near to the post where Tenney was bound to the stake.

"It's over!" Rusty called from a little distance. "There's no more danger. I'm telling these people things that will make you like a chief in this tribe. You will be every man's brother, from today."

With that, he turned and shouted a few more words to the assembled tribe. Then he stepped forward and laid his hand on Tenney's shoulder, as he spoke, and a great yell widened still further the distended throats of those Indians.

"I have told them you are my brother," said Rusty Sabin. "I told them you have given me my life. You will see, now."

There was plenty to see. Tenney, weak with happy relief, began to laugh foolishly, as scores of hands reached to take part in the work of liberating him. But even through his laughter, he could mark the tender manner in which Rusty picked up the prostrate form of the lad who had so nearly drawn the blood of Tenney. Cradling that body, mummified by disease, in his strong arms, Rusty was calling out to the happy, milling crowd of the Cheyennes. A huge, middle-aged warrior came out of the throng and laid his hands, also, on the body of the boy. He would be the lad's father, for an expression of infinite fear and care was in his face when he looked down at the boy, and infinite joy and hope lighted his eyes when he looked at Rusty.

Tenney, so suddenly freed, found himself being patted and spoken to kindly by all the men around him. Lazy Wolf, appearing at his side, found his hand and grasped it heartily.

"I thought there was to be one brave man less in this world," said Lazy Wolf. "I'm happy about you, Tenney."

"They would have had me dead yesterday, but for you," answered Tenney truthfully. "You were the one who kept them off until Rusty had a chance to come here. My God, man, when I see how they love Sabin, I don't wonder that they wanted to tear me to shreds."

"Aye, they love him . . . and they need him." The other nodded. "Put need and love together and it makes a pretty bright fire. A very bright fire, in fact. This tribe is dazzled by the light, just now. Aye, but, later on, how will they feel when they find out that Rusty can't really help these poor sick devils?"

"Aye," Tenney agreed, nodding. "What *can* he do?"

He shook his head soberly. "I don't know," growled Lazy Wolf.

"He could make a bluff, I suppose," said Tenney.

"A bluff? There's no pretending in Red Hawk. He'll do the things that he thinks Sweet Medicine tells him to do. He'll pray, and have a fool dream, and then he'll do what the dream says."

"Aye, but if the dream don't say nothing?"

"Them that are hungry to believe can always find something to believe in," answered Lazy Wolf. "We've got to find my girl, somewhere. When Red Hawk shouted to the tribe that you were his brother, and that you had given him his life, she pulled her hair down over her eyes and began to moan as though her best blood had died.

"She wants to see you, Tenney. She wants to get down on her knees and beg your pardon. If you don't forgive her for the way she talked to you yesterday, she'll cut off her long hair and slash her body with a knife, and she'll sit on a hill outside the camp and howl and mourn for seven days and nights. When a Cheyenne gets excited, there's a fire in the blood . . . and my girl's dying of grief, just now. She's afraid that you'll tell Rusty about her."

Tenney laughed.

When they came through the happy, shouting crowd to where the girl stood, drawn back against a teepee, he saw that Blue Bird had in fact thrown her hair forward over her face, and that she stood disconsolate, her head bowed. When her father spoke to her in Cheyenne, she flung her head up suddenly. And all at once, as the dark hair flowed back against her shoulders, her beauty dawned on Bill Tenney like the brightness of day. She came to him quickly, with her hands stretched out. Her knees were already bending as she tried to cast herself to the ground, but Tenney caught the hands and held her up.

"There ain't anything to get worried about," said Tenney as gently as he could manage. "And even if there was, I'd forget it. I've forgot it already, in fact. I've sure forgot it so much that I wouldn't be able to tell Rusty even if I wanted to."

What he said so filled her that her happiness overflowed in a sharp cry.

"Look," she said to her father. "He is not only a brave man, but he is a good man. How kind he is. There is pain in me when I think what I have said." She took one of Bill Tenney's hands between hers and patted it. There was strength in her touch, and soft gentleness, also.

"Red Hawk is not cruel," she said, explaining. "But he thinks very much. He can even think himself away from people. And I don't want him to think himself away from me."

After that, the night became a whirling confusion, in the mind of Bill Tenney. For wherever Rusty went, Tenney had to go with him, and Rusty had to go everywhere through the camp.

The crowd poured along with him. What happy laughter brightened the air about the returned medicine man. He had to go into lodge after lodge. He had to take a bite of the buffalo meat that would be brought out of the stew pot over every fire; he had to blow one whiff of smoke from every pipe; he had to look at the children who stared up at him in awe and yet in trusting confidence; he had to take in his hands small babies; he had to grasp the withered hands of old men and, with lifted head, offer up a prayer to Sweet Medicine to increase their strength and their remaining days.

And always, no matter where he appeared, he was greeted with looks of hushed expectancy, as though a miracle might at any moment happen.

If there was strength in belief, Bill Tenney saw, Rusty had enough power to move mountains in this camp.

It was when Rusty Sabin was turning out of a teepee that he said to Tenney: "And White Horse? Where is he, brother?"

That question stunned Tenney. He had to take a long breath and steady himself before he could answer: "He's gone, Rusty."

But the blow was so great that the full weight of it missed Rusty utterly. He merely halted and looked back at Tenney with uncomprehending eyes.

"Gone," repeated Tenney. "When the Cheyennes come on me in that gulley, where I was down out of the saddle, they scared him off. He went right up the side of the bluff like a goat . . . and . . . he's gone. God knows I'm sorry."

Rusty made a queer gesture with both hands reaching in front of him, like one who is walking through thick darkness and feeling his way.

"White Horse," he said. "White Horse. I thought that he was to be taken away only for a little while. But he is gone. Everything is gone from me."

And then, with a gentleness and a sudden movement of tact that brought the tears' sting to Tenney's eyes, Rusty laid his hand on the big fellow's arm and added quickly: "No! Not all gone. For I have you, brother. And, as for the rest, I have my tribe . . . I have the Cheyennes. I have my own people." Suffering made his face seem suddenly older, and yet his voice rose louder as he added: "They are my happiness. My people are my happiness. Ah, Sweet Medicine, make my heart so wide that there is room in it for every Cheyenne, both the old and the young. Give me the power! Give me the power to help them!"

He went, after all this, straight to the lodges where the sick people had been gathered. In three big teepees the women, the men, and the children lay, each group with its separate shelter.

Into the lodges of the children Rusty went first, and their voices rose up to greet him in a soft chirruping, like that of so many birds. It was a terrible and a touching thing to see, their trust and their perfect faith in the big White Indian. Only the lad who had crawled to Tenney's feet that evening was incapable of movement now. He lay on his back like a corpse, and the puckering of his starved cheeks made him seem to smile.

They will die, thought Tenney. *They will all die, and in some way the grief for their deaths will revert upon Rusty Sabin's head.*

Tenney drew back by the entrance flap and bowed his head. If he had known a prayer, there was that in his spirit that would have made him utter it now.

Chapter Nineteen

The women and the men who were the parents of the sick children crouched beside them, motionless. They looked like figures of doom. Well, they would probably be roused when Rusty Sabin began to dance and prance. He was a medicine man, the Cheyennes said, and Bill Tenney knew that all medicine men dance and howl and contort themselves.

But Rusty did not so much as speak. He merely stared down for a long time on the bodies of the sick. For Indians, they were dusty pale, and, above all, their eyes were strange. The whites were not luminous and translucent. They were dead white, like paint or snow.

After a moment, Rusty turned from the lodge with Bill Tenney at his heels. Right out of the camp Rusty proceeded, to a low hillock from which Tenney could look back on the entire circle of the village, thinly glowing with spots of firelight.

"What's comin' up now?" asked Tenney.

But Rusty merely raised a hand for silence. He pulled off his shirt and sat down, cross-legged, in front of a handful of fire that he had made with a few dead twigs from a bush. Into that fire he sprinkled sweet grass from his pouch, and with the thick, odorous smoke he bathed himself thoroughly. The fire died as the ceremony of purification ended, and Rusty stood up with his arms raised to the sky. He remained in that frozen attitude for a long time, silent.

It seemed to Tenney that the man must be made of metal to endure the posture so rigidly and for such a time. A sudden gasp of breath from Rusty made Tenney look quickly around him, and then, far in the east, he saw a dim hand of light that freshened quickly and became a point of white fire. This, in turn, grew into a full moon, stretching like a vast golden disk on the horizon.

Rusty, with a faint groan of content, dropped down on the ground and lay at full length, exhausted, panting, while awe such as Tenney never had known before spread over him. Magic, silent magic had seemed to be in Rusty's prayer. There was not much room for superstition in the soul of Tenney, but small cold shudders ran through his heart as he stared at that rising moon. If a prayer had raised it, might it not vanish again like a breath, an exhalation? Still it rose, shining ever more brightly, while the wavering prairie came into wider view. And Tenney, closely wrapped in a buffalo robe against the chill of the night, waited for other and stranger things to happen.

Again, again, and yet again, he saw Rusty rise from the ground and offer up that silent prayer, with upraised arms. But nothing further happened. Each time, Rusty sank back to the ground more exhausted, and the interval was longer before he could rise once more.

He spoke only once in the Cheyenne tongue, and once again in English, when he said to himself, loud enough for Tenney to hear: "Sweet Medicine, they are hungry. Teach me what food to give my children."

The poor, starved youngsters, the withered women, the skeletal braves who were wasted by the mysterious disease, all of them were the *children* of Rusty Sabin.

And why should any man choose to be a blacksmith and a common laborer among the whites when he could be a king and a father among the great tribe of the Cheyennes?

The coolness of the night began to make Tenney shiver under his robe, yet Rusty, though half naked, appeared to be unconscious of the discomfort, rising time and again to stand there until the arms that he lifted wavered with weakness and slowly sank of their own leaden weight. Then he would drop to the ground, rest, and renew his effort.

The gray dawn had begun to creep around the edges of the sky, suddenly expanding the plains to the vastness of the unbounded sea. The moon, at the zenith, had turned into a pale, strangely formed cloud, when Rusty stood on his feet again. He had been hardly a minute in this posture before he started so violently that Tenney looked up in haste, and, following the direction in which Rusty stared, he saw an eagle balancing high up, where the light seemed brighter than that which filtered down to the earth. Still higher, another eagle hid itself in distance.

Now the first one stooped. It struck a rabbit so close to the hillock where the two men were that Tenney could hear the poor little beast cry out with an almost human scream. He heard the loud report, also, as the eagle exploded its wings at the end of its stoop. Then the great bird went up with laboring wings, in slow circles.

It was not very high in the air before trouble came to it. The second pirate of the air shot down with folded wings, swifter than a falling stone. It seemed to Tenney that he could almost hear the hissing of speed. At least the eagle with the rabbit was in some manner warned of danger, and turned on his back in the air like a swimmer in water. The rabbit fell from his talons, the little body streaking downward while the two eagles, forgetting the prey, struggled across the sky with angry screaming.

Not three paces from Tenney, the dead rabbit struck the ground a heavy blow. Rusty was instantly upon it, raising it in his hands. He was so weary that he was staggering, but there was laughter in the voice that he raised to thank Sweet Medicine for this answer to his prayer.

"Is that it?" asked Tenney, almost sick with awe. "Is that the thing for the sick folks to eat? Is that what Sweet Medicine says?"

Rusty shook his head. "The Sky People talk a strange language, brother," he answered. "Their words and their signs are never what they seem. Now look at what we find. The body of the rabbit has been torn open. It is eviscerated . . . the entrails are gone. Where? The eagles have flown away with them. Ah, there is the answer, I think. It is not of the solid body but of the entrails that the sick must eat to become well."

"Hold on, Rusty," said Tenney. "Even starving folks wouldn't want to eat that."

"No," said Rusty. "That is true. They must not eat what is unclean. But the liver is clean. There are many buffalo. The plains are covered with them, and the sick must be given fresh liver after the hunting. If I am wrong, I must pray again."

The whole village was roused not many minutes later, and throngs of buffalo hunters, riding their swiftest horses, set out, with Tenney in their midst. Rusty Sabin had gone to purify the sick with the fumes of sweet grass before they were given food, but Tenney, mounted on the best of the horses of the war chief, Standing Bull, ranged with the swift hunters far out over the plains. He did not need to know the Cheyenne tongue in order to understand that these were peerless stalkers of game, and, when the surround was made and the charge delivered into the thronged masses of the buffalo, he had to admit that he did not exist as a horseman, compared with these bronze monsters.

They took their mustangs right into the midst of the herd and fired from a yard or more into the huge beasts. What Tenney lacked in skill as a horseman, he made up for with his expert handling of the rifle, and he accounted for three cows in the hunt. But he felt himself dwarfed when he saw Standing Bull, disdaining a rifle, ride into the herd like a yelling madman, armed only with a powerful bow and a quiver of arrows. One of those arrows Tenney saw driven right through the body of a cow until it thrust out on the farther side!

When the stampeding herd broke away at last, the grass was spotted with dead buffalo for miles, and the hunters were hurrying here and there to identify their kill and put their mark upon it. Those who had used arrows had signed their game with the tool that killed it, but there was some dispute over those slaughtered with bullets. Those disputes were settled by Standing Bull.

In the meantime, the women who had trooped at the rear of the hunt with the extra horses came up swiftly and set about the butchering of the meat. There came over Tenney such a sense of abundance, after the joy of the hunt, that he swore he would never leave this life. Then, with a massive chunk of meat loaded on his horse, he started back with the other braves toward the village.

There was no faith in Tenney that the eating of liver would help the sick Indians. Neither he nor any man of that day could have known that in fresh liver lay the cure of anemia such as that which had wasted the Cheyennes. But in a single day, strange effects from the new medicine were observed. The dusty look began to leave the faces of the dying. And on the second day, Tenney, with his own eyes, saw that boy who had barely been able to crawl to his feet, now erect and walking, though with staggering knees.

All doubt left Tenney when he saw this thing. A miracle had been performed, and he was amazed that the Cheyennes took it so calmly.

Lazy Wolf offered the only explanation. "They just expect it of Red Hawk," he said. "They think that Sweet Medicine hears every word of his prayers, and so they're ready for whatever happens. He couldn't surprise them, now. If he turned himself into a cloud of smoke under their eyes, they would merely grunt and cover their mouths."

"Aye, but how did he do it? How did it happen?" demanded Tenney.

"How would I know?" asked Lazy Wolf. "It must have been half luck and half chance. But the thing worked. And Red Hawk's a happy fellow just now. He sees a promise in this."

"What kind of a promise?" asked Tenney.

"Why, he was being wiped out. His father had left him . . . he had lost his girl . . . and White Horse had run away. That showed him that Sweet Medicine was turning his back. But now comes the cure of the Indians. The whole tribe is laughing, it's so happy. And Red Hawk begins to feel that Sweet Medicine is looking his way again. For him, it's almost as though he had White Horse again, and his girl on the back of the horse."

Tenney rubbed his knuckles across his chin. "You don't think there's anything queer about this, do you? You don't think that things are likely to happen . . . queer things, I mean?"

Lazy Wolf looked sharply at him. "Of course queer things will happen," he answered. "Whenever a man has perfect faith, he's sure to start doing ten times as much as any other man could do!"

Chapter Twenty

When the heart of an Indian overflows with joy, he must express his pleasure in acts of kindness. And that was what big Bill Tenney discovered before long. The whole thing began as though upon a signal.

That morning he was taking his ease in the lodge of Lazy Wolf, where he and Red Hawk were given hospitality. He had beneath him five or six folds of heavy buffalo robes to ease the hardness of the ground, and his strong shoulders were made comfortable against an embroidered backrest. Near the entrance of the lodge, Blue Bird was beading a pair of moccasins. She worked continually, smiling, her fingers apparently guided through the intricacies of their work by instinct so that her eyes were left free to travel where they would.

Now and then her glance, as she lifted her head, touched on Tenney and gave him her smile, but, more often, she looked toward her father and Red Hawk, until it was plain to Tenney that the joy in her heart sprang from Rusty Sabin's nearness. If she occasionally smiled at the stranger, that was merely because her eyes would have had to shed kindness on the entire world, on this day. And Tenney, sick with longing because of the blue of her eyes, began to hate Rusty Sabin as only a jealous lover can.

As for Rusty, he sat up, cross-legged, and listened eagerly to the words of Lazy Wolf who, as inert as his name, lounged against a padded backrest and talked at random of many things—of trapping in the cold north, or trading across the burning deserts of the Southwest, and, above all, of the scenes and incidents of his life among his own race of white men. To this Rusty paid attention of the most childish sort. He was generally simple and naïve in his manner, but, on occasion, among the rest of the tribe he could wrap himself in a very sufficient dignity. In the lodge, however, dignity was laid aside. He uncrossed his legs now, and lay flat on his belly, with his chin in his hands, staring with wide eyes at Lazy Wolf. He was like a small boy. Perhaps that was why Blue Bird now and then frowned a mere shade and shook her head.

Aye, but she loved him. And she knew that no matter how he acted, he was the savior of the tribe, the friend of Sweet Medicine, the hero of battles, and on a day the master of White Horse.

Such savage pains of jealousy disturbed Tenney that he looked around the tent, gloomily. In it there was piled all manner of Indian wealth, for in his double role of trader and interpreter, Lazy Wolf kept himself supplied with all the luxuries that an Indian camp could provide. There were whole bales of blankets and robes, still corded and untouched. Even the inside of the lodge had been painted with gaudy Indian designs. There were half a dozen rifles and some shotguns, boxes of ammunition, costly painted robes, fine willow beds decorated from end to end, fishing tackle, bags of pemmican against the winter, bales of dried meat, heaped baskets of corn and roots, a whole stack of garments for Lazy Wolf, and another for Blue Bird.

Into this scene of plenty more was suddenly poured, for a voice spoke at the entrance to the tent and Standing Bull, the war chief, appeared. The huge man was dressed in his full regalia, with a feathered shield of tough bull's hide, almost strong enough to turn a rifle bullet, a lance in his hand, his fringed shirt covered with delicate embroideries of colored porcupine quills, his moccasins and leggings flaming with the same colors. Maturity was scarring and seaming his face more than battle, but, when he spoke to his dearest friend, Red Hawk, his expression made his features seem beautiful. He said a few words that made Red

Hawk jump up in protest. Standing Bull merely smiled and left the tent.

Blue Bird let her shining eyes rest on Tenney for a moment. "Standing Bull," she translated, "says that the Cheyennes are coming, bringing gifts to Red Hawk because of the thing he has done. Red Hawk wants no gifts. *Hai!* If he were as naked as winter, he would not want gifts . . . because there is no pride in him."

For all that, Red Hawk had to go out and stand in front of the tent, for the people began coming in throngs, some bearing gifts and others to watch the presentations. Every one of the sick who was being cured was able to give some token of regard. One man brought up a whole herd of a dozen horses. Others led horses loaded with guns, axes, knives, beads, flour, sugar (that priceless treasure of the Indian), robes that were furred or tanned or painted, doeskin softer than flannel, moccasins, beaded shirts, and all the wealth that an Indian can cherish. Presently a vast heap was gathered beside the entrance to the teepee.

Afterward, Red Hawk went back into the big lodge and sat down with a gloomy face. Blue Bird carried in the heavy gifts and stacked them here and there. She was panting and laughing from the work. Her laughter was no louder than a whisper, lest it should interrupt the thoughts of the men, her masters. Tenney helped her with the weightier things.

"Thank you, brother," murmured the girl.

He had picked up a good many Cheyenne words by this time, and he had learned that all of the tribe greeted him by the same term. For, if Red Hawk called him brother, he was brother to all the Cheyennes. That was why they invited him into their lodges. That was why the children came up to him fearlessly and took his hand, just as they took the hand of Red Hawk. That was why, only the day before, a brave had stripped from Tenney's back the buffalo robe he wore and given him, in exchange, a priceless painted robe that would have made a museum piece. Other warriors had presented him with moccasins, with knives and guns, until he was already able to set up his own lodgings the moment he cared to do so. Thus he was brother, also, to Blue Bird, although *brother* was not the term he would have liked to hear from her.

When the work of storing away was ended, Tenney heard Lazy Wolf saying: "Why are you unhappy, Rusty?"

And Rusty answered: "They love me, and I love them. But all their gifts and all their kindness cannot fill an empty heart."

"Why is it empty?" asked Lazy Wolf.

"There was the white girl," answered Rusty with perfect frankness. "She sent me away. I gave her the green beetle as a sign that we loved one another, and she sent it back to me to show that she cared no longer."

Blue Bird, again at her beadwork, sat suddenly straight. "Why do you say the thing that is not so?" she demanded.

"I say the thing that is so," answered Rusty gloomily.

"She won't believe you," said Lazy Wolf. "*She* would have you soon enough. She'd be your second squaw, or your third . . . and still be happy."

The girl, her face flaming, jumped to her feet and started to leave the lodge, but Lazy Wolf stopped her by saying: "That is what I want to talk about. Stay where you are, Blue Bird, and tell me when I say the wrong thing."

She paused by the entrance. Her hands were gripped hard at her sides. Tenney's keen eyes could see the small, wild pulsation of the heart under the closely fitted doeskin shirt. Fires of shame and of love were in her, and an exquisitely cold anguish ran through the body of Bill Tenney, the thief.

"Now look at her, Red Hawk," said Lazy Wolf. "Or you don't have to look at the poor girl. You ought to see her in the eye of your mind well enough, and be able to answer me. Your father's gone, my lad. Well, it will be a long time before Wind Walker comes back to you. He's as near to the Pawnees as you are to the Cheyennes, or flesh to bone. However, I've always been damned fond of you. And if you could put up with a fat, lazy old man, I'd be happy to have you somewhere near.

"If your girl, Maisry, has left you, why do you wring your heart like a wet shirt? You can squeeze plenty of misery out of it, but too much wringing is sure to tear the garment. Let her be, then. One good woman is as like another as two peas in one pod. In color, Blue Bird's more olive than white, but she's a pretty thing, if you look at her twice. Look at her now, and tell me, Red Hawk."

Rusty Sabin got up and went to the girl. He took her hand and led her across the lodge, so that she sat down beside him.

"What is your father saying about you, Blue Bird?" he asked. "Sweet Medicine gave me eyes clear enough to see the truth . . . that there is only one maiden among the Cheyennes. *Hai!* But now you are unhappy. You look down, and there is sweat on your forehead. Tell me why you are sad? Shall I make Lazy Wolf stop talking like this?"

With the clean white of his deerskin sleeve he wiped her forehead, and the girl looked up with sudden resolution.

"I am not sad," she said. "But I am seeing so much happiness that I am afraid. Like a hunter who is thirsty in summer and is afraid that the blue water he sees may not be true."

"Good girl! Brave girl," said Lazy Wolf. "By the Lord, Blue Bird, I'm proud of you. There's no lying or sneakery about you. You see what she is, Red Hawk. The bravest and the rightest and the truest woman that a man could find . . . and loving you these many years, if you'll look back and have a thought about it. And if. . . ."

"Hush," said Rusty Sabin. "Is it true, Blue Bird? *Hai!* What a fool and a blind fool I have been. I seem to remember certain things. That time when I went out to die in the Sacred Valley and you stopped me and talked to me . . . I remember that. I remember many things now." He took her hand and patted it. His eye looked on her with a grave concern.

"Now, then," said Lazy Wolf, "since Maisry is gone from you, Red Hawk, be a wise man and listen to me. Take Blue Bird for your wife . . . and, before many years, you'll have children squalling in your lodge and you'll be as happy as any fool of a man in the world. What more do you want? Houses and carpets and glasses on the table don't make happiness. You may never be much more than a blacksmith among the whites, but you're a great chief among the Cheyennes. And here's a Cheyenne girl for you. Why don't you take her?"

The same thoughtful seriousness remained in the face of Red Hawk as he asked: "Do you want me to take you, Blue Bird?"

Tenney, with the blood roaring in his ears and aching in his temples, waited for the assent. Then he saw that she was sitting straighter than ever, staring at Rusty.

She said: "If I don't want you, why have I sacrificed every year the best beaded dress that I could make? Why have I prayed to Sweet Medicine to put me in your thoughts? But I know this about you. You had one father . . . and, when you found him, there was no other. You had many horses, but, when you found White Horse, there was no other horse. You left your people to follow your father. You will leave the Cheyennes soon, to follow the way of White Horse. Of each kind, there is only room in your heart for one. So if you make me your wife, one day, you may see this Maisry again, and then all thought of me may run out of your heart like water out of a basket made only to hold corn."

"*Hai*," said Red Hawk softly. "She speaks like a wise old man at the council. She speaks better than a medicine man. Blue Bird, you are beautiful and you are also wise. You are half white, and the Indian blood only makes you more beautiful. It is true that I keep seeing another face that comes between us. I try to think of it frowning and scorning me, but all I can remember is the smiling. However, your father is older and wiser than I am. If you can be happy with me, we shall be married."

She stared at him again through a long moment. "I don't want to paint the surface of water," she said. "I don't want my happiness to be drawn on the wind that will change. I am going out to walk and think."

With that, she got up and left the lodge.

"See how wise she is . . . and how good," said Rusty to Tenney.

But Bill Tenney could not speak; a fist seemed to be stuffed down his throat.

"She'll be back," said Lazy Wolf, "as soon as enough sun has shone on her to make her believe that this miracle is true."

But she was not back. And at the close of the day there was no sight of her. When inquiries were made, one of the young braves who circled the camp continually at a distance from the lodges, as a guard, said that he had seen her riding a pinto toward the south.

"She has gone to a little distance to think and to be alone. There's a brain behind that pretty face," said Lazy Wolf.

Chapter Twenty-One

Blue Bird rode far, because she was riding to find the truth. She rode south, which should be the way to warmth and easiness, but, because she rode to find truth, she rode also to find sorrow. That is the fate of human lives.

She was bound for the town of Fort Marston to find the girl called Maisry Lester. Once she heard Maisry renounce Red Hawk by word of mouth, then she would believe that the miracle was true.

Trouble came early on her march. It seemed as though God, out of His heaven, had marked Blue Bird down, because before the night was over He sent down a sweeping storm of rain, and then one of hail so huge and heavy that neither horse nor man could hardly live in it.

The wild mustang on which Blue Bird rode tried to buck her weight off its back, but it might as well have tried to pitch off its skin. The bronco grew tired of bucking, and the half-breed girl was still on its back.

The hailstones struck like small pebbles, thrown from an unsure hand. Some of them were roaring on the face of the prairie. Others were beating against her body. One of them, almost as big as an egg, landed squarely between the eyes on the smooth of her forehead, and split the skin so that the blood ran down. That was a blow from heaven, but she rode on.

In a great, raw-edged gulley in the badlands, she found a huge boulder, and on the leeside of that she remained with the horse. The pony huddled against the rock, and she huddled against the horse. The fear and the terrible roar of the heavy storm made horse and girl alike silent and cringing.

The water began to rise in the bottom of the gulley. It rose and flowed. It swept over her feet, over her ankles. It grew higher and noisier, and sucked and gurgled and pulled at her legs, halfway to the knee. Still she remained there, because the fury that rushed out of the sky was more dreadful than the torrent that was flooding over the earth. She looked up, and the glare of the lightnings dazzled her eyes.

She began to say, softly, loudly enough for her ears to hear her sweet voice: "Oh, god of Red Hawk, greatest of the Sky People, lord of all the spirits . . . Sweet Medicine . . . be good to me. Do not strike me down with the pelting ice. Do not burn me with the great sky fires. Let me go on to the end of my way."

Afterward, the uproar from the sky was less than the rushing noises of the water about her. Then she left the shelter of the rock and made the unwilling mustang cross the bed of the gulley.

They dropped into deep, whirling water, which swept her around and around. She could feel the pony fighting for life beneath her. But after that they gained shoal water, and found before them a sloping bank up which the mustang could climb. So they came out on the level prairie again.

Compared with the terrible beating of the hail, and the coldness of it, that pouring of the rain was like the shining of warm summer skies. There was no wetness to the water, because it was so warm. She parted her lips, and the rain stung them softly, and she laughed.

"Sweet Medicine has heard my prayer," she said to herself. "It may be that he will let me take back in my heart all of the happiness that it wishes to hold."

Afterward, the rain fell to a drizzle. Still there was darkness for a long time, and the sucking sound of the hoofs of her mustang as they pulled out of the sticky earth. They came to the sight of the dawn, which was moving in grayness out of the earth, all around the circle of the sky.

The rain stopped. She almost felt in her flesh the movement of the wind that carried the clouds away from the surface of the sky. The bright sun came up and struck at her from the due east, so that she was sure that she had held her course steadily to the south through the night.

The sun climbed higher. She felt the warmth and the sleepy comfort. As the sleepiness increased, she knew that it would not be well for her to go into the town and speak to the white girl while she was in that weary state. Therefore, when she came to a gulley, with its bank pitching out like a roof, she lay down there after sidelining her horse so that it would not wander far.

The moment that the softness of her body was stretched on the hard pebbles she was sound asleep, and smiling in her sleep. God sends this peculiar grace to those that labor hard. The lax strings of her strength grew gradually taut again, and, when they were pulling hard enough, suddenly she was awake.

There was a flaring brightness of sun in the sky. She was hot, her body fevered, and there was a sound of running water in her ears. And so she pulled off her fitted clothes, and gave one half-shy, half-laughing look about her at the emptiness of the gulley and the sky. Then she dived into the blue of a pool, and swam at her will.

She began to laugh as she sported. She dived to the bottom and touched the sticky mud and the rough, big stones. Her olive skin, tinted with rose, flashed on the surface and glided beneath again.

Afterward, she dried herself like an Indian, with the whipping edge of her hand. She was in no haste. The force and the brightness of the sun polished her legs and her swinging arms. She was as hard as any active boy, and yet Nature clad her in such a grace of curving lines that she looked softly feminine. This made her laugh still.

She knew that she was beautiful, because all women have objective knowledge of themselves. She understood perfectly how her beauty showed through the clinging doeskins in which she was always dressed, and she wondered, like a child and also like a woman, how Red Hawk could look at her calmly, and how he could take her hand and talk to her like a brother.

She knew what men are like, because she had seen a great many men, and she had learned how to be unconscious of their eyes, which is the one lesson that God teaches all good women. But she wondered about Red Hawk.

At last she mounted and continued on her way. And after a time, out of the wide flat of the prairie, she saw the flat head of Fort Marston rising from the ground. These white men, wolf-like or fox-like, were creatures to be dreaded. When she saw the pointed roofs of the houses in the town, she was shuddering.

Chapter Twenty-Two

When she came into the town, the first person she passed was a man carrying a heavy sack over his shoulders. White men work like women. In all ways, all white men were wrong. The very smell of the cookery, the very odor of the town, made her nostrils quiver with disgust.

She said in English that had only a small touch of accent in it: "Will you tell me where I can find Maisry?"

"In me," said the man who carried the sack. "You can find plenty of misery in me." He walked on, slowly, his knees giving a trifle to the weight upon his back.

Puzzled, she rode on, and presently she was in the main street of the town. The houses looked out at her with many eyes. The street was worn by a thousand interwoven ruts, all black from the rainfall, with welters of sun-brightened waters here and there. Why should men live in one place, beside one trail, when there is the glorious wide earth to wander over? Why should they fix their houses in one place, like old bulls bogged down, instead of making for themselves the light, warm, beautiful lodges that can be taken down and packed on horses, and made to travel swiftly over the plains?

Around a corner came a prancing horse, with a man in uniform on its back. Blue Bird wanted to pull a robe over her face and go on, shamefaced. But she had no robe with her, and, besides, she had to ask questions. So she lifted her right hand in the Indian salute, and her open eyes looked straight into the leering eyes of the sergeant.

"*Hau*," she said.

"Hello, sweetheart," said the sergeant.

The word struck her like a whiplash. But her face did not change.

"Will you tell me where I can find Maisry?" she asked.

"I'll tell you where you can find me," he said. "Damned if I wouldn't let you find me any day. You ask for Sergeant Tim O'Connor, and you'll be finding me. I'll be right at your hand. I'll always be there, damn my heart, if you want to ask for me."

Disgust stiffened her lips. She kept on looking the sergeant straight in the eyes, and repeated: "Can you tell me where to find Maisry?"

He was abashed. He answered: "Try the house at the corner of the fort. The cabin with the two chimneys. That's the place where Maisry Lester lives, if she's who you want to see."

He went on, the feet of his horse making sucking sounds in the wet of the mud, and the water spurting out like flames from the hollow of the hoofs.

Blue Bird went on to the house with the two chimneys. In the doorway, on the step, she saw a girl knitting, making the needles flash in the sun. Her head was bent, and Blue Bird knew that she was not very happy, this girl on the doorstep.

It was Maisry. Blue Bird knew it was Maisry before the head was lifted. She knew by the delicate round of the neck, by the glow of color like that which strikes through the skin of an Indian baby. Her brow was smooth, when she lifted her head, and on her lips was that faint smile that beauty places there. As for her eyes—well, the eyes of Blue Bird were blue, also, but the color of these was like a stain in the face.

Blue Bird swung down from her horse, and the other girl stood up. She was just the height of Blue Bird, but she was dressed in an ugly dress of printed calico. But Blue Bird knew where to look. She looked at the ankles and the hands, and the wrists, and the throat. To an Indian, beauty does not lie in the face alone, and certainly not in the dress. Blue Bird saw the other girl as the Creator had meant her to be to the world.

"Are you Maisry?" she asked.

The answer came: "Yes. I am she."

More than the name and the beauty, the voice struck cold through Blue Bird's heart, for it was a voice so gentle and so soft that it made a music that was hateful to the ears of Blue Bird. So many thoughts rushed through Blue Bird's mind, and she stood there gazing bitterly so long, that at last what she said was simply: "Do you want him?"

"Want him?" echoed Maisry. She tried to smile, but the fierce, great eyes of the stranger daunted her.

"Yes. Do you want him, or have you thrown him away?"

Maisry stared for only an instant longer, and then she exclaimed: "Are you talking of Rusty Sabin?"

"I am talking about Red Hawk, the great chief and medicine man!" cried Blue Bird. "Is it true that he ever looked at you and wanted you?"

She saw Maisry catch her breath. The change in the face and the change in the eyes worked a swift poisoning of Blue Bird's soul. She had a good knife at her belt. She wanted to drive it now between the breasts of the white girl. She wanted so much to strike her that she made a step closer and added: "Is it true that you are a fool? Is it true that you have thrown him away?"

"No!" gasped Maisry.

She was so shocked that she looked positively stupid. Blue Bird wished that Maisry would always look like this.

Said the half-breed girl: "Now you lie. For I know everything about it. He gave you the green beetle, and that is his medicine. That is half of his strength. It came from his mother. With it, he gave you his soul, but you returned the green beetle to him. You laughed and you returned the green beetle to *him. Hai!* Is there no shame in you?"

Maisry was silent, thinking about Major Marston's words. And she was beginning to grasp at another explanation that started to make her beautiful, for the dead hope revived and burned up in her.

The Indian girl was saying: "If you have given him up, I shall have him. I shall be his squaw, and his children shall grow in my body as the corn grows in the earth."

"I gave him the green beetle because he begged me to give it back to him," said Maisry. "He sent for it."

Blue Bird opened her mouth to make a harsh denial. She closed her lips again without having spoken, and it seemed to her that she had breathed not air, but fire.

"The messenger, he spoke the word that was not so," said Blue Bird.

"He? He could not lie! He is Major Marston!" cried Maisry. "He. . . ."

She hushed herself, for Blue Bird had lifted her hand.

"Listen to me," said the half-breed girl. "I sat in the lodge. I heard Red Hawk speak. I heard the weight of his heart in his words. I heard a heart heavier than the heart of a tired man. He said that you had sent him away, and that you had given him back the green beetle and his soul along with it. Do you hear?"

"I hear," whispered Maisry.

"And he told me, afterward," said Blue Bird, "that he would take me for his squaw. He took my hand in his hand. He looked into my eyes, but it was only as a brother would look. I can go back to the Cheyennes and take him for my husband. I can give him my hand and my body. I can be the mother of his children. But will you promise never to call him back, with a word or with your eyes?"

Maisry let the tears run down her face. "What can I do?" said Maisry. "How can I take him away from you?"

Blue Bird came to her with a terrible anguish and a terrible envy breaking her heart. She took Maisry's hand, close to the round, narrow wrist. Blue Bird's hand was not very soft; it had been toughened by using the fleshing horn and the hoe. The weights she had carried made her back straight, and the sense of Cheyenne glory in this world had made her heart proud. Out of these strengths she spoke, holding Maisry by the wrist.

"If I take him," she said, "how long will he belong to me? The white blood calls to the white. If I take him, how long may I keep him? The thought of you will come over him as the cry of the wolf pack comes over the tame wolf. He will lift his head, and presently he will be away through the night, and I shall never see him again. He is not a man to have two wives. He is a man with only one friend, one horse, one knife . . . and he will be a man with only one woman, also. Oh, little soft, blue-eyed fool . . . are you woman enough to be his woman?"

After she had asked this, the strength went out of Blue Bird. It drained out through her eyes, for she was staring at Maisry and seeing her beauty, and it seemed to Blue Bird that the tears that rolled down her face were from her heart, leaving it empty.

Chapter Twenty-Three

True sympathy between two women is as rare as true blue in the sky. Between this pair it seemed impossible, because, when Blue Bird looked at Maisry, she knew with an almighty knowledge that Rusty Sabin belonged to the white girl. In knowledge like this, men have no part. They are beneath such understanding.

It would have been a miracle if a man could have lost bitterness as quickly as did Blue Bird. But it was as though the tears melted the envy out of her heart and left only sorrow, which is a pure thing. Maisry put her arm, cautiously, around the slender body of the Cheyenne. She felt the strength and the big beat of the heart and the deep, quick breathing. She was awed, and she was also merciful. She felt that she was looking up, not down.

"You don't hate me?" she said.

"I am trying to. I *have* hated you. I shall hate you very soon again," said Blue Bird. After that, with exquisite lack of logic, she dropped her head on Maisry's shoulder and clasped her in her strong young arms and sobbed, silently. Indian women make no noise in their grief, unless it is for the dead.

Mrs. Lester found her daughter in that attitude on the step of the house. She cried out: "Maisry! An Indian! A frightful, red-skinned . . . Maisry, step away from her this instant! Richard, come here and see. . . ."

Maisry lifted her head. There was so much goodness in her that she was not so much rejoicing over the lover who had been given back to her as she was sorrowing for the Cheyenne.

141

She merely said: "I want to see Major Marston. I want you to ask Father to go find him at the fort."

"Major Marston? Of course I'll send for him," said Mrs. Lester. She was overjoyed. When she thought of Major Marston, which was several times a day, she always thanked God for placing such a splendid man where her daughter could see him. So she ran back into the house as Maisry led the Indian girl inside. To her husband, Mrs. Lester exclaimed: "Get Arthur Marston quickly! Bring him here at once. Maisry is asking for him. It's the first time. And . . . maybe . . . maybe this is the beginning of something. . . ."

Richard Lester looked up from his book. His lean face was filling out with health now. He said to his wife: "I'll get Arthur Marston, but never think that Maisry will see him with your eyes."

However he went quickly up to the fort and came back with the major.

When Marston heard that Maisry was taking compassion on a stranger, he was not at all surprised. She was the sort to take compassion. When the major thought of all Maisry's virtues, he knew that God had specially designed her to make him a wife and so compose a difference and fill a vacuum, which Nature abhors.

A good deal of the jump went out of the major's sprightly step when he came into the house and found Maisry in her own little room, sitting beside her bed, on which the Indian girl was stretched. But when he looked into Maisry's eyes, all his smiles went out.

She had been grave from the day when Rusty Sabin left the town. But now she was stern, also, and the upward tilt of her face, which made her more lovely, gave her also an imperious command. She said with the directness that was part of her nature: "Why did you say that Rusty had begged for the green beetle, Arthur?"

There was a thunderclap in the heart of the major. Even the hardiest liar in the world will feel that stroke when he is confronted with his lie. Perhaps that is a token that we are honest by nature, no matter how we overlay the fact with our guiles and savage distortions of instinct. However, he had the natural fertility of the born liar, also, and he merely remarked: "Why, of course he sent for it."

Here Blue Bird suddenly lifted her head; she rested her weight on her hands and arms, and looked up at the major. She had been weeping with a silent violence. Her eyes were a little swollen, her lips were thick, and her face was reddened. But the major had been long enough on the plains to think her darker skin just as lovely as that of Maisry. She said to him: "Why do you say the thing that is not so?"

There is no word in all the Indian tongues for *liar*. There is only the roundabout phrase that means the same thing, and Blue Bird had to translate her thoughts out of Cheyenne into English.

"Come, come," said the major. "What tricks and antics has Rusty Sabin been playing with this pretty young thing? What sort of nonsense has she been talking to you?"

Blue Bird leaped to her feet. "I am the daughter of the white, Lazy Wolf," she cried, "and he is almost a chief among the Cheyennes! I speak the thing that is true, and I have only one tongue! You," she exclaimed more loudly, pointing an indignant hand, "you are a man who says the thing that is not so!"

The major merely laughed. He stopped laughing at once, however, because even he could see that his laughter had a hollow and an unreal sound. Then, making himself doubly serious, and striking himself grave in an instant, he said to Maisry: "Now, let's get down to the bottom of this, Maisry. Something has troubled you. Is it something this girl has said to you? She's cut up. Don't be too hard on her. She's trying to do her best about something,

I suppose, but the right words come hard to people who don't know a strange language."

And Maisry said: "She tells me that Rusty would marry her, except that he still cares about me. He thinks that I sent the green beetle back to him as a sign that I no longer love him. Arthur, you brought me his message."

Chapter Twenty-Four

No one really knows how to pretend innocence, but the major offered a very good imitation. His color decreased but his smile was cheerful, his eye bright and steady.

"Indian heads are likely to get white ideas twisted," he said. "I know that this girl is trying to tell the truth. In fact, it looks as though she had come a long distance in order to tell it. But you can be sure that something is twisted. My dear Maisry," he added with a perfectly good and sincere laugh, "what in the world would I have had to gain by misinterpreting messages between you and Rusty Sabin?"

Maisry was about as clear and simple and straightforward a girl as one can find anywhere, but no woman was ever born so simple that she was unable to tell when she quickened the heart-beat of a man. And Maisry, looking earnestly into the face of the major, could not help doubting him just a trifle. She had seen the familiar hunger in his eyes more than once, and instinct had taught her how it was to be dreaded. But she could only say: "Of course you had nothing to gain. But something is terribly wrong. He thinks that I sent back the scarab to him . . . he thinks it was because I was through with him. What did you say to him, Arthur?"

"What did I say?" answered Marston, pretending to be puzzled. "Let me see. I tried to make the thing easy for him. He was sorry to take the green beetle away from you. I tried to smooth out the case for him and comfort the poor fellow, so I suppose I told him that you didn't care at all, and that you'd get on perfectly

145

well without a green beetle hanging around your neck. Ah, perhaps that's the catch! Perhaps what I told him on my own account
may have seemed to him like a direct message from you . . . words
from you. By the Lord, Maisry, I believe I've hit on it."

A moan of distress made her throat tremble. "How did he look
and what did he do when he heard you say it?" she asked.

"How did he look? Well, you know he's two in one . . . and,
just then, he was all Indian. I couldn't have read his mind in a
thousand years, he kept his face so immobile. But I'll tell you
how to work this thing out. I want to show you that I'm a friend
worth counting on. The thing to do, Maisry, is to send back your
pretty little Indian friend with a letter to Rusty Sabin. I'll tell you
what I'll do. The plains are covered with Pawnees and Comanches, and they'd like nothing better than snapping up a young
Cheyenne girl on the loose by herself. But I want to take my men
out for some heavy marching soon. The scoundrels are getting fat
and lazy, and their horses need work, too. So I'll take 'em out and
march them in the direction of the Cheyenne camp. I'd as soon
as not, and I'll give your little friend an escort through the larger
part of her journey."

The major had done very well, in this speech, for, after start-
ing with a defensive explanation, he had passed into the stage of
good advice, and then into an offer of assistance. He made his
handsome face fairly shine as he concluded his proffer. Maisry
was not one to hug suspicion and doubt. There was no more
deceit in her soul than in a fine summer day, and now she ban-
ished from her mind every doubt about big Arthur Marston.
She shone on him with her thanks, and the major turned at once
to Blue Bird.

"Now, I want to know just how far away your camp is," said
Marston, "and how you people happened to travel as far south
as all this?"

She hesitated a little before replying. Youth and beauty in a
man made very little difference to her. She had a true Indian

woman's worship of battle scars and battle fame, and a sour-faced old brave with one eye gone and a broken nose would have filled her soul with content, if he wore some of the stained coup feathers in his headdress. However, Major Marston was actually the war chief of the white men, and, although his uniform looked silly, and his short mustache was absurd, in her eyes, she was willing to treat him with respect. A single strong reserve remained in the back of her mind; she felt that a lie had certainly been in the air somewhere, and that the major was its most probable author.

She made her answer: "The camp is a day's march away, as a woman rides, riding steadily. We came south with our sick people because we heard that Red Hawk was in this place."

"Hello! Is he a doctor?" demanded the major, sneering a little in his smile.

"He is a great medicine man," answered Blue Bird, watching the major's eyes, and liking them not at all.

"Well, what did the great medicine man do for the sick?" asked Marston, still half bantering. He looked at Maisry, who flushed.

She was always made most miserable by any reference to the superstitions that so largely controlled Rusty's life.

"Red Hawk raised up the dying men," said Blue Bird, and a wild gleam came into her eyes and her head rolled a bit from side to side as she chanted out. "They were starving. Meat would not feed them. They dwindled. They shrank away. They turned gray."

"Anemia," commented the major, nodding. "That kills thousands of red men every year. More than bullets ever got rid of. What did Red Hawk manage to do about anemia? It's not curable, you ought to know."

"*Hai!*" cried the girl. "Not to white men. *They* cannot cure it. But Red Hawk went out and prayed to Sweet Medicine, and an eagle flew down out of the sky with the answer. There is nothing but laughter and happiness in the camp, now that Red Hawk has come home to his people."

In one respect, this stirring answer was not at all to the taste of the major. However, a new thought was coming into his mind. "How many of the sick are there?" he asked.

"Five twenties of them," said the girl.

"A hundred sick?" exclaimed Marston. He half closed his eyes, fiercely staring at this beautiful chance. One hundred wild Indian warriors, now weak as children owing to disease, but daily growing stronger, soon powerful enough to join the fight with any soldiers in the world. Why should they not be wiped out, if it were possible? To be sure, at the moment there was peace with the Cheyennes. But the major did not care about that. He could work up an "Indian outrage" in his report, and, if his massacre succeeded, there was not apt to be much investigating from Washington. So Marston added: "And how many other braves are along with the sick people?"

Blue Bird hesitated. She did not like these direct questions. Besides, all questions about numbers worried her a good bit.

As she hesitated, the major suggested, gently: "Two scores? Two twenties of warriors?"

"Three scores," said Blue Bird.

There was no doubt that sixty was closer to the truth than forty, and, as for the difference, she did not care to worry her head over the real figure, which was some two hundred and fifty braves in the full prime of their fighting strength.

That was how the major got his first misleading information.

* * * * *

He went straight back to the fort to prepare for the march. The more he thought of the thing, the more convinced he was that an inspiration had come to him. He would take a flying column of a hundred picked men, with plenty of reserves in the way of horses. With those men, he would escort the Cheyenne girl across the plains, and she would at the same time be a flawless guide to him. As for the letter that she carried to Red Hawk, it would be strange if the major could not interfere with that. His real hope, growing every moment from the bottom of his soul, was that he would be able to take that Indian camp by surprise, and that the saber of every man in his command would run red before the slaughter was over. He would become a colonel overnight, and full on his way to a general's pride of place.

Poor Maisry, in the meantime, was writing her letter, pausing over it, telling herself that it ought to be brief, but all the while tasting, as she drew the pen over the page, a strange happiness and homesick grief combined. She had thought that she would never see Rusty again. Now she blessed the words that would go before her and come under his eyes.

She worked with her head canted to one side, smiling. Now and then she looked blankly across the room toward Blue Bird, seeing not the Cheyenne girl, but only her own visions. But every time the Cheyenne smiled sadly in answer. She knew, well enough, what picture lay in the eyes of this beautiful white girl.

Chapter Twenty-Five

Major Marston liked round numbers, and that was why he had exactly one hundred officers and men behind him when he started out the next morning. He took the van, and beside him rode his voluntary and unpaid guide, Blue Bird. She, feeling the eyes of the soldiers search her, was a little pleased and a little disgusted.

The major talked to her a good deal. At first, like the others, he had in his eyes the look of a hunter, but the major was a man of intelligence, and he soon changed his manner toward her. He took on a serious air. He asked her questions that flattered her intelligence, and he listened with a keen attention and respect. It might be that now and again he said the thing that was not so, but this was characteristic of the whites, as all Indians knew. The whites had double tongues and they spoke with two meanings.

But certainly he was most interested in whatever she had to tell him about Red Hawk. And that was the theme nearest and dearest to her. She could dwell on a thousand points. But above all, she loved to enlarge on the time when Red Hawk, alone, had gone into the Sacred Valley and dared to confront Sweet Medicine in the cave on the cliff. The vastness of that daring made her pale. Then she told how Red Hawk had returned to the tribe with the broken arrow, and how he had made his famous chant before all the Cheyennes.

"Could that have been simply a common owl, and not Sweet Medicine at all, that Rusty Sabin found in the cave?" asked the major, controlling his desire to smile.

She made a fine gesture. She merely laughed to dismiss the suggestion.

"But what was that other thing?" asked the major. "Isn't it true that Rusty Sabin was afraid to go through the initiation when his time came to be a brave?"

Her face clouded, but only for a moment. "That was because Sweet Medicine wanted to lead him away from the tribe," she explained. "Sweet Medicine himself was driven out of the tribe, as you know. And so Red Hawk wandered. But when he came back, he was riding White Horse. *Hai!* How the boys screamed with happiness, because he was such a great man and belonged to the Cheyennes. The breath went out of the women. They could only cover their mouths and stare at such a man."

In her delighted eyes he read, easily, the secret of her heart, and hatred for Rusty Sabin stabbed him again.

The pace of the march was not very fast. A hundred men cannot travel like one or two. They were far from the Cheyenne camp when they had to halt for the night. The major picked out a good site for the camp. It was in the hollow lowland near a creek, sheltered at the back by a high bank.

Blue Bird, as camp was being pitched, unsaddled her mustang, sidelined it as usual, and sat down on the bank to watch the proceedings. The little dog-tents amused her. So did the utensils for cooking. So also the heavy rations that the men produced from their saddlebags. Already there were ten fires blazing unreasonably high, and there were squatting groups of men, cooking, at each fire.

Why, the smoke rolled away in sufficient volume to have told watchers ten miles away that here were men at camp. The major saw her laughing, as he brought to her a well-filled iron pan, heaped with hot food. He had filled her coffee half full of sugar, and, when she drank it, she had to cry out with excited pleasure. She was then willing to tell him why she had laughed.

"Look," she said. "When a Cheyenne war party starts out, the braves carry a little jerked meat, some parched corn in a pouch, and that is all. Sometimes they chew a little corn, and that is their food for the day. Sometimes they only pull up their belts, and that is their food for the day. Sometimes they kill game, and then they feast. But for two hundred warriors there would not be such a smoke as the white men make for ten soldiers."

The major nodded. It was true that the Indians could fade away from pursuit, because they traveled skeleton light. Their naked skins could be coat and overcoat, and in a pinch they could feed on field mice and roots.

"You shall sleep in a tent near my tent," he told her. "You can see my tent now . . . the big one down there. You shall have a little tent beside it, and then you will be safe."

"I shall be safe enough when the darkness comes," said Blue Bird.

And when the darkness came, she was not to be found. She had slipped away to a short distance from the camp, and there, wrapped in a horse blanket, she stretched out. Weariness made the ground a soft bed for her.

Blue Bird, out of a sound sleep, was awakened late in the night by the sound of beating hoofs. The moon glinted against her eyes a she sat up and saw a dim ghost come wavering toward her over the plains, followed by dusky forms. It was a whole herd of horses, she made out presently, and far, far away, behind the rattling of the hoof beats, she heard a pouring murmur that seemed to vibrate through the ground even at her feet. The noise worried her. It was like a thin, distant thunder that never stopped. Somewhere before she had heard it. But where?

The sight of the horses chained her eyes. And presently the ghostly form of the leader grew more defined. He was swinging on, straight toward her. A depression in the ground half covered him, but he emerged again out of the gloom like a leaping fish, and she saw that it was White Horse! Awe weakened her knees and made her drop down, for this was the horse that belonged to Red Hawk, and therefore to Sweet Medicine. This was the stallion that ten thousand hunters, white and red, had chased for thousands of miles, over plains and mountains, until Red Hawk went out like a god and laid his hand on the neck of the charger.

It seemed to her that the ghost of the man she loved was swaying on the back of White Horse, borne along by the long, effortless stride.

Behind him the heads of the herd bobbed rapidly up and down as they measured his prodigious paces with their shorter strides.

White Horse was hardly fifty feet from her, blinded by the glory of his own kingship and his speed and strength, before he was aware of her. He shot suddenly to one side then, and the herd streamed after him—a hundred—no, ten scores of horses!

She laughed with a strange sort of joy as she saw the monster go leaping away into the darkness. His herd was scattering too much to please him. In the distance, she saw him redouble his speed and turn into a streak that swept around to the rear, where he attacked the laggards and made them bunch up closer toward the leaders. Aye, for he had the mind of a chief, the mind that neglects not the least of his followers.

Then the herd vanished from view.

She was still peering through the moon haze after the departed herd, when the noise that she had marked before began to roll closer toward her. A low, dark bank, like a cloud sweeping along the face of the ground, was moving out of the south, toward her. Perhaps it was this that had driven White Horse through the night. Gradually she saw the cloud extending until it seemed to lie for miles to either side.

And now, thin and dim, she saw the small quiverings of moon shine, here and there. Her brain awakened from its dream that instant. She should have recognized the thing long, long before. It was a stampede of buffalo. It was one of those ocean-like herds cast into motion by a panic as strange as the powers that draw the sea in its tides. And now this immensity of thundering hoofs was pouring straight down on the camp of the soldiers. The mere forefronts of the host would be sufficient to smash the camp flat and trample to a red stain all the human lives.

She turned and raced with all her might toward the bank of the stream. She jerked up the short doeskin skirt and knotted the end of it at her waist. She ran like a boy—like the fleetest of Indian boys, with her body erect and her breath deeply drawn. And she could run very swiftly.

She reached the edge of the bank, leaped ten feet to the lower level, landed lightly, cat-like, rolled to her feet, and sent her scream into every sleeping ear.

"Buffalo! Buffalo! The stampede! White faces! Waken, waken! Brainless, stupid, sleeping calves, jump up before you die! The stampede is on you!"

But would they hear her?

The soldiers came running, half dressed, half naked, rifles in their hands. The major rushed like a wise and brave man straight for the center of the disturbance. Blue Bird caught him by the arm and dragged him up the bank, behind him a frightened stream of soldiers.

Now they could see what was happening. The moon was bright enough to show the whole face of the picture, though the rear of that thundering mass was lost in an uprush of dust, as if in smoke. The front rank of the host was composed of huge bull buffalos, humpbacked, running with their bearded heads low, their horns jerking up with each stride, and the noise of the hoofs was like a great bellowing voice, as though the earth had split apart and was uttering a cry.

"Shoot them down or you're lost!" screamed the girl. "Fire! Fire!" She seemed to forget her own safety. She was only a woman, and these were men—so many strong men, even if their skins were only white.

The major went out two steps before the rest. He was perfectly calm. His shouting voice cut through the uproar, giving orders. Twenty men were all that he had with him, properly armed.

"Stand ready!" he commanded. "Take aim. Shoot straight past me when I give the word. Shoot at the center of the herd. You on my right, shoot first when I give the word. On my left, shoot when I raise my hand again. . . ."

Then he waited. Courage, for that moment, made the hypocrite and the liar seem noble in the eyes of the girl.

He shouted, lifting a hand, and the first volley of shots struck the front of the herd like so many pebbles hurled against a cliff. Two or three bulls—no more—tumbled headlong. The places where they fell were marked by long succeeding ripples behind them, as the remainder of the herd flowed like water over the obstacles.

It seemed to Blue Bird that the breathing of the bulls was already in her face, like the spume and dash of spray before a wave. The horns, rattling together, had a metallic sound. An irresistible river of fear was pouring down on them when the second half of the soldiers in line fired, and then all of them, of a single accord, started leaping and shouting and waving their guns.

The buffalo divided, not slowly but as though the point where the three bulls had dropped in a heap was the head of a great rock that made the currents sheer off to either side. They spilled out at a sharp angle and seemed to increase their speed.

Dust, as though driven by a heavy wind, poured out into the faces of the watchers, and the rank, moist smell of the herd closed over then. But the thundering death had been diverted. Still widening the gap, the great herd sloped around the sides of the camp. They shot off the high bank in a steady torrent, many buffalos breaking their necks in the fall, many toppling and being trampled to death by the succeeding ranks, until the bank was beveled off by the compacted surface of the dead and hammered bodies over which the other thousands passed. The front ranks dashed the water of the creek to spray. The stream was dammed up by swiftly moving masses of flesh.

Up the farther bank the swarm mounted, with speed that seemed undiminished. A thick haze rolled overhead and like a little cloud made the stars small and the moon dim and lifeless. For an endless time the soldiers watched, anxiously, dreading lest the later masses of the herd should close in and sweep the camp away in the flood. But always the rear ranks followed their leaders, and still the heap of three dead buffalos made the exact point of the division from which the two halves swept away, very much like the point at which the long hair of a woman is parted.

At last, gaps appeared in the throng. The last few hundreds came scattering, and sheered away in their turn and were lost from view across the stream. Only the departing thunder of the hoofs rolled back to the command of the major.

For a brief moment, then, he looked about him to find the girl and thank her, because he knew that she had saved him as well as all the rest.

Lost in a buffalo stampede. That would have been a foolish epitaph to end such a life as his. And the girl had prevented it. He could at least thank her with a string of beads, tomorrow.

"You can sleep in the supply tent," he told her. "It will be day before very long."

He opened the flaps of the big tent, around the sides of which were stored the supplies from the pack horses that accompanied the march. And pulling down a stack of blankets, he told her to make herself comfortable on them; she was stretched out upon them with a sigh of weariness even before he left the tent.

Half an hour later, the major went back to the provision tent and opened the flap, listening until he was sure that she slept. When he was confident of that, it was still difficult to find Blue Bird, and by light touches to locate the pouch at her side.

Within it, he felt the paper of the letter, and drew it out, hushing the noisy crinkling by the stealthy movements of his hand.

Sweat was running on his face before he was outside the tent again, Then he went to his own tent and read the letter, written with a big, rushing hand that showed the words had tumbled headlong out of Maisry's heart.

Rusty, dear,

I didn't understand. I thought the major said you wanted the scarab back because you had lost your luck with it. How could you doubt me? Send it back to me—bring it back to me so that I can have you with it. The days have gone like lead walking on my heart. Come soon, and, if you love me half as much as I love you, I'll always be the happiest girl in the world.

Maisry

When the major had finished this letter, freezing cold puckered his forehead and dimmed his eyes. He could see only one picture—Rusty Sabin facing a firing squad. Then, from his pack, he got out some white paper, measured it by the letter, and cut it to the right size. After that he practiced the scrip for some time. He had a good, steady hand, and a natural talent as a penman. Presently he felt that he was able to make a forgery good enough to pass the unsuspicious eye of Rusty Sabin. Then he wrote:

Dear Rusty,

Why not try to do a little forgetting? It hasn't been hard for me, and it ought to be easy for you. Besides, you have Blue Bird. Isn't she enough?

You and I would never get on. Now that I've had time to think, I see that I never could like Indians—even white ones.

Have a good time with the green beetle.

Maisry

The major, after he had finished the writing, resealed the envelope and stole back to the provision tent. He could hear the soft breathing of the girl in the darkness. A fragrance, thin and dim and pure, rose from her, and a strange feeling of pity came over the major, a queer regret for all the things that he was not.

Then he went to waken his two captains, and took them into his own tent.

Blue Bird, not a minute after she had been left, awakened suddenly, with a fast-beating heart. She had that intimate and guilty sense that someone had been near her. The feeling choked her and made her hurry outside the big tent, free from the smell of food and blankets and gunpowder.

Then she went toward the major's tent, simply because she knew him better than she knew the rest of the command, and because she wanted to be near someone who was a friend, in this queer time of fear.

Chapter Twenty-Six

Inside the tent, a little fire sprang up. It cast a rosy light through the canvas, and sometimes a vast, wavering, uncertain shadow moved across the side of the tent before Blue Bird. The major's first words, however, struck her almost blind with terror. She only lived in the sense of hearing, after that. For Marston was saying: "Now, my friends, we've come far enough for me to let you understand that this isn't simply a practice march. The object of it is to wipe out Standing Bull's Cheyenne camp. There are only sixty braves with him, and. . . ."

"Hold on," said one of the officers. "They're peaceful, those Cheyennes."

"Peaceful?" exclaimed the major. "There's no such thing as a peaceful Indian! One of my chief jobs," went on the major, "is to put Rusty Sabin out of the way. Red Hawk, as they call him, will make trouble till he dies. Well, I want him dead before another day ends."

When she heard this, a small, faint cry came from the throat of Blue Bird. She swayed to her feet, scarcely realizing that she had called out, still half blinded by what she had been overhearing. And that was why the major found her when, in answer to that sound of woe, he sprang out of the tent. He took her by both arms and thrust her before him into the tent.

"We've got a spy with us," said Marston. "By heaven, she's a spy . . . and I've a mind to treat her as one."

Captain Dell, lean and hard of face, and with the sparkling eyes of a terrier, turned his shoulder to the scene, perfectly indifferent. But stocky Captain Wilbur's face wrinkled with pain and disgust.

"It's she who saved our necks tonight," he pointed out. "As for the plan you have . . . it's murder."

The major glared savagely at Wilbur. "Wilbur," he said, "it's beginning to be plain to me that you're not cut out for Indian fighting."

"For Indian *fighting*, I hope," said Wilbur. "But not for Indian massacres."

A deep, angry exclamation broke from the major's throat, but he was never able to finish that remark because Blue Bird, who had been standing limp and weak, as though about to sink to the ground, turned suddenly into a twisting, dodging, darting snake. She jerked her hand from the major's arm, ducked under Captain Dell's clutch, and whipped back through the entrance flap. The major, with a warning shout, plunged after her, and was in time to see her slip, a flying shadow, onto the back of his favorite black charger, which was tethered near the tent.

Marston leaped for the head of the horse, but the flash of a knife stopped him. He saw the tie line slashed in two, and then the fierce yell of the Cheyenne girl sent the big horse away at full gallop.

Chivalry was a fault, to the mind of Major Marston. He had no hesitation, therefore, in pulling his revolver and blazing away with the best intent in the world to pick that slender feminine body off the back of the horse. But the rider swerved behind a supply tent, then into brush.

"Catch her! After her!" yelled the major. "Get her alive . . . or get her dead!"

That was why the men of the Marston command were presently rushing their horses furiously across the prairie. But the black was a chosen horse, and so Blue Bird got away from those hungry-hearted soldiers, and at last the moon haze covered her.

She did not flee straight toward the distant Cheyenne camp. Instead, she angled far away to the west of that course. The day rolled on almost to the evening, and the black horse was cruelly fretted with foam and streaked with whip welts before she came into sight of the thin smoke that rose over the Cheyenne camp.

She went straight into the presence of Standing Bull, who sat in his tent, smoking a long-stemmed pipe, making his cheeks into hollows as he sucked on the mouthpiece, and closing his eyes as he breathed out the smoke. Beside him, almost as a matter of course, lolled Red Hawk, now dressed from head to foot like an Indian, his blanket thrown back from his shoulders in the warmth of the tent, and visible on his breast a hawk, very cunningly painted in red.

He jumped up when he saw the excited girl. It seemed to her that there was a flash of happiness in his eyes, like a spark, and that the toss of his red hair was like a lifting of flame.

"The soldiers are coming to murder us, Standing Bull!" she cried to the young chief.

He opened his eyes and looked wearily up at her.

"They are going to kill the sick and the well," she continued. "But there are only five twenties of them." She was clapping her hands above her head, and exclaiming: "You can swallow them up with your braves! You can swallow them as a snake swallows a mouse!"

Chapter Twenty-Seven

It was infinitely beneath the dignity of Standing Bull to be startled by anything that a woman might report to him. He drew another long puff from his pipe, rose slowly, laid the pipe aside with certain ceremonial gestures, threw a buffalo robe about him, took up a seven-foot spear, by way of a staff. Then he left the lodge in silence.

Intimate though the friendship was between him and the young war chief, Rusty had not dared to speak until Standing Bull had made his exit. Then he grasped Blue Bird by both wrists, hard enough to hurt her, although she only smiled back into his face, as though she loved the pain.

"And Maisry?" he demanded. "And Maisry? Maisry?"

She bowed her head as she took the letter from the pouch, so that he would not be able to look too closely into her heart and see the pain that was rising there. When she raised her head again, her face was calm. There was enough Indian in her for that.

He tore open the letter in a frenzy. She, held by a perverse torment, waited to see joy spring into his face. But she only saw the widening of his eyes, and the color leaving his face. He read aloud, slowly, in a breathless voice no bigger than a whisper:

Dear Rusty,

Why not try to do a little forgetting? It hasn't been hard for me, and it ought to be easy for you. Besides, you have Blue Bird. Isn't she enough?

You and I would never get on. Now that I've had time to think, I see that I never could like Indians—even white ones.

Have a good time with the green beetle.

Maisry

He lowered the letter with a jerk of his arm, and stared at the girl. His eyes were as empty as the eyes of a child. Certainly there was not enough Indian in him. And shame struck the girl deeply as she saw the grief in his face. She, woman though she was, knew better how to manage such things.

"But what is it, Red Hawk?" she asked. "The white girl was happy. When I talked about you, her eyes shone, and she laughed."

"Aye," said Rusty slowly. "She laughed." He dropped the letter into the small fire that burned under the stew pot. It threw up one flare of brightness that died at once, and left a small dance of gray ashes over the coal.

After that, Rusty lifted his head again. "The whites," he said, "are not like the Indians. They are not true. Look at me, Blue Bird."

He extended his hands into the smoke that rose above the fire, expanding lazily before it was sucked up through the vent above. In that smoke Rusty bathed his hands, his arms, his face, and then his body, with half-imaginary handfuls.

"I wash away the white that is in me," said Rusty gravely. "I become now a true Cheyenne. All my blood is Cheyenne blood. All my heart . . . all my heart is . . . Cheyenne . . . and . . . all my. . . ." His voice broke.

Blue Bird, dazed, looked suddenly down to the ground lest she see tears in the eyes of this great chief and medicine man. She was so overwhelmed that she did not even see him leave the tent. But when she looked up again, he was gone.

He was gone into the open, with the sunset making a great bonfire of the sky, and the wind softly blowing the flaming clouds in the zenith, where the deepening blue dissolved them.

166

A great voice shouted behind him. It was Tenney, beating a huge hand on his shoulder.

"Have you heard the news, Rusty? The soldiers are gonna tackle us. They're gonna try to wipe us out. Oh, God! Oh, God! If only I can get the sights of my rifle lined up on the major. If only I can get him hugged small, inside my sights." With his powerful arm, he brandished his rifle on high. Then he laughed, and smote Rusty's shoulder again. "What's the matter, Rusty?" he said. "Ain't you one for a fight? Does thinking about the guns make you kind of fade out inside? Aye, a lot of pretty good men feel that way. But when the shooting starts, they're all right. I've found out in a lot of fights that them that look the most scared are the ones that raise the most hell. That's the way you'll be."

Rusty said nothing. He looked at the huge man beside him, and saw what appeared to be an Indian. Clad in trousers of fringed deerskin and a beautifully decorated shirt that dropped as low as his knees, with a tuft of feathers in his long hair and beaded moccasins on his feet, all the trappings of an Indian dignitary, only the paler face of Bill Tenney showed that he did not belong to the tribe.

He was happy in this Cheyenne camp, and the happiness had modified the wolf look in his face. He seemed fatter now, but it was merely because he was less hungry in spirit. He had lived among people who gave to him as though he was the son of every brave in the tribe. He was the brother of Red Hawk, and therefore he was the brother of every Cheyenne in Standing Bull's band. He could do no wrong. If a feast was given, he was sure to be asked to it. If he desired to make a speech, he had by this time picked up almost enough Cheyenne words to make it, and, where he failed, Lazy Wolf filled in the gaps, making a flowing, smiling translation. In that way, he had been able to tell of his own land of Kentucky, and of certain feats that he had accomplished there. And the braves would mutter their approval, for nothing that he had ever done could possibly be wrong. Was he not the brother of Red Hawk? It was like being the brother of a god.

This atmosphere of approval had fleshed the very spirit of Bill Tenney and made him stand straighter. His eyes seemed to be larger and calmer. And so Rusty looked at him with approval now, though there was a sorrow in him that misted over all other things.

"If there is fighting," said Rusty gently, "I don't think I shall be sad." In fact, he felt just then that death was such a small thing that he was even able to smile a bit.

Tenney saw that smile, without understanding it. His mind was rushing on to other things. The powerful grip of his hand seized Rusty's arm and almost surrounded it. For the arm was not large, although it was packed with tough, nervous fibers of muscle that for a time had enabled him to swing a fourteen-pound sledge all day long—had even enabled him to swing it up and feather it down, backhanded, until its cold face kissed his chin, and then was swung back again.

Tenney said: "Is it right? Is it true? Is Blue Bird back in the camp?"

"It's true," said Rusty. And he peered suddenly at Tenney, and saw the man blush. "Do you want her?" asked Rusty Sabin.

"Want her?" said Tenney. "I'd die for her. I want her so much that she gets between me and the taste of stewed buffalo tongues. And God knows they're good eating. She gets between me and the game I shoot at. I can even forget how a mustang's bucking under me, when I think about her." Tenney's face was working with emotion.

"Is it that way?" said Rusty. He said it dreamily, and Tenney stared at him. "Well," Rusty added," she *is* beautiful. I know that. When I look at her, I can keep on looking for a long time. There is softness all around her mouth. Have you seen that?"

"Have I seen it? I ain't blind!" cried Tenney.

"And there is strength all around her chin. Her forehead is big and free, and there is space for thinking inside it. She is brave, but she is not sad. Sometimes, when I think about her, I could laugh . . . because thinking about her makes me happy."

"Does it?" snarled Tenney.

"But there is only one knife that fits the hand, and only one horse that fits the mind, and only one woman that fits the heart. That is why she could never belong to me," said Rusty Sabin. "And if you want her for your squaw, go ask her father for her, brother. If Lazy Wolf wants a price, I have a great many possessions, and they shall all be yours. Now let us go on and see why the warriors are shouting outside the camp."

It was a miracle to Tenney. He knew where Blue Bird surely belonged—fitted into the hand of Rusty Sabin. And yet the man was flinging her away. Well, he was not one to ask for reasons or motives. It was better for him to accept the good that he found, and where he could find it.

They went on past the outskirts of the camp, and now they saw the rest of the Cheyennes proceeding forward, while shouts came ringing out of the distance and a small, sweeping thunder rolled toward them across the plain.

Then they saw the dust cloud—not thick, because there was not much dust, but rather only a haze to be knocked out of the grass at this season of the year. Under the cloud ran the body of the herd of horses—led by a shining shape.

"White Horse!" cried Rusty. "White Horse!"

There was no doubt that it was the stallion, driving like a shining spear point over the plain. And after him came a whole torrent of horses.

"What's he doing?" demanded big Bill Tenney. "Gone out fishing . . . and brought home the whole catch?"

It looked that way.

The Cheyennes began to laugh and shout. Some of them looked at Red Hawk, shaking their heads and wondering. It would be another miracle that they would attribute to him forever, if White Horse actually brought back the stealings through which he had built up his herd.

The camp horses, in the meantime, seeing the approach of this mass of their kind, bunched together more closely. The boys and the young braves who had been guarding them at their grazing spread out to allow the strangers to be incorporated into the whole. It looked as though riches were about to be showered upon Standing Bull's tribe. Only Rusty Sabin was murmuring: "Has he really come back to me . . . or is he here to be a thief?"

White Horse seemed to stand up from the dark of the plain like a great light, and, as he came close to the Indian herd, he threw up his head and sent a whinny before him, a rousing blast that stirred both beast and man.

A moment more, and his lofty, tossing crest was sweeping through the Indian horses. They spilled this way and that. They fell into a whirling confusion, through which rushed the great wave of the strange ponies. Then the whole mass staggered and wavered, and, with a thousand neighings and squealings, the mixed herd bolted in a headlong stampede.

The trumpet call of White Horse gave direction to the flight. He had swept through the entire crowd, and, issuing on the farther side, he had gathered behind him the rush of the stampede. He was again the glistening point of the spear, and behind him moved a huge, flying wedge.

All of this had happened so quickly that not even the horse herders who were nearest the place were able to move to prevent it. Such boldness as this in a wild horse had never been seen before. It was as though White Horse's familiarity with men had now made him despise them.

The whole body of the Cheyenne ponies was in headlong flight. There were not a dozen horses left to the camp—and half of these were being frantically ridden by the herders in pursuit of the fugitives.

But man-ridden horses have no chance of overtaking unweighted ponies, half wild by nature, and soon made all wild by a good, stirring example. From the very first, the herders were losing ground. The great, thundering crowd of horses rushed off into the dusk, and they were only half seen when, for the last time, the triumphant neigh of White Horse rang faintly back upon the ears of the watchers.

Chapter Twenty-Eight

At any time, that loss would have been a major calamity. But now it was a direct blow, and a curse from heaven. For if the camp broke up and drifted away in pursuit of the horses, it would have to move as slowly as a wounded snake, because in it there were fully a hundred invalids, rapidly gaining strength, but still quite incapable of making prolonged marches. And if a selected number of braves started off on foot, and with the few remaining horses, the camp would be stripped of a part of its remaining force at the very moment when Major Marston's soldiers were about to strike.

In five minutes the truth was realized, and the howling of the women began to rise in their lament. Even the dogs of the camp sat down and added their voices.

As for the braves, those heroes of the plains were suddenly turned from lions to bloodless curs. The camp could be made defensible, perhaps, but the only walls with which the prairie Indians were familiar were the blue walls of the horizon, between which enemies could skirmish and charge, and through which the defeated could fade away. They were not accustomed to steady fights behind fortifications, nor was fighting on foot the Indian's talent. To be without a horse was almost as bad as to be without legs.

They greatly outnumbered Major Marston's soldiers, but what good was that? If they tried to charge on foot, the cavalry would retreat at ease, and then cut to pieces the rear of the Cheyennes as they retreated. Provisions were not plentiful in the camp, and all hunting would become impossible. Worst of all, heavy stores of ammunition had not been brought along on this southern march, and two or three days of brisk skirmishing would probably exhaust the supplies of powder and lead. After that, the Cheyennes would lie at the mercy of the whites, like a huge, helpless body that could be worried until its power of resistance was entirely gone. It was the sort of a game that Major Marston would know how to play to perfection. That was why the heart was gone out of the warriors. That was why the Cheyenne braves stood about, stupidly.

To make the blow more paralyzing, it had fallen upon them through the horse of their great medicine man—through the horse of Red Hawk himself. The thing was not to be understood, and the braves, looking up at the flaming, darkening sky for help from Sweet Medicine, saw no hope.

Finally, across the plain, the little troop of their herdsmen was seen slowly returning. And almost at the same time, out of the south as if to take full advantage of every chance, the long, thin column of the cavalry hove in view, little ant-like figures crawling against the red glow of the horizon.

Standing Bull, powerful and intelligent chief though he was, was helpless now. It was the white man, Lazy Wolf, who became the greatest force in the camp. He roused the braves with a small speech, and set the leaders in motion. He dispatched his daughter to speak to the chief squaws. And presently, under the supervision of Lazy Wolf himself, men and women and even the children were busily scooping out a shallow trench all around the camp, and raising a low bank outside it. The invalids, those who were well enough, came and gave their feeble best to the work. Men sat on the ground and, for lack of better tools, slashed and stabbed at the earth with their knives.

Lazy Wolf, calmly puffing a pipe, went here and there, giving advice and corrections. He was instantly obeyed. Under ordinary conditions, he had little to say about the management of the tribe's affairs, but, when unfamiliar and dangerous circumstances arose, he was looked to with great expectancy, because the fertility of his invention had been proved over and over again.

Already there was a shallow trench—a low bank sufficient to shelter prone riflemen when the darkness fell completely.

After that, out of the darkness, a voice called in clumsy Cheyenne, such as a trader might have picked up. It was a messenger from the camp of the soldiers, inviting Standing Bull to advance fifty paces into the dark and there converse with the war chief of the whites.

Standing Bull took a rifle, mounted one of the few remaining horses, and straightway rode out from the camp. He could be seen dimly against the stars, at a little distance from the edge of the camp, and another rider could be seen coming toward him from the distance. This was Major Marston himself, happier than he had ever been before in all his days. He opened the conversation by going at once to the point. Through the interpreter he said: "You people are helpless, Standing Bull. Your horses are all gone. We saw them blown away like the dust. Now, if you prefer to bring this thing to a fight, you know that you're lost before you begin. I've started patrols riding around the camp. Your men won't be able to get away. In a few days, you'll be starving, and, soon after that, you'll be dead. Do you see that you're helpless?"

Standing Bull answered: "We have been friends. There is no war between the Cheyennes and the whites. Why do you come here to harm us?"

"Dogs and wolves can never be friends," said Major Marston, borrowing a touch of Indian picturesqueness for his speech. "How many white trappers and settlers have your people cut off and murdered with tortures? But now we have you fast, and we're going to keep you that way. If you want to show that you are friendly, give me two men out of your camp."

"Which two men?" asked Standing Bull.

"Rusty Sabin, who you call Red Hawk, and the other white man, Bill Tenney."

Standing Bull's reply came in those words that are still remembered in certain parts of the West: "Red Hawk is my brother. His eye is my eye. His heart is my heart. His blood is my blood. *Hai!* To all the Cheyennes, he is a father and a brother and a strong hand in evil days. Ask for the teeth out of my mouth and the fingers from my hands, but do not ask for Red Hawk."

When the major understood this reply, he was in a fury. He shouted out: "If I can't have him living, then I'll have him dead! Go back to your camp, you fool . . . and tell the women that they had better start their howling again. They're dead, and the men are dead. I'm going to write my name in Cheyenne blood . . . write it so damned deep that it will never come out of the earth. Go back and tell your red-skinned dogs to howl. It's the sort of music I want to hear."

That was the word that Standing Bull carried back to the camp, with a heavy heart. When he asked for Red Hawk, he was sent to the lodge of Lazy Wolf, where he found all three white men. Lazy Wolf was now smoking, as usual, and calmly reading a book. Bill Tenney lay on his stomach, with his chin in the palms of his hands and his eyes fixed constantly on the face of Red Hawk, who had purified the teepee with the smoke of sweet grass and was now praying to Sweet Medicine in a murmuring voice. In one corner crouched Blue Bird, all eyes for the actions of the great white medicine man.

Standing Bull himself, overcome with awe, sat down on his heels and did not venture to interrupt the prayer.

Chapter Twenty-Nine

Far away, and then nearer and nearer as many voices joined in the lament, the women of the Cheyennes were raising the wail again, a blood-curdling cry of hopelessness. But inside the tent, the murmuring voice of Red Hawk was barely audible.

At last he folded his arms on his breast, dropped his head, and seemed to fall asleep. In that posture, he remained for a long time, but there was never an interruption from the others. In that lodge there were no doubters of the miraculous powers of Rusty Sabin—with the exception of the skeptical Lazy Wolf.

But pray though he might, Red Hawk heard no answering voice and saw again and again only one thing—the image of White Horse as he had appeared through the sunset, like a racing, crested wave. If Sweet Medicine were speaking now, why should it always be to send this image?

At last it seemed to Rusty that he understood. He rose and said briefly: "I must go to White Horse. Sweet Medicine is sending me."

"Good!" grunted Standing Bull. "But how do you go? The moon is shining now. The plains are as bright as day. The white men are riding around and around the camp, with their rifles."

"I must go," said Red Hawk. "If Sweet Medicine calls to me, he will turn the bullets away from my body. If he calls me to my death, perhaps it is time. There is no great happiness in me, oh, my friend. My father has been stolen away from me. White Horse runs free. The woman who should have come to my lodge is laughing at my name. I think I am ready to die."

Blue Bird covered her head and began to weep. Her sobbing made a small, musical sound of woe.

"Well," said Tenney, "if you're gonna run the lines, I'm going with you, partner."

"And I must stay here to die with my people!" exclaimed Standing Bull. "Red Hawk, do you take this man with you?"

Red Hawk turned with a strangely gentle smile toward big Bill Tenney. "He is my brother. If he must go, he must go," said Rusty.

Outside the tent, the pair selected, of the wretched dozens of ponies remaining, the best and the swiftest pair. Only when he was mounted, Rusty said: "Will the Cheyennes say that I am running away from them in the time of their trouble?"

The voice of Blue Bird cried softly and swiftly: "If ever a Cheyenne speaks against Red Hawk, the ground will open at his feet . . . fire will fall on him from the sky."

The larger and the stronger horse had been given to Tenney, because of his greater bulk. They rode now to the very verge of the camp, and across the skyline they saw four of the cavalrymen jogging quietly to make the rounds of the camp.

"As soon as no one is in sight, we start," said Rusty to Tenney. "We ride softly for a little while, so that the hoofs of the horses will not make a great sound. When we are seen, we whip hard."

Tenney nodded.

Standing Bull lifted his great arm higher than Rusty's head. "We are about to die, brother," he said. "But the happy days we have spent together will be waiting for us in the hunting grounds. Farewell!"

It seemed to Rusty, as he looked at the huge man, that the worst pain of death had already gone past him. But his throat was filled so that he could only mutter a formless word. Then, since the white patrol was out of sight, he jogged his horse forward at a dog-trot.

Watched by only two pairs of eyes, and their departure unde-tected by the rest of the Cheyennes, Tenney and Rusty left the camp behind them. The moon was very bright over their heads. To right and left they saw no danger, so they quickened their horses to a lope that set the ground swinging back in regular pulsations beneath them.

If only there had been a gulley, or one of those dry draws that the spring rains cut here and there into the plains, they might quickly have been out of all danger of pursuit, but the moon seemed brighter than the sun at midday, and the plains stretched away with hardly a ripple, a becalmed, a frozen ocean.

Tenney's voice, low, hurried, struck suddenly into Rusty's mind.

"They're coming! Run, Rusty!"

Red Hawk heard the pounding of the hoofs at that instant. Behind, and to the right, he saw five riders streaking through the moonlight. Behind and to the left, the other patrol of four was racing toward him. Big Bill Tenney already had his horse at full speed, and Rusty's pony followed without urging. They drew away.

Looking back, Tenney marked the way the patrols had bunched together, making one streaming body behind them, and he laughed.

"They'll never catch us, Rusty. We're leaving 'em behind. . . ."

In the midst of his exultation he was jerked out of Rusty's sight. Horse and man toppled headlong as the poor mustang put its foot in a hole in the ground.

Rusty, with a cry of despair, rounded his own pony back to the spot, but it was only to see the fallen horse clumsily trying to rise on three legs, while big Bill Tenney remained senseless, face down on the ground. His head was twisted sharply to the side, as though his neck were broken.

There was no doubt in Rusty's mind that that was the case, and, as he wheeled the pony near the spot, he cried out with a great pang of loss. He threw up a hand into the bright arc of the moon, calling: "Sweet Medicine, have mercy on his spirit! Take him to the Cheyenne Happy Hunting Grounds. Let him ride with us again in the buffalo hunt!"

Behind him, he heard the deep, united shout of the pursuit, and he allowed his nervous horse to dash away again over the prairie. When he glanced back, he saw that two men had paused beside the fallen body of Bill Tenney. But seven more kept on the chase without interruption.

They were well mounted. It was not for nothing that Major Marston hand-picked the horses that were kept at the fort. Out of every ten Indian ponies, he bought for the government only the best one of the lot. He chose them for size and conformation and proved speed, and now all seven of the troopers were keeping fairly close to the quarry. To Red Hawk, accustomed to the immense sweep of White Horse, it seemed as though his mount were bobbing up and down, unable to leave a single spot.

Then he saw that the enemy gradually was closing in on him. They came up close enough to open fire, and now and then a chance shot purred in the air close to his head.

But the cavalrymen were not wasting their efforts in this manner; they merely fired often enough to keep his nerves on edge.

A short half hour from the camp, it was perfectly clear to Rusty Sabin that he was lost, for his mustang's head had begun to bob. And now, at the very moment when his cause was already lost, his way was blocked by a dry draw that clove a winding way across the prairie, with ten-foot sides as straight as a masonry wall.

He had to turn, groaning, as he did so, to ride up the edge of that ditch. But before he had gone two jumps, a big caliber carbine bullet smashed into the mustang with a heavy, chugging sound. The poor beast swerved in its agony, and leaped blindly straight into the draw.

Chapter Thirty

Rusty had quickness enough to leave the back of the horse. Then came the shock of the impact that knocked him headlong. It was a rolling fall, or he would have been knocked witless. As it was, he got dizzily to his feet and staggered around the next bend of the great ditch.

Above him he heard the loud yelling of the cavalry. He could see the heads and shoulders of two galloping riders as he sank down behind a bush that thrust out from the side of the bank. Sounds of scattering gravel told him that the men had found a way down into the draw. Then, with a mighty crunching of small rocks underfoot, three riders hurtled past him.

The noise diminished in that direction; it grew up again, and thundered past him. They had only to give one fixed look to the little bush that half sheltered him with its scattering leaves, in order to discover his place of hiding. But they went on past, leaving a thin reek of horse sweat in the air. And Rusty heard a voice thundering: "Back the other way! He's not up here."

Then the storm of hoof beats roared away.

And so Rusty stepped from his concealment and ran for a minute or so over the stones of the draw. He climbed the northern bank, but from its top he could see nothing. The horsemen were totally swallowed in the depths of the little ravine. Then he stood up and began to swing straight north with that long, reaching, effortless stride that only Indian runners or Finns know how to use.

If only a darkening cloud would blow before the face of the moon. He had thought he was ready to die, but Tenney, Standing Bull, his father, Maisry, White Horse—all that he had lost—began to seem small compared with the sweetness of bare life itself.

But there was not a cloud in the sky, and the brilliance of the moon drowned all the stars near it and made thin the glittering of the little specks of light along the horizon.

Far off to the right, he saw a small, dark figure moving. That was one of the riders, sent to scout for the fugitive. He stared behind him to the left, still running. There, in spite of the joggling of his head, he could make out another dim shape.

Would it be wiser to cast himself flat on the ground and try to escape detection in that manner? No—for if the cavalry had started its search so systematically, they would cut for sign all across the ground, and the grass was hardly longer than the nap of a deep velvet. Hiding would be impossible.

A sudden uproar to his right startled him. Then, out of a shallow depression a quarter of a mile away, he saw the source of the thundering. A great herd of horses had been startled by the approach of the first rider that Rusty had spotted. It was veering straight across the line of Rusty's flight, and in its midst he saw a shining shape, like the foam on the crest of a great dark wave. White Horse!

Then, as he ran, he shouted. He headed straight on toward the running mass. There might be danger in that. Wild or half wild horses that will flee from a mounted man will often despise a man on foot. But the gleam of the great white stallion had maddened him.

A great shoulder of the flying herd poured down at him, perceived him, veered suddenly away. He yelled at the pitch of his voice, but the noise of the beating hoofs, and of the squealing, grunting horses, utterly drowned the sound.

He tried to whistle, as he stood fast, but for an instant his panting made that impossible. Then, looking wildly about him, he saw the rider from his left cutting straight toward him, with head lowered to jockey his horse into fuller speed.

Once more, Rusty tried to form his lips to send the familiar signal shrilling through the moonlight toward the stallion, and this time the blast went out with a thin, high quaver that seemed utterly futile against the roar of the herd.

But an ear keener by far than that of any human being had marked the sound. Red Hawk saw the lofty head of the stallion veer through the flying crowd of horses, and, as he whistled again, the mighty shape emerged from the herd like the moon from among swiftly blowing clouds. It stood there for an instant, head high, glorious of front, with the tail bent aside by the wind. Then, with a rush, White Horse came at him headlong. His hoofs skidded over the turf as he swung himself in beside his master. And in another moment Rusty was on the familiar, sleek-muscled round of the stallion's back.

He wound one hand into the mane. Behind him, he saw the cavalrymen riding erect, heard them shouting with amazement. Off to the right came the second pursuer at the full bend of his pony. But Rusty laughed like a madman now. They might as well try to catch him as try to catch the far-flinging thunderbolts from heaven. It seemed to him that White Horse could outdistance even a bullet in full flight.

He shouted, and instantly the stallion was plunging deep into the sweeping masses of the herd, a river of horseflesh that streamed about Rusty. Here and there, the broken end of a lariat tossed wildly in the air—a sign that Indians had once owned all of these horses that the stallion had reclaimed for the wilderness. And by the grace of fortune, Indians would once again sit on their backs.

In the meantime, the rush of the herd left the manhunters far to the rear. From the high back of White Horse, Rusty could see the cavalrymen pull up their horses and sit and gaze.

He let the herd pour on for a half hour or more. Then, gradually, he sent the stallion up into the lead. There was no bridle to control the monster, but no bridle was needed. All he had to do was to speak—or to pull on the mane, as on reins connected with the sharpest of controlling bits. The mere sway of his body or the pressure of his knees would guide White Horse.

All the while, as he drifted the big fellow up and down across the face of the herd, he could feel the ecstasy of that reunion springing through the great body of the stallion. Gradually it was slowed, then halted. After that, by degrees, Rusty began to range the herd on the back march. He worked them slowly, because he knew that the main point would be the moment of pouring them into the Cheyenne camp. He had no means of warning the tribe of the treasure that he was bringing. And it would be only with a rush that he could hope to send the mass of mustangs flying through the white patrols.

And once they were started at such a pace, might not their momentum carry them out again on the other side, and so flinging away across the prairie again? Or, before he came near the camp, would the outpost of the white soldiers see him and plunge in at the horses, scattering them?

He knew how those chances lay, but he could only go on, keeping the horses ranging to hold the herd compact. Thought of the wailing of the Cheyenne women filled his mind like a wind.

Chapter Thirty-One

Bill Tenney did not have a broken neck. He almost wished that had been the case, when he found himself in the hands of two cavalrymen, with his hands tied behind his back. They drove him before them, and one of them, with a drawn saber, pricked him in the back if he went slower than their pleasure. The other one occasionally flicked him with a quirt, and both would laugh as he freshened his pace.

"The major's gonna be right glad to see you," they kept telling him.

And the major was right glad, indeed. Joy, rather than anxiety, was what had kept him from sleeping that night. For with his patrols posted, he had not the slightest doubt that the game was in his hands. If the Cheyennes had had their horses, he would have been in a bad pickle, to be sure, for it was plain, the moment he had sight of the camp, that it contained many times more than the three score warriors that Blue Bird had told him of. He would have put it down as a village capable of sending out two or three hundred fighting men, numbers enough to make his retreat to the fort a desperately dangerous affair. But he was confident that since the men were on foot, the soul was gone out of them.

There was also the lamenting of the women to make the soldiery savage with confidence and to pass like the sweetest music into Major Marston's soul. As he listened to it, it inspired him. The bleating of sheep would not have been more delightful to the ear of a hungry mountain lion. He could not resist leaving his tent and walking restlessly up and down, all his nerves a-tingle.

He had rushed an Indian camp more than once. He knew what it meant to spit human bodies with a straight sword thrust. He knew what it meant to bring down the sword in a great over-hand sweep, until the edge closed through flesh and shuddered home against bone.

The thing to do was to make a clean sweep. The soft men he had carefully weeded out of his command. The men who remained were chosen cut-throats. They were the riff-raff of the frontier— thieves, sharpsters, man-killers who he had gathered up and of whom he had robbed the gallows to fill out the numbers of his command. If there were a few honorable natures remaining, they would be carried away by the example of the rest, when it came to the final pinch. And he expected to kill man, woman, and child, when he stormed the Cheyenne camp.

First, however, there would be long, sweet days of peace and plenty in the soldier lines, while the Indians gradually starved. The red men had neither the skill nor the nerves to endure a siege. Their ammunition would soon be spent. And their hearts would wither faster than their bodies. Every day, they would send out deputations begging for terms. The women would come screaming for mercy.

But the major would drive them back again. He hated the Indians, one and all, with the hatred of a conqueror and with the passionate aversion of one race for another. Above all, he saw ways of torturing this battle into the fairest flower of his fame.

No wonder that the major, filled with these prospects, was still awake when the first fruits of his victory were brought to him in the person of the escaped thief, Bill Tenney.

The major was sitting at his little portable desk, drawing up a first draft of the long lie that he would write to Washington. The light from the small lantern was not bright, but his eager mind did not need comfort at a time like this, when his shoulders were already being weighted with the insignia of a general. For after such a deed had been reported, it could not be long before the statesmen who chewed tobacco in the capital city would reward him with that which he desired.

Then he heard the footfalls. the knock at the door, and. . . .

"Night patrol with a prisoner, sir."

He looked up with a smile and commanded the party to enter. A corporal and a private came in with Bill Tenney driven before them.

The major did not continue to smile. The joy he felt was too savage and too deep for mere smiling. Instead, the corners of his mouth began to twitch just a little, and his eyes burned bright.

"Ah! My old friend Tenney," he said.

Tenney said nothing. He could only wish that the fall from the pony had been fatal to him. The death that the major gave him would be a masterpiece of consummate torment, of that he was certain. But as he had faced the same prospect in the Cheyenne camp, so he was able to face it now.

"There was a couple of 'em bolted out of the camp. This here was one, sir," said the corporal. "We took after 'em . . . Number One and Two Patrols. This here come a cropper when his horse busted its leg. The other one went on. But the boys was closin' up on him, the last I seen."

"Well done," said the major heartily. "This is the sort of service that's easily remembered. I won't let you two get out of my mind in a hurry. We're going to have the bones of that camp to chew on, before many days, and I'll see that you two have some with marrow in 'em."

The corporal saluted. The private could only grin like an ape.

"Now, Tenney," said the major, "tell me where you were heading with your friend . . . and who the other fellow was. How was it that the Indians let the pair of you go off on two of their precious few horses?"

"Why," said Tenney, finding his tongue with amazing ease, "there wasn't no trouble about that. Him that I rode off with . . . they'd give him their hearts in their hands, if he as much as asked 'em for their blood."

"Is he their chief? You mean to say that their chief was running away from trouble in the pinch?" demanded the major.

"Him? I ain't talking about their chief. Standing Bull is considerable man, but he ain't the first man in *that* outfit."

A cold thought struck through the breast of the major. "Do you mean, by any chance, Rusty Sabin . . . that rat of a refugee from justice?" demanded the major.

"Him is what I mean."

The major turned white about the mouth. It would be the undoing of the sweetest half of his plans, if Rusty should escape from him. For if ever he came to meet Maisry again, one look between them would undo all of Major Marston's plots and counterplots.

"You mean to say," he thundered suddenly, "that just as I'm closing my hand over the camp, the man I want the most is squeezed out of it?"

"They'll get him," declared the corporal. "They was sure closin' up on him, sir, when I last seen 'em."

"Why didn't you go on?" shouted the major. "When you knew the chief prize was right ahead of you, why did you stop for this poor fool?"

"We didn't know it was Rusty Sabin, sir. Besides, we was detailed by the sergeant."

"Damn the sergeant! Are you sure they were closing on him?"

"They sure was closin' on him, sir."

"If they don't bring him back, God help their souls," said Major Marston. He turned his attention suddenly back on Tenney. "Where were the pair of you headed?" he demanded.

"Across the plains," said Tenney.

"Where were you headed?" snapped the major again.

To Tenney, it was as though the pain of the whip had again eaten into his back. He remembered the lie just in time to speak it. "There's another outfit of Cheyennes lying off there . . . some-wheres," he said. "Spotted Antelope . . . or somebody like that."

"With how many braves?" asked the major.

"I disremember how many," said Tenney easily. "The Injuns don't count like we do. Spotted Antelope, and I think there was about ten twenties of braves with him, the way they reckoned it in the camp."

"Two hundred men!" exclaimed the major.

"Something like that," said Tenney carelessly.

"And you were to send them word?"

"That was the idea. The gang, here, under Standing Bull, was to keep to the lodges and wait till dust started up on the edge of the sky. Then they was to come out and begin peppering you with rifles, while Spotted Antelope and his boys come up unnoticed and took you from behind. They reckoned on fetching in a lot of scalps, that way."

"You infernal, damned ruffian," said the major.

He had a quirt lying across his desk, and he snatched this up and raised it to strike Tenney across the face. Then a thought came to him, and arrested his hand. He looked over the body of the big, wolfish man for a time, and then ordered his men to tie Tenney, guard him securely, and wait for further orders. After that, he took himself to his thoughts.

It had been very strange to find a band of Cheyennes as large as Standing Bull's outfit as far south as this. But they had a definite purpose in their errand; they had come to find Rusty Sabin in the role of a healer for the sick among them. But what could have drawn down another hand of an almost equal size? The thing was strange, and it might be a lie. Tenney had looked like a man capable of cool-witted deception, no matter what his own danger might have been.

The major was still pondering this problem when the second part of the patrol arrived, and the sergeant, a man with a weary and a troubled face, made his report. He talked slowly, for his tongue was still thick with awe. It had been he whose horse had frightened the wild herd. And he had had a close view of the fugitive calling the stallion out of the herd.

"He sort of waved his hand," said the sergeant huskily, "and the horse come out to him. He slid onto the stallion, and away he went. The wind never blowed as fast as they traveled, sir."

"Damn the wind . . . and damn you, too!" shouted the major. "Damn the pack of you for a lot of half-witted dummies! My God, if I could only have a few *men* in my command! Didn't you have the wits to try a few shots at him?"

"Yes, sir. I dropped to the ground and lay flat, like regulations, and I put in three shots at the big horse. But it was kind of like shootin' at a wave in the sea. I sort of knew that the bullets couldn't do no good."

"You did, did you? Are you one of these fools who believe that Rusty Sabin can do witchcraft?"

"I don't know, sir. All I know is what I seen. And I don't want to see nothin' more just like it . . . not while I'm alive, sir. It looked kind of ghostly. There was that run of wild horses, like a river . . . and the white of the big horse in the middle . . . and Rusty Sabin lifts his hand . . . and this fast white horse comes runnin' out to him . . . and away they go. It didn't look nacheral. It looked spooky."

"Get out of my sight!" cried the major, and the sergeant slunk away.

But Major Marston, left alone, no longer could bring his wits to bear on the smooth report that he was planning to send back to Washington. If it were true that another band of Cheyennes lurked somewhere on the prairie, then Rusty Sabin on White Horse would soon be among them, and the whole gang of red-skinned fighters would be charging across the plains to find the white men.

In such a cause as this, even children would grow strong and would strike as hard as men. For Marston had tried to betray the

Indians, and he knew that treachery, once it is discovered, multiplies and reinforces the strength of an enemy.

He began to plan on throwing out a detachment of ten men, to be posted in pairs toward the west, in order to give early word of danger approaching from that direction. But at this moment, new trouble descended on the head of the unlucky major.

Outside of his tent he heard shouting voices. Then an uproar broke out all through his camp.

"Indians! A thousand of 'em! *Indians!*"

He heard shouting and he heard cursing, in the high-pitched notes of fear. Then he ran out into the light of the dawn.

* * * * *

There was no other time between day or moonlit night when Rusty Sabin could have worked his throng of horses so close to the Indian camp, undetected by the white guards. But he had cannily held the crowd at a little distance until the moment came when the dawn light and the moonlight wove together into a mist, obscure and difficult for weary eyes that have been on watch half the night. It is the time, also, when men are expecting nothing but the coming of day. At just that moment, he was sweeping the great herd in toward the Cheyenne camp, not at the frantic gallop of a stampede, but simply at an ordinary canter that the Indians would be able to stop.

And that was what the major saw from the edge of his camp. He peered for a single instant, and then he shook both fists above his head.

"They're not Indians! They're simply the horses that the stallion picked up. Look, you fools! There are no riders on those backs. 'Boots and Saddles'! Bugler, sound 'Boots and Saddles'! To horse, you yammering, yapping, yelling rats! Head off that herd! Where's the damned patrol? Is everyone asleep?"

As he shouted, he saw White Horse at the rear of the flowing mass, working to this side and to that, hurrying up the laggards and giving momentum to the entire herd. And on his back there was a rider, and that rider was the man who the major hated most in this world, for the simple reason that we cannot help hating those who we have injured.

The major himself was already flinging himself on the back of his horse as he saw his two extra patrols rush in front of the sweeping horse herd. But the flow of those hundreds of half-wild animals was too much for the nerves of the soldiers. They started shooting, but instantly they became the targets of riflemen who ran out from the camp and dropped to the ground to take steady aim. So they retired to this side and to that, scurrying, leaning low over their saddles, and the huge herd flowed easily in toward the camp of the Indians.

Chapter Thirty-Two

Every Cheyenne in the camp had been wearing his scalp lightly, through that night. But now, with the dawn, horses were being poured in upon them—and hope—and a chance to fight, not for their lives only but also for the sake of the sweetest of revenges. They had been pegged to the ground by the lack of their swift-footed ponies. Now there were horses and to spare, for every man! Each man could be mounted three times over—and more—and more. A ceaseless tide of horse wealth was flooding in upon them.

The tribesmen came out with rawhide ropes. The men were the first, and the young, deft-handed boys. But the old, the invalids, the women, even the little children, helped with the work, fishing in that flood of horseflesh until every hand was rewarded.

"No Cheyennes on their backs . . . only horses," the major was saying as he watched the spectacle. "Yet they broke through my patrols. My God, I haven't any men under me . . . I have nothing but fools and cowards. Strike the tents! No, damn the tents! And damn the whole camp! Boots and saddles, and away. We'll have two or three hundred devils after us in no time at all. Rusty Sabin . . . he's done the trick. The devil burn him. And I'm a ruined man."

Dead was what he meant to say, instead of *ruined*, as he saw horse after horse rapidly prepared and mounted.

Out of the Cheyenne camp there rose up now, in place of the long, wolf-like howling of the mourners, a new sound—a sort of double shout, repeated over and over again, with the voices of

193

women in it and the outcrying of jubilant children and the deep-throated cries of the men.

"What are they yelling, damn them?" the major demanded of the interpreter, who was agape like a stunned man.

"Red Hawk. Red Hawk. Red Hawk," said the interpreter. "That's all they're saying. That's Rusty Sabin's name among 'em. He's a god to 'em. Maybe he's more'n that."

He was more than that, just then. For as the braves snatched at and caught horses and commenced mounting, not one forgot to turn toward the figure on White Horse and, brandishing a rifle high over his head, shout: "Red Hawk!"

The name itself had become a song of praise. They could be cruelly jealous of the fame of other men, but Red Hawk was not merely a man; he was a holy vessel that the Sky People poured full of light and power. That was why he shone out among all the tribes. He healed the sick who were dying. He rode through the ranks of the enemy and drew back from the prairies the far-scattered herds of horses in the time of need. Sweet Medicine himself was hardly greater—he was no more, say, than an elder brother to this giant soul.

So those fanatic Cheyennes screeched.

As Rusty Sabin dismounted, a squaw, huge with fat, came waddling up to him and touched him gingerly with her forefinger, and then she began to leap and flop about in a mad ecstasy, waving her arms, screeching his Indian name.

Others came, even more shining with worship, but a great deal more useful. They carried Standing Bull's finest horse blanket and fixed it on the back of the great white stallion. They drew a beaded headstall over the animal's head.

Blue Bird, tossed in the throng, seeming to run over the others, brought her father's best and newest Sharps rifle and placed it in Rusty's hand. Through the dust that rose from the trampled ground, and through the dimness of the dawn light, he peered into her face.

"They are given into your hands, Red Hawk . . . great brother," she was crying to him. "Now wash yourself in their blood. The traitors. Make yourself red. Make yourself Cheyenne forever. After today, you are one of us in your heart and your hand."

He smiled vaguely at her, and mounted the stallion. Of all the many scores of warriors, he was the very last to find his place on a horse. And the rest had not yet moved from the immediate vicinity of the campgrounds. They were swirling this way and that. Racing their horses on the outskirts of the crowd, braves were hacking at airy images with their hatchets, and stabbing them with knives, and, in eager anticipation, they were flourishing imaginary scalps in their raised hands.

But all the wild mass was awaiting the leadership of Red Hawk. When the Sky People have given a leader to the men on earth, when they had endorsed him so many times, is it not true that he should be followed and no other?

Standing Bull, war chief though he was, felt no jealousy. Hideous in his war paint, which he had hastily daubed on his face and his powerful, half-naked body, he waited on his dancing horse, close to Rusty Sabin. He cried out: "When your word is given! When you speak, Red Hawk, we charge them! They are ours!" And then, maddened by the battle enthusiasm like the others, he began to shout: "Red Hawk! Red Hawk! Red Hawk!"

And all the great chorus that was yelling the same name—"Red Hawk!"—at that moment, looked across the brightening plains and saw the column of the cavalry in retreat from a camp where the tents were still standing. It was a retreat in good order. The column, as he watched, was forming gradually into a moving hollow square. They would fight well. But courageous as they might be—well-disciplined, enduring—they simply had not the numbers to withstand the first charge of these hordes of inspired madmen. There would be little time for the exchange of volleys.

Indians rarely wish to charge home. But these Cheyennes, on this day, wanted nothing else. They would close—they would break those ranks with the weight of numbers. For every cavalryman there would be two or three huge Cheyennes, savage with eagerness to count the first coup, to take the scalp, to die or to be gloriously revenged for Major Marston's cruel treacheries.

All of this was clear to Rusty Sabin. But was it just? With the cream of Fort Marston's fighting men gone, the fort itself would quickly be a prey to the attack of the massed bands of the Indians. That outpost of the white civilization would be rapidly rubbed out. Perhaps the check would be sufficient to stop the westward march of the white man forever—and then the plains would be freed from the pollution of whiskey and the white man's diseases.

There was little knowledge in Rusty of the great cities and the closely peopled farm lands of the white men that stretched for twelve hundred miles to the east. Perhaps, on this day, he could change the way of history, he thought. Perhaps he could make himself glorious forever in the annals of all the Western tribes.

And were these Cheyennes not his people, thundering his name into the heavens?

He looked aside. He saw Lazy Wolf waving his hand with a book in it, shouting unheard through the din, and vainly striving to press closer to the hero of the moment. Lazy Wolf would try to dissuade him from sending home the crushing attack. But Lazy Wolf was merely a white man who was too inert to join the red men. He, Red Hawk, was indeed all red!

He made his decision in that moment. Maisry and her family—he would manage to save them, somehow, when he delivered the terrible attack on Fort Marston, later on. As for the rest, where had he ever found kindness and decency among them?

The fat saloonkeeper—he would be spared, also. But the rest deserved to die. Scheming, lying, cruel, cunning—they were foxes, born to steal. They deserved to die. Anger had waxed big in Rusty's heart—and determination, by the time he came to the edge of the great, swirling mass of warriors.

He raised his hand. Instant silence fell on those around him. To the rear there was a brief repetition of the shout: "Red Hawk speaks!"

Then they were hushed. It seemed to Rusty's excited mind that the very dogs of the village, at this moment, had ceased their clamoring.

"Standing Bull!" he called. The chief instantly appeared beside him. "Range them in two halves," said Rusty. "I will take the first half forward . . . you carry the rest to the rear of the white men. When they see us, they will have to halt. And then. . . ."

"*Hai!*" breathed Standing Bull.

The chief was trembling like a terrier in a fever of anxiety for battle and blood.

" . . . and then," cried Red Hawk, "when I give the signal, and when you hear the men of my party shout all together, you charge with us! We will strike them from the two sides at once.

"He that dies in this fighting rides on the ghost of his horse, straight to the Happy Hunting Grounds, there to eat buffalo tongues and hump meat the rest of eternity!"

Chapter Thirty-Three

Major Marston had one hope, and one hope only. This was that the Cheyennes, charging in their first mad enthusiasm, would come on so blindly and so headlong that their first ranks might be blotted out by the first steady volleys of the soldiers. Once thoroughly checked, if they were like other Indians the major knew about, they would not have the courage, or the rashness, to push their other charges home. They would merely begin to demonstrate in fake charges, skirmishing up and down the length of the hollow square.

But now he saw one mass of the Indians sweep away across the prairie, and among them sped the man on White Horse. The whole body of horsemen, yelling like fiends, described a half circle, and then halted in front of the white soldiery. Here they formed not in a single line, but in three dense ranks. Indian brains were not apt to think of this device in pushing home a charge. This was the work of Red Hawk!

Looking to the rear, the major saw the other half of the Cheyenne warriors ranging in the same manner.

That instant the major felt that he had come to his last day on earth. Maisry—military glory—all that fame or money could give to a man—these were as nothing compared with the sweet breath of life. But life was to be taken—that he saw. Always savage, brave, and determined fighters, the Cheyennes individually far outmatched the whites. Through lack of discipline, they could be beaten like other Indians, when they were opposed by an orderly resistance. But here there was no chance of digging in.

If the cavalry tried to lie down behind their horses, they would be washed over by the first charge; if they kept their saddles, they would be hammered down just as quickly.

He halted his command. It had seemed a powerful unit to him, when he had left Fort Marston with the design of massacring two or three score Cheyennes. Now it seemed a mere handful.

His men, moreover, knew what was coming. They looked steady enough, but their eyes were shifting from side to side, and they were pale. They were silent, too, and that was the worst sign of all. They should have been cursing silently, as they handled their guns and picked out their individual targets. But they were as still as death. Only a single voice roared out of the ranks close behind the major, as if in answer to the shouting of the Cheyennes. That voice cried in Cheyenne, also, and it was from the throat of big Bill Tenney.

The major wheeled in the saddle and stared grimly at the prisoner, who sat on horseback, with his feet lashed together beneath the belly of the mustang. Marston had almost forgotten him, but he could remember now.

"When you're dead, we'll have one less enemy, Tenney," he said. "What did you yell just now?"

"Red Hawk," said Tenney fearlessly. "Put a bullet through my head and be damned to you. The Cheyenne dogs will be gnawing your bones, ten minutes after I'm dead."

There was an uncomfortable truth in this that sent a slight shudder through the major's body. And his shifty brain went to another side of the possibilities that were locked up in his prisoner.

"You called out more than Red Hawk," he said. "What was the rest of it?"

"Nothing more. Just Red Hawk . . . my brother. Him and me are brothers."

"Brothers?" said the major.

"He says so, and that makes it so," answered Tenney joyfully and carelessly. "Go ask through the Cheyenne camp. Who are the brothers of Red Hawk? Why, me and Standing Bull, the war chief. They rate me kind of high in their camp, Major."

"Wolf knows wolf!" sneered the major. "And after you'd ridden away on White Horse? That didn't make any difference?"

"They're a queer lot," said Tenney. "Anyway, I guess Red Hawk knew that he'd get White Horse back, one of these days. And he's got him now. And may God rot your soul, Major."

The major had something else to think about, and he endured the insult without so much as a change of color.

"You're a poor tool, but I may be able to use you, Tenney," he said. "There's only a small brain in Rusty Sabin's head, and I think that I can addle it now."

That was why he went to the head of the column, nearest Red Hawk's ranged men. He could see Rusty Sabin passing between the ranks, speaking to this man and to that. He could see the set, savage faces of the warriors. They looked like so many crouched panthers on horses.

The major took out a white handkerchief and waved it over his head. Then, three of his aides following him, several yards behind, he rode straight out from the ranks of his own men, still waving the handkerchief. A howl of hatred and derision greeted him from the Cheyennes, and several of the braves jerked up their guns to take advantage of the excellent target. But a shout from Rusty Sabin made them lower the guns unwillingly.

Red Hawk himself came out on the grandeur of White Horse to take his part in the parley, followed by Standing Bull and two lesser chiefs. Or was it surrender that the major had in mind, rather than a parley?

Marston settled that doubt with his first words. "Mister Sabin," he said, "you have us in a bad corner. It's a tight place. If you insist on fighting the thing, a lot of men are going to die. These fellows of mine are outnumbered, but they'll account for an Indian apiece before they go down. They're well armed. There's a Sharps rifle for every man, and they know how to use 'em. If you charge, we'll blow the head off your battle. You may clean us up afterward, but do you think it will be worthwhile? Some of your lodges will be singing because they've got a fresh scalp inside, but the rest of 'em are going to be howling because they've got a dead man. Have you thought that over?"

It cost the major a good deal to talk in this reasoning vein. His mouth kept pinching in, and his nostrils kept flaring out. He could not help remembering that Rusty Sabin had once been at his command, helpless, inside Fort Marston.

Rusty looked at him with strange eyes such as never had stared at the major before. There was little hate and much disgust.

"You are not a man," he answered. "I am sorry for some of the others. But if you had had your way, the Cheyennes would have died one by one. They would have starved until they had to charge on foot, and then they would have died under your rifles. Why do you talk to me about the numbers of Cheyennes who may die? We are *all* ready to die if we can kill the white men."

"Sabin, you're a white man yourself," said the major.

"My skin is white, but today my blood has turned all Cheyenne. They are my people . . . they are all my people. Now, when I look at you, I know that you must die. There is a voice in my throat that tells me that I shall kill you."

He spoke so solemnly that the major was silenced for a deadly moment, while fear slid into his soul like the blade of a knife.

"You throw away Tenney, then?" he asked.

"Tenney?" exclaimed Red Hawk angrily. "He is already dead. He fell from his horse and he now lies dead on the plains. Afterward, I shall see him buried on a platform of high poles, and I shall kill your best horses under the platform, so that his ghost may ride happily through the sky. For it was your men who killed him."

"They haven't yet," said the major. "But they'll certainly send the first bullet through his head if you start a charge. If you doubt that he's here with us, look for him. There he is, behind the first ranks. You can see him, taller than the rest. That's Tenney. He was only stunned by the fall, Sabin. He wasn't killed. He was brought in and treated well, thief that he is."

Rusty raised himself high and stared with a glad but startled eye.

It was true. He saw the big fellow turn his head and distinguished clearly the wolfish outline of the face. Tenney was not a ghost wandering through the air, but a living man. And suddenly Rusty Sabin was smiling with happiness.

"It is true . . . he is there!" he exclaimed joyfully.

"He's living now. But he'll be the first dead man when the fight starts," said the major. "Think it over, Sabin. He calls you brother. What do you call him? Dead man?"

The great breath that Rusty drew proved how the blow had shaken him. But after his glance had wavered to this side and to that, he answered: "And you? How are you to die?" He held out his hand, pointing steadily at Major Marston's breast. "There *must* be battle between us," said Rusty.

"I'll be glad when the time comes," said Marston untruthfully. "But my first duty is to get my men safely back to the fort. After that, I'll meet you. I'll meet you alone, Sabin, and we'll have the thing out."

"Many times," said Rusty slowly, "you have said the thing that is not so. Why should I trust you now?"

"Because," said the major, his hatred and rage bursting from his throat loudly, "there's nothing under the sky that I want so much to see lying dead on the ground as you, Sabin! Will you believe that?"

"Good," said Rusty, for he could feel the truth in the emotion of the major. "Now I believe you. But where can we meet . . . and when?"

"Three days from this," answered the major. "Up the Tulmac and the first creek that runs into it from the north. That's a place where men never go. We could be alone there."

Rusty made a long pause as he considered. Then he looked up, suddenly, and raised a hand to the sky. "Sweet Medicine," he said, "give me wisdom." But all that he could see, in his mind's eye, was Arthur Marston's face, convulsed, dying. To Rusty Sabin that vision appeared as the most beautiful of pictures.

"It must be true that I can trust you to come. Will you go there alone?" he asked.

"Alone," agreed the major.

"At dawn, on the third day from this. On the third morning I am to meet you in the valley of the creek?"

"At dawn, on the third day," said the major. And already his subtle brain was scheming.

"You give me Tenney now?"

The face of the major writhed suddenly with rage and pain as he answered: "Yes. I give you Tenney now."

The agony that that speech cost him was purest pleasure to Rusty Sabin.

"You give me Tenney . . . and you swear to meet me on the third morning. With your right hand raised . . . so . . . with your sword in your hand . . . facing the sun. You swear it?"

The major drew his sword. "On the third morning. In the valley of the creek. I swear to meet you."

He faced the rising sun as he spoke, and Rusty sighed with relief.

"You give me Tenney," he repeated, after the saber had been sheathed again, "and you give what to the Cheyennes?"

"To the Cheyennes? What should I give to them? What have I to give?"

Rusty pointed. "You have rifles and ammunition . . . you have good horses . . . very good. You have blankets and tents left behind you, but you have many other things . . . and money. You will put everything on the ground and then march away?"

"To be massacred?" shouted the major. "Do you think I'm such a fool, Sabin? Am I going to disgrace myself forever, man? What are you asking me to do?"

"Ah. . . ." Rusty Sabin nodded. "Now I see that a man can lie and cheat and be ready to murder sleeping people at night, and still he can be proud. That is a very strange thing. But you won't be massacred. Not one of the Cheyennes will stir to hurt you. Besides, you will all keep your revolvers."

"And get back to the fort how?"

"You have good, strong legs," said Rusty. "I, also, have made the journey on foot."

"Damnation!" groaned the major. For he saw the clear picture of the future. It would be a disgrace to the service, one that would cancel all of the major's past services. He would certainly be demoted; he might even be discharged from the Army. Then he would have to walk the streets of a city dressed like other men, no longer drawing admiring glances. Men would not come and go at his bidding. In a sense, it would be the end of his life.

And all of this wretchedness was to flow upon him through the agency of this naïve young white savage of the gentle face and the still more gentle voice. The major felt a sudden horrible conviction that there *was* an unearthly power operating behind his enemy. There must be.

It's a thing that never can be done," said Major Marston. "My men . . . they'd rather die."

"No," answered Rusty gently. "They are not ready to die. I can see that they would be very happy to live. They will be glad to walk away from this place. Afterward, perhaps they may have sore feet . . . but that is a small thing."

He smiled a little, contemptuously, as he spoke. And the major, looking earnestly into Rusty Sabin's face, knew that the thing would have to be as commanded.

Then the major, with a groan, turned his horse suddenly and rode back to the ranks. He could hardly speak to give the commands. He could only, with bowed head, mutter the necessary directions to Captain Dell, and then turn in haste, so as to blot out from his eyes the white, horror-stricken face of his subordinate.

"We are all ruined men," muttered Dell. "And it's better to be dead than shamed, Major Marston."

"Obey your orders . . . damn you!" shouted the major suddenly, and he swung his horse aside.

Chapter Thirty-Four

The news of that compact brought a great groaning from the Cheyennes, but the older men pacified the younger ones quickly enough. It was not hard to see that a hundred trained fighting men would cause a frightful havoc before they were cut down to the last unit. Moreover, if these men were destroyed, other whites might come. That was the old story of the plains. A single Indian victory would for years be followed by a series of raids executed by the white soldiers. Villages would be destroyed, standing crops of corn burned. War against the whites meant bitter summers and starving winters, and, before long, a voice of lamenting in nearly every lodge.

But there would be no such aftermath to this bloodless victory. Lazy Wolf saw to that, for he drew up a paper written out in a clerk's neat hand, stating that the Cheyennes had been peaceful, that the soldiers had been the aggressors throughout, that chance and Red Hawk had put them at the mercy of the Cheyennes, and that the Cheyennes, instead of taking blood, had merely exacted a proper tribute before sending the whites safely away. This precious document, which would ensure continued peace for the Cheyennes, Lazy Wolf gave to Rusty, dwelling on its importance for the future. Then he made him force the major to sign.

It was a moment like death, for Marston, for in the signing of that formal document he was calling himself for all time a traitor, a liar, a night raider, and a murderer. His face was haggard and old; it was frozen in miserable hate as, at last, he traced his name at the bottom of the paper.

He said to Red Hawk softly: "It's not the killing of you that I have to worry about . . . it's the manner of the killing that I have to consider. Ah, Sabin, if you had the life of a brigade of troops in you, it wouldn't be as much as I'd like to feed into the fire."

"Why do you talk like this?" said Rusty simply. "What you want to do may be very clear, but you can only accomplish what your Great Spirit wishes."

That was how he left the major.

In the meantime, that wretched retreat began. The hundred soldiers who had come out so hot for blood and plunder and fame stacked their good rifles, took off their ammunition pouches, laid down all their little possessions, and went off on foot, leaving their saddled horses behind them. They kept only their revolvers, with which they threatened the insulting clouds of the small Cheyenne boys who raced about them, raising a dust that covered the ranks, clothes and face.

But the rest of Standing Bull's band, forgetting their own blood hunger, soon were contenting themselves with the plunder. It was no indiscriminate plundering. Standing Bull saw to that, distributing a share to each individual. Above all, the bright spurs, many of them gilded, were treasures beyond the rest of the loot, in the eyes of the simple Indians.

But Red Hawk himself took no share in the rejoicing, after that victory of his contriving, that famous and bloodless battle of the plains. He went into Lazy Wolf's tent and sat with a robe over his head, and the noise of the dancers—the singing, the shouting, and the laughter—covered the sound that was made by Blue Bird in entering. She spoke, close to him, before he looked up. Little of his own face was showing as he looked at her, but he knew surprise at the misery that he saw in her eyes and mouth.

"If you love the white girl so that your heart is always empty, Red Hawk," she said, "go find her again. Whatever she may have written on the paper, it was not in her voice when she talked to me about you. When I heard her speak six words, I was sure that one day you and she would be happy together. Go back to her. Happiness is not a tame dog. It will not come to your feet whenever you whistle."

"If I go back, she will laugh at me," said Red Hawk. "And then I shall have such pain that I shall wish to die."

"But you will not die," said Blue Bird. "Love is a very great pain, but it won't kill you."

"Ah, do you know about it?" asked Red Hawk.

"It is a great pain," said the girl, putting her hand on the spot, "somewhere between the stomach and the heart. Also, it makes the throat dry. But if she laughs at you, you will not die. You will only come back to the Cheyennes again and become truly one of us. There will be no white left in you, once she has laughed at you."

"True," said Rusty Sabin. "Now go away from me, Blue Bird. Because whenever I see you, I begin to think about her. Sometime, after she has laughed in my face, I shall want to sit down in front of you for a long time, until the thought of her is rubbed out forever and I can see only you, very clearly."

He started for Fort Marston the very next day. No one knew his destination. He went out of the camp as if for a bit of hunting, riding west. Not till he was beyond the sight of the lodges did he turn toward the south, and Fort Marston.

He could not know of things that were happening behind him, or of how big Bill Tenney sat in the lodge of Blue Bird and Lazy Wolf, his legs crossed, his pipe fuming. He had a habit of blowing out and then drawing in, so that the pipe bowl of red stone grew burning hot, and the bowl gave out more smoke than his mouth, even. He made his speech very well, quietly, evenly. He said: "Blue Bird, you want Red Hawk, but you'll never get him. He doesn't change his mind, much. He only gets one idea at a time. And that idea lasts him all his life. There's something about him as hard as the green beetle, the one he wears around his neck. He won't change. But look here. I'm a kind of a swine.

I want all I can get. But I wouldn't take nothing from Rusty. I don't think I would."

He lifted his wolfish head and stared at the smoke that was gathering in the top of the lodge. Lazy Wolf, with his near-sighted glasses pushed high on his forehead, peered without malice at the big man.

"No," said Tenney, shaking his head as if in wonder. "I wouldn't take nothing from Rusty, even if I could. Partly because I'm scared of him . . . partly because of him . . . what he is, I mean." He wondered to hear himself speaking like this, admitting fear of any other man. He felt as though there was a new soul in him. "Are you listening, Blue Bird?" he said sharply and suddenly.

"I listen," said the girl, and she looked up at him, dreamily.

"What I was driving at," said Tenney, "was like this. I ain't much to look at, but I'm kind of fond of you. You give me a chance, and I could be pretty good to you. Look at our kids. They'd be one-quarter Cheyenne. Think of it that way. And if things change, they could be white. If things didn't change, they could be red. I mean, being practical. . . . You see what I mean? Well, I'd like to have you . . . for a wife or a squaw, or anything you want. White marriage or Indian marriage, or both. Now, you think about it."

Blue Bird lifted her head and smiled a strange smile. She had, in that lifting of her head, the wonderful grace of those who bear burdens without being broken by them. She looked at her father.

He said: "You think it over, Blue Bird."

He was grave as he spoke to her. She widened her eyes at him.

Tenney saw her surprise, and broke in: "Look here, I ain't comparing myself with Red Hawk. Nobody is like him. Only, I mean that I might be better inside than I look outside.

"I might be better than I know. I might be better, because damn my heart if I ain't *wishing* to be better. You Indians . . . you've taught me something. About not wanting what the other gent has . . . except his scalp. I dunno how to say what I want to say."

Blue Bird turned to him with a beautiful smile. He wished that the smile had been less beautiful. He wished that it had been more conscious of him, rather than of something inside him. Her bright, big eyes, blue as her name, were looking through him and beyond him.

"Well," she said. She liked that little word. It was new to her. She felt it was a very good word to use. "Well . . . Bill . . . I have a love for Red Hawk." She paused. "If he raised his hand, I would go running to him. You wouldn't want a squaw like that?"

He considered. Her face burned. "No," he said at last.

"You want me for a wife," she said. "Do you want me more for a wife than you want Red Hawk for a friend?"

He had to consider again, head bent, thoughtful. He thought of a great many things.

"My God," he said. "There ain't nobody else like him. He wanted to butcher them soldiers, and Marston along with 'em. But he gave that up because of me. When I come to him to say I was pleased and grateful, he put a hand on my shoulder and he sort of smiled on me, surprised. He says . . . 'What are they, compared to you, brother?' Brother! He calls me that. Him as clean as clean . . . and me what I am. My God! He says to me . . . 'What are they, compared to you, brother?' Like that he said it, sort of surprised, and smiling on me. And my eyes begun to sting. All at once, I seen that there was nobody like him.

"'Brother,' says he to me. And now you ask me . . . no . . . you don't mean to me what he means. You ain't ever died for me, and give me back my life, like he has. No . . . I'd see you . . . in hell before him."

The sweat streamed down Bill Tenney's struggling face. He was amazed, after this implied insult, to see that the girl was smiling tenderly at him.

"Well," she said, "someday it may be different . . . but now I only want to help him. *You* can help him, too, Bill. You go and help him."

"Why, he's right here in the camp. He just went out for some shooting."

"I think he went to shoot a man," said the girl. "You go . . . fast . . . to Fort Marston. Maybe you'll find him. Don't let him see you, but go to Fort Marston. He may need help."

Bill Tenney jumped up. "What man would he be shooting?" he asked.

"When he speaks about Major Marston, there is something in his eye," she said. Then she added: "I saw a squaw once, killing a mouse with a great club. I think that Red Hawk looks like that when he thinks about the white war chief."

"You think that? Then I'm going, and I'm going fast," said Bill Tenney, and he left the tent quickly.

Chapter Thirty-Five

Under the very eyebrows of the night, and before the light of the day had been shut out entirely, Red Hawk came close to the town of Fort Marston and saw the big, square shoulders of the fort rising out of the plain. He dismounted then, and in a growth of willows near the bank of the stream he made the stallion lie down, well knowing that White Horse would not rise again until his master summoned him.

After that, he stripped himself and dived into the stream. The current plunged in, here, close to the shore. He had to fight it with all his lithe might, in order merely to stay even with the bank. And this made him think of that day when he had been swept down the stream with White Horse. He thought of big Bill Tenney, also, and of how Tenney had rescued both horse and rider, and he was still thinking of Tenney when he climbed up the bank and whipped the moisture from his body.

Afterward, he took sweet grass out of his pouch, kindled a tiny blaze, and turned it into smoke as he sprinkled the dry grass over it. In that smoke he washed his entire body, ceremonially. When he was purified—because the thought of Maisry was in his mind—he pulled on his clothes, which stuck to his damp body. When he was dressed, he went up the bank to the place where the stallion was couched, and stood for a moment beside him. His hand, blindly in the darkness, found the trembling stiffness of the ears and trailed through the mane and over the hard velvet of the neck. And White Horse snuffed inquiringly at him.

Then Rusty went straight to the house of Maisry Lester. Voices stirred beside the house, hardly bigger than whispers of the wind, and he hunted them down and crouched in the brush. When he made sure that it was Major Arthur Marston, he could hardly keep himself from rising and leaping and driving home his eighteen-inch knife. But he waited until he could hear, surely, for Maisry was saying: "I know what the town talks about. But disgrace doesn't mean much to me, I've been through such pain. Even if they take your command away from you, even if they expel you from the Army entirely, that would make no difference. It's another thing that keeps us apart, Arthur."

"Aye," he said huskily, after a moment. "That other one, eh?"

"That other one," she said.

A queer, quick-born hope leaped up in Red Hawk's breast. Then he drew back and bowed his head a little, so that he could not hear what more was spoken between them.

Eventually he saw the major go away; yet the girl remained there, close to the wall, almost unseen.

Red Hawk stood up then. He gripped the handle of the great knife until some of the strength from his arm flowed into his heart. After that he came close to her and said, clearly: "I have come to speak to you . . . not to take you. Don't be afraid."

There was only a wall of silence to greet him, blank as the wall of the house. He came a little closer. He said harshly: "I didn't come like a dog to whine around your feet, for I know that you are a bad woman. The Cheyenne girls are better. When I got the green beetle, and knew that you had thrown me away from you, I was sad. When I had the letter that you sent by Blue Bird, telling me that it was easy to forget, I tried to hate you. But I am not a very strong heart. Instead of hating you, I kept on being sad. And when I came near this town, just now, I wanted to speak to you again. So I am here, speaking. Tell me again that it is easy to forget."

She went right up to him. An angry man might have moved like that. She went right up to him and stood but a few inches away. "Did Blue Bird tell you that it was easy for me to forget?" she asked.

"*She* would not say such a thing. There is pity in her," said Rusty Sabin. "She told me that there was love in your eyes when you spoke of me . . . but, after I had read your letter, I knew that it was only laughter."

"Do you know what my letter said? Shall I tell you? It said that I loved you, and I waited for you."

"I am not blind. I read the words!" he declared.

"Then they were not my words," said the girl calmly.

That was what shocked him—the calmness with which she said it. He could not disbelieve her. He seemed to be touching her with a thousand hands. He was staring through the darkness, and he could see her eyes glimmering. There was nothing but truth in them. He knew that. There never had been a thing but truth in them.

"Sweet Medicine," he prayed faintly, "written words are but the foolish shadows of the truth. The real voice speaks out of the heart. Tell me now that I can believe her."

"Rusty," said the girl.

The strength went all out of him then. He put his hands out and rested them on her shoulders. He bowed his head beside her head. "*Hai,*" he whispered. "I am as weak as an old man, when you speak my name. It drives knives through me. If you are saying the thing that is not so, still continue to speak it. I am happy . . . and weak."

"Do you believe me?" she asked.

"I have two brothers. Tenney and Standing Bull. I am ashamed, but I believe you as I believe them."

She began to laugh. There was a flutter and tremor in the sound that burned his soul like a shaking flame, quivering up in the wind.

"Rusty," she said again.

The mind went out of him, after his strength. "This is good," was all he could say.

She pressed close to him. "Rusty," she said once more.

"This is very good," said Rusty Sabin. "I feel as if the Sky People were laughing and happy all about us. I feel as if you are my squaw, and as if I am your man."

"It will be true," said the girl.

"I feel as if our child is already in your arms," said Rusty Sabin. She answered: "Ah, what a long time he has been in my heart."

"I believe," said Rusty. "In you I believe. In you I trust. Sweet Medicine, give me a greater strength to trust you forever."

There was a sort of blasphemy in this. She closed her eyes. He was not very much taller, but a greatness swept out from him like a rising smoke and humbled her. Out of her soul she looked up to him.

"What you read in my letter was wrong. All that I wrote there was love," she said.

"Hush," answered Rusty. "Talking will not say it. There are not words to fit it. I would as soon try to tie a saddle on the wind. I would as soon try to make the wildflowers breathe out of the palm of my bare hand. I would as soon try to build the mountains and level the plains as to tell you what is in me. It is in you, also. The Sky People, they breathe about us. They breathe as you breathe. There is one thing for me to do. Afterward I shall come back to you."

"Come back to me," she said.

"I shall come quickly. There is still blood between us. I shall clean it away, and then I shall come back to you. Ah, my brothers, I am leaving you . . . and yet I am happy."

After that, he drew away from her a little. She held up her face, but he knew nothing of what that meant. To an Indian, a caress is in the eyes and the voice.

"Wait a moment," said the girl, closing her eyes. "I want to say something. . . ."

She stood there for an instant, but, when she opened her eyes and began speaking, he was gone. She ran forward a few steps and called out softly. The darkness swirled like water before her face. She breathed of fear, and it choked her. He was gone, and she was left teetering, falling forward from a height and into nothingness. If he could be reached. . . .

At that, she screamed out his name. The blood rushed up into her head, and the beating of her heart shook her. She told herself that out of the distance he had answered, faintly, but she knew that was wrong.

Her father came rushing around the corner of the cabin. He stumbled into her and was frightened, then he caught her up close.

Maisry," he said, "what's the matter? Why did you call out for Rusty like that? Why did you yell out like that just now? Rusty isn't here. Come inside, Maisry, darling. Let me help you. Rusty isn't here. Maisry, what's the matter?"

He got her into the house, and her mother jumped up as swiftly as a child, so that her sewing spilled all over the floor.

"Ah, Richard," she whispered, staring at Maisry. "Ah, God. What's the matter?"

"She called . . . she was calling for Rusty . . . out in the dark of the night," said Richard Lester. "Look at me, Maisry. Do you see me, dear? Would you please look at me, Maisry?"

"Stand away from her, Dick," said Mrs. Lester, approaching the girl with both hands held out and her face terrible with fear. "Let me have her. Maisry, I want you to lie down, darling girl. Everything is going to be all right."

"Don't!" said the girl. "Don't talk to me. I want to be alone. I don't want you. . . ." She turned toward her father and steadied herself by holding to his arm, but there was no sight in her eyes.

Mrs. Lester thudded down heavily on her knees. "Go on talking, Maisry," she said. "It's going to be good for you. Just let everything come out. I don't care. I love you. If you hate me because I was against Rusty, say it all right out. I want you to say it all right out. Don't be silent like this. Don't keep it in. . . ."

Her father took her by the shoulders and shook her a little. "Maisry!" he gasped. "Don't look at me like that. You're going to have Rusty. We're going to find him and tell him. We're going to get Rusty for you. You're going to be happy . . . always. Do you hear me? We're both sorry. We only want you to be happy. . . ."

She pushed away from him and went to a chair and sat down.

She heard her mother say: "Get some hot water, Dick. I'll watch her and stay with her. Ah, God of mercy!" Then she came stealing up and stood just a bit behind Maisry. She began to wring her hands.

Maisry said: "I'm not going to scream any more. I was out there talking with him. . . ."

"Yes, darling, yes," said her mother in a rapid, trembling voice. "Of course you were talking with him. Of course he was out there. I know he was out there. I . . . I could hear him talking. And everything is going to be all right."

"Then he seemed to disappear," said Maisry. "He seemed to go out into the night. Was it something I dreamed? Am I going crazy? Was he really there?"

"He was there. Of course he was there. I heard him. And it's all right," said Mrs. Lester.

Maisry touched her mouth with light fingertips. "But if it had been real, he would have kissed me. Yet he didn't kiss me."

"Maisry, don't jump up like that . . . for pity's sake!" pleaded Mrs. Lester. "Don't look around you like that. There are no ghosts in the room. Everything is going to be all right. There's just your father and your poor mother, who love you, darling!"

Maisry stood with one hand against the wall. She kept her eyes closed and her head leaning against her hand. "It's all right," she said. "I'm not going to do anything. Women never do anything. They just wait. I can wait, too. God keep me from hating. I'm only going to stay . . . and wait . . . and wish I were dead."

Chapter Thirty-Six

Major Marston, who knew that he was to meet Rusty Sabin in the dawn of the next morning, up Culver Creek, consulted the practical side of his very sound wits. He was to meet Rusty, and one of them was to die, but the major saw no particular reason why the dead man should be himself. He did not fear Rusty's strength or Rusty's skill with weapons, but he argued that Rusty was a fanatic and that it was as foolish to tackle a fanatic, man to man, as it would have been to try to handle a madman.

During the night, therefore, the major left the fort and met three men with whom an appointment had been made the day before. Poison was what the major needed to use, and therefore the three were the purest poison that he could find. He had known about them for a long time, and they pleased him, in a curious way, because they were so perfectly evil. They were three brothers who bore the name of Lavier, and ever since their childhood they had done everything together. They had hunted and trapped and stolen in company. Three times, they had all taken Indian wives in different tribes, and three times they had left their squaws. Together they had made enemies; together they had murdered them. They were frontier spawn—Dan, Bob, and Lew Lavier—and their cunning combined in their souls all the evil of the whites and all the evil of the Indians, as well as a certain special hellishness that was their own brewing.

It was easy for the major to talk with them. He could show his mind as freely and easily as a man can stand naked under the eye of Mother Nature only.

When he found them under the dark of the tree, he broke right into his thread, saying: "I'm going up into Culver Creek, at dawn. I want you to be there. Rusty Sabin is going to meet me there to fight a duel. Before he starts fighting, I want you to fill him full of lead." He waited a moment.

Dan Lavier, the eldest of the three, parted his lips with a smacking sound. "How much?" he asked.

"A hundred dollars," said the major.

"A hundred ain't enough."

"A hundred dollars in gold."

"Maybe that'll be all right. Gimme the money."

"I only brought fifty with me. You'll get the rest when Rusty's dead."

"What kind of fools you maybe think we are? You pay now, or we don't budge."

"I wouldn't cheat you boys. I'm not stupid enough to cheat you. I don't want to go to sleep with a bullet through the head, someday."

The three Laviers laughed, making snarling sounds high in their noses.

"All right," said Dan. "Gimme the fifty, then."

The major counted out five $10 gold pieces. He made them clink, one on the other. He talked a little more with them.

"I'd be scared of him, maybe, too," said one of the Laviers. "But him not expecting us, we'll kill him dead easy. So long."

The major went back to the fort, and slept like a child until his orderly wakened him. The night was still black when he dressed. He put on warm clothes. In spite of the Laviers, he might have to do some fighting before the morning was over, and there is nothing like warmth to assure the steadiness of the hand.

His horse was ready for him, and so he rode out at once toward the mouth of Culver Creek, three miles to the northwest.

* * * * *

Big Bill Tenney had not dared to enter the town of Fort Marston. Instead, he had skirted around it, cautiously, so cautiously that, unseen, he was able to spot White Horse in the distance as it left the place, carrying Rusty toward his meeting in the valley. And Tenney followed on.

Now that he had so luckily discovered Rusty, he bided his time before coming up to his friend, and he got a sort of relish, a strange happiness, out of the thought that in a sense he was the disposer of the fate, the guardian of the life of the great medicine man of the Cheyennes.

What was in Tenney's breast he could not recognize. For, plainly, he had nothing of a practical value to gain. The girl had begged him to come, and yet she would never reward him except with friendship. The rest of his pleasure would be in service.

But when he thought of this, he had to shake his great head, amazed. By nature, he was a taker, not a giver. If he followed another man, it ought to be for pay or for vengeance. Instead, he was keeping this trail, to whatever dangers it might lead, in the hope that Rusty Sabin might have added cause to speak a few words to him in that gentle voice—words of praise—words of happiness.

Bill Tenney's mind was heavily involved in these thoughts as he kept after White Horse, but he had to drop farther and farther behind because, as the dawn light increased, it was more and more likely that his leader might turn and spot him.

He made out the place where White Horse paused, and then dipped over the edge of the cañon wall. When, in turn, he came to the same place, he found beneath him a pitch, down which he would never have dared to venture with the mustang he was riding. It was the finest horse in Lazy Wolf's string, yet it could not be trusted down such a pitch. Even a mountain sheep might have grown dizzy here. Farther up the valley, there were other places easier in descent.

He was about to go to one of these when he saw that Rusty had dismounted, on the bottom of the valley, and was advancing on foot. And looking down toward the other end of Culver Cañon, he saw Major Marston in person, also on foot, with a horse left well behind him. Rifle in hand, he was marching toward Rusty Sabin.

The heart leaped in big Bill Tenney's breast. In an instant, he was off his pony and drawing a sure bead on the major. Then something in his mind made him jerk up the muzzle of the gun.

They were about to fight a duel, those two bitter enemies. And the major, since he had lost his fame, his honor, his good name in every way, would now lose his life as well. But why should it be taken by a rifleman lying at a secure distance? Was it not better to trust all to Rusty, and to the machinations of the mighty spirit, Sweet Medicine?

That sense of awe that had troubled Bill Tenney more than once, recently, flowed through him again. He began to smile, as he looked down on the wide shoulders, the tapering body, the long, red hair of Rusty Sabin. Red Hawk had come like an Indian to what might be his final field. From his head flowed a great ceremonial dress of feathers. His body, naked to the waist, was so brilliantly painted that even at that distance it startled Tenney's eye. Rusty was all Cheyenne, as he prepared for the fight.

At sixty or seventy paces, the major had halted. Red Hawk paused in turn. They stood for a moment with their rifles at the ready. And now for the stroke that would lay the major on the earth.

Bill Tenney looked up, half prepared to see some wide-winged owl, the bird of Sweet Medicine, floating above the valley. But he saw nothing. He only heard, while his glance was still in the upper air, the sudden clang of three rifles, fired almost in a volley. The sound did not come welling up from the bottom of the ravine. Instead, it hammered right across from the opposite lip of the cañon. Tenney saw the wisps of smoke rising, and three men clad in deerskins rising from behind the rocks that had sheltered them so securely. Was it murder?

Into the valley Tenney's eye plunged, and saw there the medicine man—the hero—the glory and the ideal of his eye—lying prone on his face. The major was running forward.

Across the valley rang the shout of the three marksmen, and up from the floor of the cañon drifted the triumphant yell of the major.

He was the nearer, the more vital danger, and so Bill Tenney, rifle jerked to the shoulder, sent a slug straight for the body of Major Marston. The major side-stepped like a dancer, and flung himself down behind a rock. In fear of the plunging fire from above, he dared not look out and try to return the bullets. He had simply to hug the back of the big boulder that shielded him.

From across the valley, three rifle bullets sped at Bill Tenney and smashed upon the rocks about him. He crawled behind a split rock that would serve him like a breastwork with a loophole in it, and through that he fired at the first target that offered.

There was ice, not blood, in Bill Tenney's brain now. The thing that he had seen, that most foul murder of Rusty Sabin, was like boyhood recollection of a tale told on a winter evening.

It was not Rusty who lay prone, down there—Rusty could not be killed. Sweet Medicine would turn those terrible bullets with the invisible flat of his hand.

Tenney looked down again, and indeed the prone body had stirred. It was still moving, lifting its head, and a thin signal whistle sped down the ravine. That whistle brought White Horse on the run. But it would also bring a fresh rain of bullets from the three murderers on the opposite height.

Bill Tenney, as he reloaded his rifle, caught sight of a head and shoulders rising from behind the shelter of the boulders near the rimrock, taking aim. Without time for care, he used a snap shot. He knew, as he pressed the trigger, that the bullet would strike home. In fact, the tall man in deerskins leaped up and dived into the thin air over the brow of the rock, jumping as if into water. His arms were extended stiffly above his head, his body twisted into a knot of pain. But halfway to the ground all that tension went suddenly out of him, and it was a loose, dead thing that Tenney saw strike the floor of the cañon. He saw, and he heard it. And he heard also the thin yells of the Laviers as they plastered more bullets on the rocks about him. Well, if they could be kept from firing on the wounded man down in the valley, he did not care how much they drilled away at him.

He saw White Horse kneeling down beside the master. He saw Rusty with small agonized efforts drag himself over the back of the stallion, wind his hands in the mane, and collapse. He saw White Horse rising, gently, head turned as though watching the weight that hung loosely on him. Then, at a smooth lope that was like the swaying of an easy wind, the great horse went down the valley. Had Rusty been saved for another chance at living?

No, for a yell of savage pleasure came from across the ravine, and Tenney saw that Rusty was slipping far to one side, inert, with life and power only in his hands to keep him on White Horse. Then a shoulder projecting from the main valley wall screened Rusty from sight, although it was plain that in another moment he would be falling.

Chapter Thirty-Seven

On the floor of the valley, the major, risking gunfire, was darting back to catch his horse and resume the chase. Of the trio of murderers, the two who remained were vaguely glimpsed by Bill Tenney as they withdrew from their covert. No doubt they would be taking covert, also, and trying to come up to the quarry. And Bill Tenney's place was down there in the thick of the thing—down there with Rusty Sabin.

He flung himself on the back of his mustang. The yell that came out of his throat was a Cheyenne cry. He hurled his pony along the verge of the cliff. A steeply slanting, dangerous slope appeared before him. He sent the horse down it. The poor little mustang cringed, but he spurred it savagely. He lifted it with his whip, a stroke that drew blood, and presently it was sidling, slipping, dodging, and swerving down the devil's slide. Twenty feet from the bottom, the ground jumped out from under its feet, and horse and man toppled headlong onto the valley floor.

But the horse was a cat and the man was a tiger. Tenney was in the saddle again before the tough little bronco was on its feet, and he raced the horse up the ravine to the rescue.

Rescue? No, that was not the thought that was in his mind. One man, even one man like Tenney, could not deal with three expert fighters. He rode so furiously—well, he could not have told exactly why. It was not to save his brother. It was rather to see that Rusty Sabin did not die alone.

Just around the big, projecting rock at the side of the valley he found Rusty, toppled on the ground, his limbs twisted together.

The great horse stood over his fallen master. He lifted his head. Surely it was a note of appeal that he sent thundering to Bill Tenney.

There seemed no life in Rusty. He lay half on his back, his eyes partially open. On his lips was a faint smile. That was the way the dead look, thought Tenney, and he dug his hands into the hair of his head and tugged.

God . . . I'm pullin' my hair out like a woman, he thought to himself. He was blind. He was sick.

Then he saw that Rusty's wounds were still bleeding. There were three of them—shoulder, side, and thigh. They were still bleeding freely, and dead men don't bleed. The heart stops pumping, and there isn't any flow.

Bill Tenney flung up one hand to the sky at that. If he had known enough Cheyenne, he would have made his prayer to Sweet Medicine to stop the gaping mouths of the wounds and prevent Rusty's life from flowing away. But the Sky People, if they were worth anything, would be able to read even a white man's mind.

Then he picked up the body. It was limp. The head and legs hung down. He had to shift the weight, and the shifting made the blood well suddenly from Rusty's side. It flowed down over Bill Tenney's body. He could feel the warmth of it.

"My God . . . my God," said Tenney. "If only I could run some of my blood into you, brother."

He saw how the rock was cloven away at the base, receding twenty feet or more, the outer lip fringed with boulders as with teeth. That was where he would find a refuge and tie up the wounds. He ran then, flexing his knees, and turning up his feet so that he would not stumble. White Horse was following, snuffing at his master, flattening his ears, and shaking his head threateningly at Bill Tenney. White Horse followed right into the cave beneath the cliff.

"A hell of a cave," said Tenney. For the great mouth yawned open on all three sides, inviting invasion, and the hoof beats of the running horses down the valley drummed soft on the sand and loud on the rocks.

After putting Rusty down, his clothes became like paper in Tenney's hands. He ripped them off and made them into bandages. He bound the bandages around the wounds, after he had clogged the mouths of the rifle holes with loose, dry dust.

Rusty, with his eyes slightly parted, lay on his back, moving only as Tenney moved him.

Then a gun boomed, and it seemed to fill the ears of Tenney with thunder. It drove a red rod of pain across Tenney's back, all through the thick muscles of his shoulders. Glancing across the shoulder blades, the bullet had sliced its way, and the blood ran out.

"I've got him!" shouted Major Marston's voice. "Now in . . . and finish 'em both. Now in at 'em. Come on, boys!"

They came. The major ran with a silent grin that showed his teeth. The two Laviers came screaming, almost as though they were shrieking in fear. But they were merely mad for the kill.

Tenney knew that. He had to move slowly. There was not much strength in his arms. The nerves seemed to have been cut. There was not much strength in his back, either.

He sat up and swayed to his knees. From the ready, he fired a slug into the breast of one of those screaming men who were charging, and the fellow spilled sidewise across the course of his brother so that he tripped him flat. Tenney smashed the butt of his rifle into the skull of that second man.

But then the major was at him. His rifle was empty because he had just sent its bullet into Tenney's back. Now he gave the big fellow the barrel along the head, and whacked him back against the face of the rock.

It might have brained another man. It only knocked red sparks and jumping flames across Tenney's eyes. And the blood ran down in one gush across his face.

"Now for you, Sabin!" he heard the major yell.

But Tenney grasped with his great arms at the legs that were striding past him, and the major stumbled and fell. Then terrible blows began to rain on Tenney's head. They merely cleared his eyes, however, and he was able to see Rusty rising on one elbow—rising as if out of death, and smiling a little, still in pain, with a smile that was like death. He sat up, and in his hand there was the curving sheen of the great knife that he had forged with his own hands, long ago in the blacksmith shop. And the man prayed—even in the midst of battle, one swift lifting of hand and eyes to Sweet Medicine.

The major, kicking himself loose from Tenney at last, swung his rifle to brain Rusty Sabin.

"Now down . . . damn you!" screamed the major.

Rusty leaned forward on his left hand, and with the right, he thrust out the length of the knife into the body of Major Arthur Marston. The rifle came smashing down, but not on Rusty's head. It hit the rock just behind him, and the stock snapped off.

The major staggered. He got hold of Rusty Sabin's knife hand, and he seemed to pull the knife deeper into his mortally wounded body. Perhaps he was only steadying himself for the second stroke, to be delivered with the bare barrel of the heavy rifle. But as that stroke heaved up above his head, and, as Rusty raised a hand to ward off the blow, the major's knees buckled both to one side. He came down on them with a lurch. He twisted himself over and tried to pull out the knife, but he merely succeeded in widening the wound horribly, slashing it to the side.

"God," breathed the major. "A . . . a damned . . . a white . . . Indian. . . ."

The major was dying, and Tenney knew it. He dragged himself past the soldier with a rush, and got to Rusty. Rusty was struggling weakly to sit up, but all the strength suddenly went out of him and he slipped down on his side. And Tenney's great hands were dangling loosely, helplessly. What could he do with them?

Once, he had been able to break the back of a man with those hands, but now he could not find a grip on the fleeing soul of his friend. He could only drop to his knees and peer into the white face. The hair above it seemed like a weltering flame. The blue eyes were not pinched with pain; they were wide open—clear and full of unspoken words.

Rusty made toward Bill Tenney a gesture of infinite gratitude and affection. He smiled in the face of the man who was known as a thief. But he gave him no words. Because, of course, there was no need of words between them.

"Maisry . . ." he said.

Bill Tenney slid a trembling, weak arm under Rusty's shoulders and supported half the weight of that body. It was not a great weight. There had been a time when Tenney despised all except big men, huge-handed men like himself. But that was in the distant past, in that small, obscure portion of his existence before the days of his companionship with Rusty. Now he knew that there is a thing of mind and of spirit that is even greater than flesh. Here, with the strength of his hand, he was upholding a worker of miracles who still would have to submit to the last and greatest miracle of all, the coming of death.

"Aye . . . tell me about Maisry," said Bill Tenney softly.

"Tell her that I died thirsty for her," said Rusty. "I am thirsty for her. More than summer and long marches ever made me thirsty for water. And if. . . ."

His eyes closed. A slight shudder went through him, and Tenney, with a leaping agony in his heart, was sure that even as quietly as this, like a breath of wind through a door, like a gleam of light over a river, his friend had left him.

But with closed eyes, Rusty spoke again: "Where are you, brother?"

"Here . . . here," said Tenney. "Rusty, don't be wasting your breath on Maisry. No woman is worth it. No man, either. Think of your Sweet Medicine. Go on and say a prayer . . . to him that's helped you so much. He can help you again."

But Rusty would only say: "You know the blue of water at the end of a long march, when the horses are staggering and the men force themselves to grin, because of the pain in their throats? I feel that way about the blue of her eyes. Tell her that, brother." His eyes were still closed.

"Rusty, will you hear me?" groaned Tenney. "Make a prayer now to Sweet Medicine."

"There is no need to pray to him," said Rusty. "He is near enough to see me. I hear a rushing sound in my ears, and what can that be except the wings of Sweet Medicine? But speak to Maisry. Words from a friend who is far away are better than food. Words from the dead must be better than honor given by a great tribe. Tell her that I have loved her . . . she has loved me . . . and the love of two people must go on living, even when they are both dead."

"Those are hard things to remember," said Tenney. "But I'll never forget. The love of two people . . . you mean it goes on like a ghost that walks."

"Aye. Like a kind ghost," said Rusty. "Tell her. . . ."

His head fell over, suddenly, weakly, against Tenney's arm, and a faint sigh ended his words.

Tenney laid the loose body on the ground, softly. He pressed his face close to Rusty's heart, and heard no beat. Was he dead? The eyes of dead men should remain half open, it was said, and yet Rusty's eyes were closed.

"He's dead," said the major's voice, stepping into the broken current of Tenney's thoughts. "He's dead . . . the red rat. D'you think I'd pass out without taking at least one life along with me?"

Tenney lifted his dazed head and saw that the major had managed to put his back against a rock, had at last managed to jerk out the knife. Now he held his two hands over the rent in his body, but still the blood forced its way rapidly out between the fingers.

Tenney picked up the dripping knife.

"D'you want to hurry me out?" said the major.

"No," said Tenney. "I wouldn't hurry you. If there was life worth saving in you, I'd tie you up and nurse you back to strength, so that I could kill you all over again. I'd make you last. I'd make you last days . . . and days. . . ."

The major nodded. "You and I could understand each other," he said. "But that red-headed fool on the ground, there . . . nobody could understand him. He's a cross between a baby and an old man, with a lot of the fool mixed in all the way. You never could get anything out of him."

"He called me brother," said Tenney slowly, and then he added: "I wish to God there was a way of holding the life in you till I've done what I could think of doing to you, Major."

"It's too late," said the major. "The blood's draining out of me, and my eyes are getting dim. I can still see the red of Sabin's hair, though."

"Aye, and your lips are blue."

"That's because there's the taste of death on them," said the major.

His voice was a little fainter now. A grim curiosity carried Tenney's mind even away from his grief.

"How does it feel?" he asked wonderingly.

"Like lacking air. Like the middle of summer. And not enough air. But it'll soon be over . . . I could take my hands away from the cut, and I'd go out like a breath. . . ."

"You're a cool man . . . and a brave man," said Tenney, willing to admire even the man he hated most. "And if you'd let Rusty work on you the way he worked on me, you could have been a good man and a right man, before you passed out."

"Let him work on me? He's worked enough on me," said the major. "I've had my hand closed, almost, on the woman I wanted.

And he's forced my hand open, and taken her away again. I've had a reputation in my grip, and he's smashed it like an egg, and made a fool of me. He'd broken my life before he ever ran his knife into me. That's the work he's done."

"Because you stood against him like a fool. Like a log trying to swim up against a river. That was you."

"Aye," said the major, suddenly submitting to the idea. "And maybe you're right, after all. But where did he ever get his strength?"

"Out of the sky," said Tenney credulously, lifting his hand to point.

The major attempted to laugh his scorn at that answer, but the blood burst out of him, suddenly, and he began to choke. He fell on his face and kicked at the sands. He hit at the ground like a mad dog. And that was how he died, with Tenney staring, overwhelmed, seeing in this a fresh miracle, a blow struck by the sightless hand of Sweet Medicine.

Big Bill Tenney was still looking down at death when he heard a murmur behind him, and turned with a gasp of terror. For in fact he thought that the god of the Cheyennes, in ghostly person, would be seen standing behind him. And those who see the gods, unless they are like Rusty Sabin, cannot live long.

But there was no strange vision before him. The sound came from Rusty's parted lips, the words stumbling slowly from them—words that had no meaning. But there was the breath of life behind them, and Bill Tenney shouted suddenly, gone mad with joy.

Somehow, Bill Tenney got Rusty into a better place, away from that terrible slaughter. He laid him on saddle blankets, heaping sand under the top end for a head rest.

Sometimes Rusty seemed dead, sometimes he seemed merely to sleep, but whenever life came into him he would begin to speak, and the first word that he said was always: "Brother. . . ."

Then the life would slide out of him again.

* * * * *

The hounds got the trail and ran it down in the middle of the day. Captain Dell found the dead man on the floor of the valley.

"One less Lavier in the world," he said, and thanked God audibly.

Then he went on behind the dogs, to the place where the other three men lay dead. Rusty's knife lay near the major's breast. After that, he came to the spot where Bill Tenney lay like a giant, a ragged bandage about his face and his body dripping with blood.

Tenney stood up and barred the way, a rifle in his hands. But the captain merely said: "I'm putting down my arms, you see, Tenney? Tell me what's happened. Tenney, is it murder? God help your soul. You see I've got twenty men behind me. There's no use resisting."

"Murder! Aye, it's murder!" cried Tenney. "The Laviers and the major . . . they've murdered Rusty Sabin. They've killed the only man in the world. They've murdered him that's a brother to me."

* * * * *

Swift help was coming from the town, also. The word went wide and far, like the running of quicksilver. Men saddled their horses rapidly, but none so swiftly as Maisry Lester. Swift horses and keen riders rushed out along the river trail, but none as swift as Maisry and her pony.

She rode it with a merciless heel and hand, for it seemed to her that the beast stood still, running on a treadmill, and that the only movement was the terrible, hour-slow drifting of the hills along the horizon.

She had no hope, as she raced, that she might come to him in time to save him. But the prayer that left her lips in ragged fragments of words was only that she might reach him in time to see the last brightness of life in his eyes. For she felt that light would come into her like a new soul into her body.

Of the townspeople, she was first in the valley—she was first up its hot sands—she was first to reach the group of soldiers who moved clumsily here and there, trying to help and not knowing what to do.

When Bill Tenney saw her, he lifted up his bloodstained hands in a gesture of surrender.

"He won't live for me," said Tenney, "but maybe he'll come back for you, Maisry. By his way of thinking, murder ain't as strong as love."

* * * * *

Well, Rusty Sabin was not murdered, after all. He was not going to die. The doctor who came out from the fort said so at the end of the long examination and the agony of probing that turned Rusty Sabin green. He would not die. He would live—if he could be kept quietly where he was and not moved for at least a fortnight.

Keep him where he was? The Lesters, mother and father, smiled. Already, they had sent back for two tents. Already, Maisry was installed as chief nurse. Richard Lester was taking charge.

And later, while Rusty lay flat on his back on a soft cot, he said: "I can see your head in the middle of the sky, Maisry . . . all blue around you. It's mighty sweet medicine for me. And you are happy?"

She merely smiled. It would have been foolish for her to try to say it in words.

"Where's Bill?" asked Rusty.

The big man came near and leaned slowly over the bunk.

"Aye, Rusty?" he said tenderly.

"There was never any chance of me dying," said Rusty. "Sweet Medicine wouldn't let me, because he knew that I could never tell you about yourself, Bill. He knew that it would take years more living before I could make you understand, brother."

He put his hand in Tenney's, and Bill Tenney held it softly, saying nothing. . . .

THE END

About the Author

Max Brand is the best-known pen name of Frederick Faust, creator of Dr. Kildare, Destry, and many other fictional characters popular with readers and viewers worldwide. Faust wrote for a variety of audiences in many genres. His enormous output, totaling approximately thirty million words or the equivalent of 530 ordinary books, covered nearly every field: crime, fantasy, historical romance, espionage, Westerns, science fiction, adventure, animal stories, love, war, and fashionable society, big business and big medicine. Eighty motion pictures have been based on his work along with many radio and television programs. For good measure he also published four volumes of poetry. Perhaps no other author has reached more people in more different ways.

Born in Seattle in 1892, orphaned early, Faust grew up in the rural San Joaquin Valley of California. At Berkeley he became a student rebel and one-man literary movement, contributing prodigiously to all campus publications. Denied a degree because of unconventional conduct, he embarked on a series of adventures culminating in New York City where, after a period of near starvation, he received simultaneous recognition as a serious poet and successful author of fiction. Later, he traveled widely, making his home in New York, then in Florence, and finally in Los Angeles.

Once the United States entered the Second World War, Faust abandoned his lucrative writing career and his work as a screenwriter to serve as a war correspondent with the infantry in Italy, despite his fifty-one years and a bad heart. He was killed during a night attack on a hilltop village held by the German army. New books based on magazine serials or unpublished manuscripts or restored versions continue to appear so that, alive or dead, he has averaged a new book every four months for seventy-five years. Beyond this, some work by him is newly reprinted every week of every year in one or another format somewhere in the world. A great deal more about this author and his work can be found in *The Max Brand Companion* (Greenwood Press, 1997) edited by Jon Tuska and Vicki Piekarski. His Website is www.MaxBrandOnline.com.